# PLAYING with FIRE

MYSTERY

"A sizzling good mystery series."
—Lesa's Book Critiques

INCLUDES RECIPES!

## J. J. COOK

BERKLEY
PRIME
CRIME

**$7.99 U.S.**
$9.99 CAN

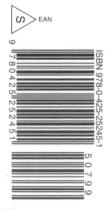

"John." Stella [...] something in [...] was. He was [...] usually meant he wasn't happy about something.

Doug sized up the other police officer and got to his feet. He was taller than John but John was stockier, with broader shoulders. "I'm Officer Douglas Connelly from Chicago."

"Nice to meet you." John glanced at him, then turned to Stella. "I have some bad news."

"Not too bad, I hope." Stella felt guilty that she'd wished it when he'd come up to the table.

"Bad enough. Mace Chum is dead. They found him off of the main road a few minutes ago. It looks like he lost control of his truck and camper. Chief Rogers wants the fire department on-site in case there's a problem getting the truck up."

"Oh no . . ."

# Praise for

# That Old Flame of Mine

*Berkley Prime Crime titles by J. J. Cook*

**THAT OLD FLAME OF MINE**
**PLAYING WITH FIRE**

# Playing
# with Fire

# Playing with Fire

## J. J. Cook

BERKLEY PRIME CRIME, NEW YORK

**THE BERKLEY PUBLISHING GROUP**
Published by the Penguin Group
Penguin Group (USA) LLC
375 Hudson Street, New York, New York 10014

USA • Canada • UK • Ireland • Australia • New Zealand • India • South Africa • China

penguin.com

A Penguin Random House Company

PLAYING WITH FIRE

A Berkley Prime Crime Book / published by arrangement with the authors

For information, address: The Berkley Publishing Group,
a division of Penguin Group (USA) LLC,
375 Hudson Street, New York, New York 10014.

ISBN: 978-0-425-25245-1

PUBLISHING HISTORY
Berkley Prime Crime mass-market edition / January 2014

PRINTED IN THE UNITED STATES OF AMERICA

10  9  8  7  6  5  4  3  2  1

Cover art by Mary Ann Lasher.
Cover design by George Long.
Logo by Shutterstock.
Interior text design by Tiffany Estreicher.

# Chapter 1

~~~~~~~~~~

Sweet Pepper Fire Chief Stella Griffin stood in the middle of a field of red, yellow, and green hot pepper plants that looked as though it went on forever. The August sun beat down on her head and made her question why she'd worn long jeans, instead of shorts, on this outing.

Sweet Pepper, Tennessee, was known for growing the hottest, sweetest peppers in the world—the small mountain town's main source of revenue. She was supposed to be a tour guide during the Sweet Pepper Festival—if she stayed that long. The festival wasn't until October. That seemed a lifetime away.

Muttered swear words came from Mackie Fossett, the farmer whose field she stood in, as he tried to get his tractor started. It had broken down after Stella's lesson in growing Tennessee Teardrop peppers. She had no idea where they were or how long it might take to get back to where they'd started.

Her father was swearing too, all the way from Chicago. This was the second call from him this morning. His Irish temper was getting the better of him. Stella held the cell phone slightly away from her ear.

How his call had managed to find a cell tower while she was outside of town was a mystery to her. But if anyone could do it—

"I don't see what good you're doing there now, Stella," Sean Griffin said—*again*. "You've been down there since last November looking for this dead fire chief's killer. You don't sound like you're any closer to finding out who it is. And frankly, you're going to lose your job up here if you're not back soon. I talked to Chief Henry yesterday. Your three-month leave was up a long time ago."

"I know, Dad." Her voice was as flat as the sound of the bees droning across the peppers in the hot, dry air. "I can't leave yet."

"Are you planning on *staying* there?" His tone was incredulous. "Your family—your friends—your *life* is here. Is a man involved? Is that the issue?"

"Yes, Dad. A dead man."

"Be serious, Stella. Are you involved with someone, you know, romantically?"

It was ironic that her ride home picked that moment to circle overhead in his helicopter. She'd been seeing the pilot, Zane Mullis, recently. They'd had some good times together. Nothing serious. He worked with the forestry service in the Great Smoky Mountains National Park, which backed up against Sweet Pepper.

She waved to Zane. He waved back. He couldn't land in the pepper field. Probably wanted to let her know that he was there. He'd land in the flat open area beside Mackie's barn where he'd dropped her off.

But it wasn't Zane who'd kept her there so long after her original contract with the town of Sweet Pepper had expired. She'd signed on to help get the town's new fire brigade going after they'd lost county protection last year. She'd done that, and more, since last fall. She should have been home by Thanksgiving.

How could she explain to her father that the ghost of the dead fire chief needed her help?

Eric Gamlyn was supposed to have died a hero in a fire forty years ago. Instead, he'd been shot in the head and shoved into a wall in the old fire station.

"Believe me," she answered her father, "I'm not involved with anyone here, not like you mean. I want to do what's right for the old chief. I can relate to this as a firefighter, Dad. You should be able to relate too."

His tone softened. "You know I love you, right? And you know your mother loves you too. This is driving us both crazy. When your mother is crazy, so am I. Come home, Stella. We need to see your smiling face."

"What did Chief Henry say?"

"That he couldn't keep holding your job open. What else?"

Stella knew that Chief Fred Henry was always more than fair with his people. She also knew he needed a full station house. She was a battalion captain with ten years of experience. The very thing that made her valuable to Sweet Pepper also made her valuable to Chief Henry. She didn't want to take advantage of that knowledge, but she needed more time.

She had to admit that it had been a long ten months of reading through old documents and questioning everyone she could think of about Eric's death at the grain silo back in the 1970s. She didn't feel any closer to an answer about how his body got in the firehouse, or who'd shot him.

Maybe she was wasting her time. Yes, Eric was depressed about losing his status as a local hero to become a murder victim. He was also dead. He might just have to get over it.

It was a long time ago. No one had any ideas about what had happened to him—or was willing to help find those answers.

Sweet Pepper's chief of police, Don Rogers, had been no help at all. She'd all but begged him to exhume the coffin that Eric was supposed to be buried in, but he'd continued to refuse.

There was a stream of reasons for his refusal: it wasn't important enough, it was too expensive, what happened forty years ago didn't matter anymore. Her favorite was: he wasn't police chief back then.

He'd said he was working with the Tennessee Bureau of Investigation, looking into Eric's death. Clearly, someone had made a mistake when they thought they'd buried the old fire chief.

And that was that. Nothing she'd said or done had swayed the chief. She'd even gone to a judge for a court order but nothing had come of it. The skeletal remains they'd found in the firehouse, after it had been gutted by a fire, had been sent to a crime lab at the state capital. There were no results back yet.

Maybe her father was right. She knew she could be stubborn sometimes when she got caught up in something. It wasn't like she could save Eric's life with the information. It was terrible that he'd been murdered instead of dying in the line of duty.

She wanted to help, but she seemed to be spinning her wheels. What could she really do for him anyway?

*Justice.*

Last year that's what she'd told herself she wanted for him. She still did.

On the other hand, she had a life back in Chicago that she'd put on hold almost to the point of it disappearing. Was she willing to give up *her* life to solve the mystery of Eric's death?

Mackie finally threw his tools down in disgust. "She's

not moving anywhere today." He wiped his greasy hands on his denim overalls and looked up at the sun. "I'll have to bring the big tractor out tomorrow to get it. Sorry about the walk back."

They started walking through the neatly drawn rows of peppers and red dirt alternating through the field. Little swirls of dust flew up around their feet.

"Stella? Are you still there?" Her father's voice barked out of the cell phone.

"I'm sorry, Dad. You're probably right." Her hand tightened on the phone with the admission. She didn't like being wrong. "I'll come home."

"When?"

"I'll look at my calendar and set a date as soon as I get back to the cabin."

"We both know there won't be a convenient time. Set a date right now. I'll tell Chief Henry."

"I have to go back to the cabin first." She didn't really need to look at a calendar—she needed to tell Eric her decision. She hated to think how he'd take it.

*I don't want to leave him this way either.*

"You're right. Go back to the cabin and pack a bag. Hop on the Harley and leave now. No time like the present."

She groaned. "I don't know how Mom has lived with you all these years. You're relentless."

"Ah, sure and she loves me, darlin'." He switched to his never-far-away Irish brogue, which she remembered so well from her childhood.

If there were anyone she should have been able to tell about her ghostly housemate and his predicament, it should have been her father. His hearty Irish family was always telling ghost stories and relating terrifying family encounters with *pookas* and the little people back in Ireland.

She *wanted* to tell him. It just wouldn't come out. It was one thing for Great Aunt Nan to recall how her great aunt, also named Nan, met up on a dark road with a creature of the night a hundred years ago. It was another for it to be happening today.

In Sweet Pepper, Stella had found that people still lived with their ghosts—no apologies. They accepted that Eric haunted the cabin and that a ghost from an 1820 carriage accident was still looking for her head on a local bridge.

There was also old Tom Swift who sometimes grabbed unwary visitors along some mountain passes, and a witch who'd been killed in her house who appeared on the anniversary of her death.

It was disconcerting at first to live with people that related stories of the supernatural the way friends back home talked about baseball. Stella had gotten used to it eventually. It would be strange now to go back to Chicago and not hear people talking about such things.

"I can't just leave, Dad," she said finally. "I'll have to set things up."

"You'll at least call tonight with a firm date on when you're leaving Sweet Pepper," her father persisted. "I'm only asking so your mother knows."

"Yes. Tonight. I'll either call or email tonight. I have to go now. My ride is waiting. Talk to you later. Give Mom my love."

The helicopter was down in the field as Stella and Mackie finally walked up. Zane was already out and talking to Mackie about the hot, dry summer they'd been experiencing. There had been countless small brush fires, and one large fire in the national park. Stella's firefighters had participated in all of those fires. Everyone was praying for rain.

Zane was about the same height as Stella, about five-foot-six. He had a shaved head and stocky build. He'd played football through high school and college. His dark eyes always seemed to be laughing. He was a good-natured, easygoing man—uncomplicated—which was what she needed after her last two relationships.

Stella freely admitted that she wasn't uncomplicated like Zane. Her lightly freckled face, stubborn chin, and brown eyes hid a wealth of deep commitment to her career and the people she served. She had been brought up to be responsible, and to know that sacrifice frequently came with her calling.

"Ask me anything about growing peppers," she said to Zane. "I know it all."

Mackie took off his baseball cap with the name of a local feed and seed store on it. He wiped his sweaty face and head with an old red rag that had been tied around his neck.

"Ain't no way. Nobody knows it all—exceptin' maybe the mountain. She knows everything about life, and peppers. But she changes every season."

"Okay. Then I at least know enough to get by during the Sweet Pepper Festival," she said, even though she'd just said she'd be back in Chicago before the event.

Stella knew she'd have to contact Myra Strickland too. Myra ran the festival. She'd have to find another tour guide to take her place. It was one thing on a long to-do list, *if* she decided to leave.

She'd have to make that decision first. It wasn't going to be easy.

Zane put his arm around Stella. "I have to get moving. There was a report of smoke over on the north end of the park. I hope it's only a misguided camper who didn't see the burning-ban signs."

"Me too." She turned to Mackie and shook his rugged, old hand. He'd been farming peppers all of his life, taking it up from his father when he was only twelve. "Thanks for your help. I really feel like I learned something today. Maybe not everything, but enough."

"Well, you give me a call if you have any questions." Mackie smiled, his deeply tanned face splitting into thousands of wrinkles. "And don't be a stranger, hear?"

Stella promised she would let him know how it went. It might be an empty promise if she left before October when the festival took place.

She reminded herself that she hadn't come to Sweet Pepper for the festival. She'd done the job the town hired her to do. They had a new fire brigade.

Maybe it *was* time to go home.

Stella and Zane got into the helicopter. She was in no hurry to get back to the cabin and share her news with Eric. She told Zane it was fine if he went and took a look at the area where smoke had been sighted. Keeping the area safe had to take precedence over everything else.

Zane chattered away about how much fun he'd had the night before when they'd gone to the VFW Night Under the Stars Charity Dance. They'd had dinner and danced until after midnight when their hosts had called an end to the festivities.

That was late for the people of Sweet Pepper, who tended to go to bed by nine p.m. Not much usually stayed open in town after six.

Not that Stella was a party person or got to stay out late much in Chicago either. Her job was demanding. Most of the time she was either too tired to party or she was working. Some of her friends seemed to manage both—like her ex-boyfriend Doug.

He was a cop, but could party with the best of them. That probably should've been a clue to her that they weren't compatible. They'd made their relationship work for a long time—until she'd caught him in bed with a friend of hers from high school.

Stella had punched him and litigation ensued, union reps negotiating. Doug had wanted her kicked out of the fire department. The *snake*!

Chief Henry had been stern but fair. He'd told her to get out of town for a while and it would all blow over. It had been good advice. She'd also been injured in a fire a week before that and couldn't work anyway.

It had been the perfect storm to bring her to Sweet Pepper, where she was supposed to sit around, sipping iced tea and watching volunteers train to fight fires.

*Ha! That hadn't happened.*

Instead, she'd fought fires and investigated arsons. She'd gotten caught up in everything going on in the small town. Now she wasn't sure how to get out of it—or if she wanted to.

"I don't see anything." Zane took the helicopter down close to the trees on the mountain ridge. "Might have been some fog. You know how it goes when it gets dry. Everybody sees smoke."

Stella hadn't known how it was until this summer of very little rain. Seeing a forest fire up close made her understand why people were nervous. A fire in the mountains could mean the destruction of Sweet Pepper, and all the other little towns around the area.

It had been frightening seeing the red and yellow flames eating up the hundred-year-old trees. She'd been terrified that they wouldn't be able to contain it.

Zane swung back around and landed the helicopter near the new Sweet Pepper firehouse.

He kissed her before he left. "I have to get back to the ranger station and make sure everything is all right. I'll see you tonight at Scooter's for supper, right?"

*One last date, maybe?* "Six p.m. Meet you there."

She got out of the helicopter and ran over to the building to get out of the way. Zane waved again as the chopper lifted into the air. Stella decided to see who was on communication duty that day before she went back to the cabin.

*Any excuse not to have to face Eric with her news.*

"Excuse me, Chief Griffin." Sheriff's Deputy Mace Chum stepped out of the shadows created by the overhang of the roof. He wasn't dressed in his usual brown uniform.

He looked *different*—it wasn't only his clothes. There was something about his face and the nervous movements of his hands.

"Deputy Chum." She nodded. "What can I do for you?"

"Well, ma'am, I'm not a deputy anymore. I retired today. But I might be able to do something for *you*. I've heard people say you've been investigating the death of the old fire chief, Eric Gamlyn. I might have some information for you. Could we step inside?"

# Chapter 2

Stella was excited at what Chum might have to say. This felt like the break she'd needed in the case no one else wanted. Chum had served in the county his whole life. He'd hinted before about secrets he couldn't tell her.

Their first meeting had been nothing short of weird. Chum had stopped her for speeding into town on her Harley. She'd taken off her helmet as he was getting ready to write her a ticket—he'd run away like he'd seen a ghost.

Stella realized later why that was.

The "ghost" had come to life for her when she'd learned that her mother had been born and raised in Sweet Pepper. Barbara Carson had never mentioned her origins, even when she'd known her daughter was on her way to work there. There had been a rift in the Carson family when Stella's grandmother, Abigail, had died. Barbara had abruptly left home and had never contacted her father again.

Chum had thought Stella was the ghost of her dead grandmother. She'd understood why when she'd seen a portrait of Abigail. She could've been the other woman, except for the red hair she'd inherited from her father. She actually looked more like her grandmother than her mother.

Chum had explained later that Abigail Carson's case was his first investigation after he'd joined the sheriff's department. He'd only been eighteen at that time and had never forgotten it.

Stella could relate—she'd never forgotten the face of her first fire victim either. Fear and death became part of you as a police officer or a firefighter. They never went away.

She had Chum sit down and closed the door to her rebuilt office in the firehouse, wondering what he wanted to say.

He stared at the filing cabinet to her left but didn't speak.

Stella took the initiative. "So you know something about Eric Gamlyn's death?"

"A little." He sniffed and rubbed his nose then squirmed in the ladder-back chair. "I know what I *saw* that night, is all. I was at the silo fire when the chief died. I saw him run in, and I saw Ricky Hutchins run out without him."

"You were on duty that night?"

"Yes, ma'am." He nodded but still appeared uncomfortable with being there. He kept glancing back at the closed door.

"And the chief never came out of the silo so everyone thought he died there."

Chum glanced around the office, his fingers nervously drumming on his leg. "But he came out, all right. I saw two men take a body out of the back of the silo before the roof collapsed. As far as I know—or anyone else knows—the chief was the only one still inside."

"Who were they? Could you identify them?"

"They were firefighters. Or at least men dressed like firefighters. They were wearing the red Sweet Pepper Fire Brigade T-shirts, like they did back then. Neither one was wearing any protective gear. I wouldn't even have noticed them with everything else going on, but I heard a radio playing and I looked back there."

She sat forward, twirling a pencil, as her thoughts raced. "What did they do with the body?"

"They put him in the trunk of an old Chevy Impala. Then they left with him. Now we know they shot him in the head and put him in that wall out there."

The skeletal remains they'd found out in the garage had been gone for months but that didn't keep either of them from looking out the window in the door as though they could still see them.

"Do you have any idea why someone would want to kill Chief Gamlyn?" She hoped an answer would pop out of his mouth and solve the whole mystery so she could go home with a clear conscience.

"Yes, ma'am. He gave the county hell about taking over the fire service for Sweet Pepper. He wanted to keep the fire brigade local. He fought as hard as he could—until they stopped him."

Stella had heard that story before. It was part of the Eric Gamlyn legend to many people in town. Over the forty years since he'd died, he'd become a folklore hero. His deeds were larger than life—a bit like Paul Bunyan. Eric had even been a lumberjack for several years. The myth grew like hot peppers in the summer sun.

"Why would anyone kill him for that? How could he have stopped the county from taking over? He was only one man."

"People said that the chief had friends up in the state legislature that were looking into making it illegal for the county to take over the local fire departments. It would've been a good thing, I guess, since they had to back out later. It was exactly like Eric said, too expensive, and they couldn't get equipment up here to fight fires fast enough."

"So, if Eric had lived, he might've been able to stop the takeover? There had to be more than that."

"How about thirty million dollars? That's a chunk of change, even today." He leaned closer to her, across the desk.

"You're right. Where did the thirty million dollars come from?"

"It came from the state, funneled through a federal program. The county was supposed to get the money for taking over the local volunteer fire departments, extra expenses and whatnot."

"I see."

"There were some big names involved locally, if you catch my drift. Most of that money never went to the county either. The county firefighters had to struggle on just as they were."

"Where did the money go?" She glanced sharply into his worried eyes.

"I can't say for sure."

Stella digested that information. At least what he said made sense. If Eric had been about to blow someone's big deal, she could understand why they'd want him dead.

"You're talking about my grandfather, aren't you?" She was used to the Carson family being blamed for everything that went wrong in the area.

Personally, she hadn't witnessed anything of the kind from her erstwhile family but there always seemed to be doubts about Ben Carson being involved when bad things happened.

"I ain't saying for sure one way or another." Chum sat back with his arms crossed over his thin chest. The motion accented his red-and-yellow plaid, button-down shirt.

"But you *think* you know, right? Why not say?"

"I'm only saying this much right now because I'm leaving. I already sent my wife on ahead." He played with the plain gold wedding band on his finger. "Most of the people who knew about Chief Gamlyn's death are dead too. The rest—let's say I don't want to take *any* chances."

"You never told anyone about those men taking Eric's body out of the silo?"

He stood up slowly, his old knees creaking. "No, ma'am. And I probably should've kept my mouth shut now. But you still remind me of *her*, of Abigail. I wanted to set you straight before I left. I think she'd want me to."

Stella wished she could think of something to say that would make him sit back down and finish all the sordid details of the story. There was probably some way to play on the fact that she still reminded him of a ghost.

She didn't know what that was. As Eric frequently reminded her—she was a firefighter, not a police detective.

"This isn't much for me to go on." She looked at the pitifully small file she'd started for the investigation into Eric's death.

"I know. And I'm sorry for that. It's hard. I stayed alive and kept my job for the last forty years by keepin' my mouth shut and not looking at what I shouldn't see." He stared at his hands. "I'm ashamed to admit it, but there's the truth."

"Well, thanks for telling me what you could." Stella stood up and shook his hand. "I hope you'll be happy with your new life. I won't tell anyone what you said about Eric."

"I appreciate that, ma'am. I wish I could be more help. I truly do. I hope you figure out what happened to the chief. He was a good man."

Stella was sure she saw tears in his eyes and wondered who or what was chasing him away from Sweet Pepper. She felt sure he didn't really want to go.

"Be careful, Chief Griffin." His thin lips quivered. "There are those who might kill again to keep their secrets quiet."

She watched him leave her office, not closing the door behind him, and sat back in her chair, frustrated. This had to mean something. Chum was scared. He wouldn't have told her if he hadn't been leaving. Clearly he believed someone would kill him if he told the truth.

*But what did it mean?* Would there be enough to follow up on?

That had been the problem since she'd first started looking into Eric's death. It had happened so long ago, most of the people who might know something about it were dead, or said they couldn't remember. Some had moved away without telling anyone where they were going—like Chum was about to do.

Maybe, like Chum, they were scared too. If they believed Eric was killed for someone to get their hands on thirty million dollars, she didn't blame them. There was an answer to what had happened that night at the grain silo. She hadn't dug deeply enough yet.

*Are you making excuses for staying in Sweet Pepper instead of going back home?*

She didn't believe that. It wasn't that she didn't *want* to go back to her old life—the idea of leaving before this was settled was what bothered her. She wanted to find the answers for Eric, and for the rest of the people in Sweet Pepper. They had a right to know.

She left her office when she heard the sound of an engine starting up in the garage.

She was never sure, without consulting her calendar, who was on duty in communications that day. They had to run eight-hour shifts, with one person on duty at all times, to relay emergency calls to firefighters, and to keep their designation as a fire department.

Ricky Hutchins Jr. was there. He was one of her chosen second-in-commands. He was funny, dedicated, and hardworking—not to mention good with trucks. He'd been on her doorstep the first morning she'd interviewed volunteers. After that, he had become indispensable.

"Is there a problem?" Stella stuck her head under the large hood of the fire engine/ladder truck.

She had to yell over the sound from it, and the loud music

coming from inside the cab. "Why does the music have to be as loud as the engine?"

"If you think that's loud, you should hear my dad's music." Ricky laughed. "Thank goodness he's got earbuds now. Like father, like son."

"And it has to be loud?"

"I guess so."

"No problem with the engine?"

"No, ma'am. She sounds great!" He revved the big engine to demonstrate and then hopped into the cab and shut it down. "That new belt made a world of difference."

"Good. Glad to hear it. It was expensive enough. I expect someone from the town council to come and inspect the old one to make sure it was bad."

He laughed as he closed the hood. "Let 'em come. I've still got it out back. And if they could put it in any cheaper, I'll be glad to step aside and let one of them take care of these babies. But I don't think so, do you?"

Stella laughed with him as she thought about *any* member of the town council climbing under the hood to work on an engine. "It was an expensive month. They'll get over it."

"Yeah. Hey, speaking of expenses, Jack Carriker was here before. He said he left a bill on your desk for the repair work on the drywall. You should probably back-charge Royce for putting that ladder through the wall."

"Thanks for the advice. You know it wasn't his fault."

"Yeah, right." Ricky grinned. "How's your bike doing?"

"Fine. Your friend did a good job putting it back together. I don't think my dad will be able to tell the difference when I go home."

He cleaned his hands on a greasy rag as he studied her face. "You know, everyone is wondering about that."

"Wondering when I'm going home?"

"Wondering how much longer you're going to be here, Chief."

"Trying to get rid of me?"

Ricky was a few years younger than Stella. He smiled his little-boy, girl-chasing smile. She was sure it had melted many girls' hearts.

His curly blond hair left one curl on his forehead, like Superman, and his deep blue eyes searched hers. "No. I wish you'd stay."

"It's gonna be hard to make chief that way." She joked though she knew he was serious. "I'm not that much older than you. You've got a while before I think about retirement."

"Yeah. I don't care. You pull us together, you know? Sweet Pepper needs you. I think you need us too."

"Thanks, Ricky." She looked up at the freshly painted white ceiling in the garage. Everyone, including her, was asking the same question.

"You could stay," he suggested. "Sweet Pepper's not Chicago, but it's got a lot going for it."

"I know. I like Sweet Pepper. It's a great place. But it's not home. I've got friends and family in Chicago. I've got a job too—if I go ahead and get back to it."

"I hear you." He tidied up his work area by the engine. "Why are you staying then, Chief? I know you're not here because we found Eric's old bones in the wall. That's a mystery that probably won't ever get solved."

Stella knew she *could* tell Ricky about Eric's ghost. He'd been one of the first people to tell her the cabin was haunted. She could explain that she didn't want to leave Eric until she knew what had happened to him. Ricky would certainly understand that.

She didn't say it.

It was silly, but her relationship with Eric was weird and sort of private. She knew if she told anyone in Sweet Pepper about him being there, he or she would ask after him every time they saw her. While she was willing to acknowledge, after a lot of doubt, that he was haunting the cabin, she didn't want to discuss it with anyone else. The whole supernatural phenomena didn't sit as well with her as it did with others in town.

"I know. I guess I feel bad about it. I'm living in the house he built and working with his fire brigade. Not to mention that I'm a Sweet Pepper fire chief too. We have a connection. I don't want to end up dead in a wall someday."

Ricky impulsively hugged her. "You don't have to worry about that, Chief. I won't let that happen to you. If you need to go, you need to go. You've worked on this for a long time. I don't know how much more you can do."

"Thanks."

"One thing I was wondering about—Dad was wondering too. Chief Gamlyn is supposed to be buried up at the cemetery. If that was him in the wall, who's buried there?"

"Good question." She frowned. "I've been trying to get Don Rogers to exhume that coffin since last fall. He won't do it without a court order. The thing is—he won't go after one, and every time I've tried, I've struck out."

"Doesn't surprise me. Probably those same people who had Eric killed in the first place are still trying to keep it under wraps. They're out there, you know. Dad said everyone knew Eric was killed because he fought the county taking over the fire brigade. No one could prove it."

"So everyone said."

Ricky's father—Ricky Senior—owned the Sweet Pepper Café with his wife, Lucille. Ricky Senior was the last man to see Eric alive. He was the one Eric saved in the silo that night, a member of the original fire brigade.

Stella had talked to Ricky Senior first when she'd begun her investigation into Eric's death. He said he'd only seen Eric briefly in the burning building, where he'd almost been overcome by smoke. Eric had given him his face mask and sent him out of the silo. Ricky thought Eric was right behind him when he'd made it to safety.

They had all waited, but Eric had never come out. After the fire was contained, a crew from the coroner's office had located Eric's charred remains inside. The roof had collapsed on him during the fire.

She'd read the accounts of it, written by members of the fire brigade and others. It had been a difficult fire, lasting for hours. Large amounts of dry grain had burned through the night.

Eric never had a chance once he was trapped in there. They'd brought what was left of him out and there was a huge memorial service for him.

Now they knew the truth and the question was, how did he get into a wall in the firehouse with a bullet in his head?

Frustration filled Stella. With Chum's statement about seeing two men take a body out of the silo, more questions were raised without the first one being answered.

Mace Chum wondered if he'd made a mistake going to see Chief Griffin before he'd left town. He glanced into his rearview mirror. There was no one behind him. The road stretched out empty before him.

He was nervous. No reason for it. They'd never expect him to tell anything. Not after all these years. He was gonna be fine.

A black car came out of nowhere. One minute, Chum was alone. The next, the car was speeding up beside him.

He looked out the window, his heart racing.

There was a popping sound.

Then the old truck, and the trailer it pulled, crashed down the side of the mountain.

# Chapter 3

～～～～～

**I**'m going up to the cabin," Stella finally told Ricky.
She needed to talk to Eric about what Chum had
said—and about her leaving Sweet Pepper.

He'd known from the beginning that she wasn't going to
stay. She didn't want to spring it on him right before she
walked out the door.

"I expect you'll find Hero waiting for you up there,"
Ricky said. "I saw him running up Firehouse Road. I think
he likes it better up there ever since we had to rebuild the
firehouse."

Stella thanked him for the information and went in back
to get her Harley. She knew he was right about Hero, the
fire brigade's adopted Dalmatian puppy. Well, not so much
a puppy anymore. He wasn't a year old yet, but he was getting big.

She knew why Hero liked it at the cabin—he liked being
around Eric. She was fairly sure Eric liked the puppy too.
In fact, she believed Eric used some kind of ghost telepathy
to call the dog up there every day.

It was all right with her that Hero spent his time there—unless there was training going on. Hero and his mother, Sylvia, were training for their own certifications as rescue dogs. It was good for them to work with the volunteers. At some point, she hoped the dogs would go out with them on calls.

Hero was going to have to be added to that ever-growing list of things she had to take care of before she left Sweet Pepper. Eric would have to stop calling the puppy up to the cabin when no one was living there. The volunteers couldn't go after him all the time. It would probably mean that he wouldn't see Hero anymore.

Something had happened after the firehouse was rebuilt. Eric couldn't get down there anymore. She had no idea how that worked, though she thought it might be the trauma of seeing his own bones in the wall. *What would that be like?*

Her ghostly roommate didn't understand it either and had refused to discuss it. Eric could out-stubborn her anytime.

Stella put on her helmet and sat down on her father's old bike. The eighty-inch black Harley was one of the last made with a kick start. She and her father had rebuilt the engine and added a super E carburetor before she'd brought the bike to Sweet Pepper. They'd found some old fiberglass saddle-bags, which had held everything she thought she'd need from home.

She wasn't supposed to buy extra things, but of course she did. A lot would be going home via FedEx.

The bike started easily and purred through the firehouse parking lot. The transmission was getting a little tired and clunked into first.

She passed the new red Jeep Cherokee the town had purchased for the fire brigade last year after she'd wrecked her bike. She knew it was for everyone, but right at that moment, the driver's-side door said *"Sweet Pepper Fire*

*Chief, Stella Griffin.*" It always made her smile when she saw it.

*Ego?*

Probably. She'd never be fire chief back home. She might as well enjoy it while she could.

Once she got her Harley repaired, she never drove the Cherokee unless it was official business. She still liked her bike better anyway, but it had been great having the town look out for her that way.

They'd never found the hit-and-run driver who'd left her in the ditch, unconscious. It seemed there were a lot of mysteries for such a small town.

The bike took the curves on the road up the mountain as though it had been born to do it. Her father had taken the bike across the country when he'd graduated from college. He'd seen the Rockies and driven through the desert. The Harley did okay for all of its adventures. She hoped she'd be in that kind of shape when she was its age.

Stella knew she would never forget the smell of the pine trees and the cool shadows on her way up this road. She'd never forget evenings sitting on the back deck of the old cabin, looking down at the Little Pigeon River. Even though she'd only been there a year, there were many memories she'd hold forever.

*Like Eric.*

She reached the log cabin too quickly. She'd wanted to have words prepared to tell him that she had to move on. Nothing had come to mind while she'd followed the road. It wasn't going to be easy to say goodbye.

The log cabin was two-story, built with large, rough-hewn pine logs. It wasn't huge—there was one big bedroom, a large living area with a fireplace, and a small kitchen.

She spent most of her time, even during the winter, on the big deck in back. It had required some serious layering to be out there while it was snowing and the winds were howling down the mountain, but it had been worth all the effort.

Eric had laughed at her for wearing two sweaters and wrapping a blanket around her. Of course, he didn't feel the cold anymore. He claimed he was warm-blooded when he was alive and wouldn't have needed that much covering then either.

Another piece of Eric Gamlyn's mythology. It was always weird thinking that he'd been dead before she was even born.

She parked the Harley and heard Hero barking inside the cabin. The front porch light was on. Eric always turned it on when she went out. It had been one of the first things that had made her wonder what was wrong with the cabin.

Stella paused before she went inside. She realized that one of the reasons she felt guilty leaving Eric without answers about his death was because he had saved her life.

When the old firehouse, the one he'd built at the same time as the cabin, had caught on fire last year, she didn't expect to make it out. It was Eric who'd come for her. He'd helped her out of the smoke and flames, fulfilling his image as a local hero, even after his death.

How could she leave before she found answers for him? Where she came from, you repaid your debts.

But what if Ricky was right and the answers never came? Was she willing to live her whole life here trying to figure out the mystery?

The front door opened. Stella walked up the short flight of stairs, past the bear-proof trashcans, and inside the kitchen. Hero was jumping around and barking, happy to see her. Eric was indulging in his new pastime—cooking. It seemed that when he put his mind to being able to do something physical, he could do whatever it was.

In this case, since the discovery of his bones in the fire-house, it was cooking. Thankfully, the kitchen was small, otherwise there was no telling how much food he could make in a day.

As it was, she came home to three different types of cakes on the tiny table located between the kitchen area and the sofa. Eric had baked macaroni and cheese the night before.

Obviously, he was trying to work out his frustrations over losing his dying hero status in the community. That was *her* diagnosis anyway. He'd claimed it didn't matter to him how he died. She knew better.

Eric hadn't sulked after what had happened—he'd talked more than ever. Not about anything to do with the discovery of his true death or what had caused him to lose his ability to travel down to the firehouse to hang out. She had no idea how he really felt about the important things.

"Stella! I'm making baked custard. I saw it on a cooking show today. I'm afraid we're out of milk now. I have that, and some other things, on a list for when you go back out. I'm thinking about pickling my own fish. What do you think?"

"I think everyone is enjoying all the food you're making—that they think *I'm* making—but we're not really dealing with the issues. Can you put the custard down long enough to talk to me about a few things? I have some news."

Eric was tall, well over six feet. He had broad shoulders and a wide chest. He'd been thirty-five when he died. He would always be young. His longish blond hair would always be tied back with a leather thong at the base of his neck. It seemed he was also doomed to go through the afterlife wearing a red Sweet Pepper Fire Brigade T-shirt and jeans. The outfit worked for him, though, emphasizing his muscled chest and arms.

He had the most brilliant blue eyes Stella had ever seen. She wasn't sure if that was because he was dead or if he'd always looked that way. The only pictures she'd seen of him were in black-and-white.

"I'm about to put the custard in the oven. What do you want to talk about?"

"I had a visitor today at the firehouse." Stella sat down on the chair beside the sofa. "It seems Mace Chum is retiring from the sheriff's department and moving away."

She explained what Chum had told her. She could see the thundercloud coming over his still handsome face.

"That's ridiculous. There's no way fire brigade members took anyone out of the silo and stuffed him in a trunk. That goes for me or anyone else. Deputy Chum must have had a problem seeing through the smoke."

"Eric, someone took your body and moved it from the silo to the firehouse. You don't have any idea who that was?"

"I told you before, I don't remember anything after I gave Ricky my face mask and watched him run out through the smoke. I don't know what happened after that."

"Well then we have to assume that Chum knows more than you about what happened that night. Can you think of anyone who would have wanted you dead?"

"I'm sure there were plenty of people I made angry down through the years. I wouldn't have thought I made them angry enough to kill me—with one exception."

He gave her a knowing look and she smiled. "Except for Ben Carson, right? What did you do to him that he might want to kill you?"

"It was the whole thing with the county taking over the fire brigade. We didn't need them, and I knew they couldn't fulfill their part of the bargain." He grinned at her. "Which is why *you're* here."

"There was a lot of money that the county was supposed to get for taking on the new fire departments that went missing too, according to Chum. Did you know about that?"

"I guess that was after my time. When I died, they were

starting to talk about appropriating money for the project. How much was involved?"

"Chum said thirty million."

He whistled. "That's a lot of incentive."

"Why blame my grandfather? He was already wealthy. He didn't need that money."

"There's no such thing as a wealthy man who doesn't need more money."

They were about to get off-course, as they always did when they talked about Ben Carson. Stella steered them back to the important questions.

"None of this seems familiar to you? Nothing that jogs your memory?"

"No. I told you, I have no recollection of anything happening after helping Ricky Senior get out of the silo."

The timer went off on the stove and he rushed to take out a pan of brownies before putting the custard into the oven.

Stella thought it was probably just as well that he couldn't remember what had happened to him. It seemed to her that it would be more painful to remember his death than to suddenly find out he didn't die the way he thought.

It still left her with the same problem—no answers.

"Chum told you this because he's leaving town?" Eric looked at the brownies.

"Yes. He said he never told anyone else because he was afraid of the consequences."

"That doesn't surprise me."

"Eric—" She wanted to tell him that she might not have the time to make sense of the whole thing and that she might have to go home if she wanted to keep her real job.

A knock on the door interrupted them.

"You should hide," she whispered.

"Really? You're the only one who can see me, except for Tagger."

"Sorry. Sometimes I forget."

It was Walt Fenway on the doorstep. He was the retired chief of police for Sweet Pepper and had been a good friend of Eric's.

"Hello, Stella." He looked around her and into the kitchen. "Eric? Are you here, buddy?"

Walt couldn't see or hear Eric but he believed his ghost was there. He'd visited frequently since she'd told him she could communicate with his friend.

Walt was different than Ricky Junior and some of the others in town. He was a hard-nosed, good-hearted man who believed in ghosts but wasn't crazy about it. He wouldn't go around spreading the word that the stories about the cabin were true.

"He's here." She moved aside for him to enter. "He's cooking. It seems to be his stress reliever. Please, take some food with you."

Walt laughed. He was barely five feet tall with a pelt of yellow-white hair that resembled an old bear rug. If it ever saw a comb or brush, Stella hadn't seen it.

He lived at Big Bear Springs, an unincorporated community outside of Sweet Pepper, served by the fire brigade.

Stella and Walt watched the brownie pan float by from the stovetop to a cooling rack on the table.

Walt didn't bat an eyelash. "Smells good. I heard someone mention the other day what a good cook you are, Stella. Guess it wasn't you, huh?"

Eric laughed. "She can barely make toast."

"I can cook." She frowned.

"What did he say?" Walt asked.

"Never mind," Stella said. "Let's say Eric fancies himself a gourmet chef now because he's watched so many cooking shows."

Walt sat down at the table in front of a three-layer chocolate cake. "This is something! I think you should give these cakes to the church for their bake sale."

"Good idea," she agreed. "Coffee?"

"Please." Walt glanced around the room as he always did, not sure where Eric was. He wanted more than anything to see his old friend. He would've been satisfied just to hear him. Since he couldn't do either, he had to let Stella tell him what Eric said.

It was one thing to sit around and talk about ghosts and another thing to really *know* one was there. Craziest darn thing he'd ever encountered—and he'd seen some dillies while he was police chief.

"Heard some news today, Stella," Walt said. "The coroner received word back from the state. Those were definitely Eric's bones in the firehouse. Looks like they have no choice but to dig up his coffin and take a look inside now—whether they want to or not."

# Chapter 4

~~~~~~~~

"The coroner, Judd Streeter, is a friend of mine. We go way back. He actually did the autopsy on—" Walt grimaced and looked around the room. "Well, let's just say the *remains* that were taken out of the silo forty years ago. He said that was Eric at the time. Now he's saying that was Eric in the wall. The state doesn't like those kinds of errors."

Stella watched Eric turn away. She guessed no amount of baking could make this any better. The sooner he acknowledged what had happened to him, the better. He kept saying he couldn't remember. She wasn't sure if he was telling the truth or simply didn't want to talk about it.

"Whatever helps us figure out what happened." She wished they didn't have to talk about it in front of Eric. She knew it had to be hard for him.

Walt didn't like discussing Eric's death either, knowing his friend was standing around listening. "Hope you're okay, buddy. I don't know if I'd want to be here with someone talking about me being dead."

"How could Eric's bones have ended up in the firehouse

instead of his coffin? No offense to your friend, but was he drinking or something?"

"Judd is the most sober man I've ever known." Walt defended Judd. "It was a mistake. Everyone makes them."

"So how did my body end up in the firehouse wall?" Eric stalked back and forth through the cabin, moving right through the furniture as though it wasn't there. "And who's in my coffin?"

Stella translated for Walt. "Eric is a little upset about the mistake."

"I knew it was either that or we're having an earthquake." Walt grinned. "The whole place is moving around."

"He's got a good point," Stella said. "It's what I've been saying to Chief Rogers for months. Now that we can actually prove the remains in the firehouse belonged to Eric, we should get some answers."

"Personally, I think he expected to find Eric in that silo, like we all did, and it colored his judgment. He said there's a notation in his report about a metal rod in the leg of the remains he found in the silo. You didn't have a rod in your leg, did you, buddy?"

"You mean the whole thing was a mix-up?" Eric struggled to understand. "Judd identified the wrong body as mine—and then I was buried in the wall?"

Stella didn't think that was it. Chum's description of that night made what happened more evident.

"I don't know how that second part happened," Walt said. "Judd is kind of convinced there's another body in your coffin. He thinks the mortuary made the mistake."

"Which still doesn't explain Eric's bones in the firehouse," Stella reminded him. "I don't think the mortuary put him there after he was shot either."

"I know. I didn't say it made any sense. I plan to be there when they dig up the coffin." Walt slurped his coffee. "I want to make sure it's all on the up-and-up this time. You planning on going since you championed that cause for so long?"

Stella nodded. "I'll be there. I'm sure there must be some kind of explanation for all of this. I hope exhuming the coffin gives us some answers. Then all we have to do is figure out who pulled the trigger. I think that's usually the toughest part."

Walt agreed. "I hope we find some answers too. You stayed all this time because you were looking out for Eric. He saved your life, after all. You have a reason to be grateful to him."

Eric stared at her. "That's why you stayed?"

"I stayed because I wanted to know the truth about what happened to you," Stella said. "Not out of gratitude, although I'm grateful to you for saving my life. I might have to go home soon, though. They won't hold my job forever, and my parents are getting worried."

"I understand," Eric said. "I didn't expect you to stay this long, and certainly not on my behalf. I'm *dead*, Stella. There's not much anyone can do to hurt me, or help me, anymore."

"What's he saying now?" Walt asked.

Stella was too busy debating with Eric to relate his words to Walt.

"Don't pretend you aren't upset about the idea that you were murdered instead of dying in the silo fire saving Ricky Senior's life. I know you haven't wanted to talk about it, but I could tell you were covering up." Stella defied Eric to disagree with her about it.

"I wasn't covering up. What difference does it make to me now? I think you should go back to Chicago. You've done what you came to do. I'm grateful to you for setting up the new fire brigade. That doesn't mean you have to stay here the rest of your life."

She stood as close to him as she could. It wasn't exactly

like standing next to a living person. He was light and energy, crackling like electricity in the small space between them.

"Why are you grateful for the new fire brigade if nothing matters to you? Your legacy is safe."

He towered over her. "It's not only about my legacy. I want what's best for my hometown. You did that by setting up the new fire brigade. I'm grateful. You can accept that and go home."

"That's exactly what I'm going to do." She folded her arms across her chest. "I guess that means we're even. I saved your stupid fire brigade and you saved my life. That's it. We're done."

"That's right. We're done." Eric disappeared in a puff of smoke that felt like warm fog on her face.

"Nice trick." Walt was only able to see the aftermath of the argument. *It must have been a doozy.* "You'll have to teach me to do that when I pass over, buddy."

"He's gone," Stella told him. "At least I can't see him. Do you want me to tell you what he said?"

"I think I got the idea. You're going home. He doesn't want you to go."

"I don't think that's it. He doesn't want to admit that it bothers him that someone killed him. After all, he's the Paul Bunyan of Sweet Pepper. How could someone kill him? Not good for the myth of Eric Gamlyn."

"I know I only heard one side of the conversation, but that's not what it sounded like to me. Excuse me for asking— I know I'm good at sticking my nose in where it doesn't belong—have you got feelings for Eric?"

*"Feelings?"* Stella thought about it. "You mean *romantic* feelings? He's dead, Walt. How could I have feelings for him? Talk about relationships that can't go anywhere."

Walt shrugged. "It wouldn't be the first time someone fell in love with the wrong person. Eric is a ghost, but he's still got that same charisma that always made the ladies flock to him."

"I don't think so. And trust me, if he ever *had* charisma, he's lost it. He's so stubborn. He always has to be right, not to mention that he's the worst roommate in the world. He doesn't clean up after himself and he has no respect for my privacy. If I have feelings for him, it's pity because he's stuck up here alone."

"Well, it's best that you don't have those type of feelings for a dead man anyway, Stella. You need a nice *living* man so you can have some kids and settle down. You know that's never gonna happen with Eric, right?"

"I don't have those types of feelings for Eric." Her voice was as resolute as any command she'd ever given on the fire line. "I'm dating Zane Mullis. He's a nice guy. I'm not staying, so nothing will come of it. He's alive and breathing. You don't have to worry."

"Okay. You don't have to convince *me*." Walt winked at her. "When are you thinking about leaving Sweet Pepper?"

"I don't know. Probably sometime soon." Unconsciously she glanced around the room in much the same way Walt did when he spoke to Eric. "I have to tie up a few loose ends. I feel like I should be here for the exhumation since I pushed so hard for it, even if it doesn't clear up all the questions."

"Let me know. I'll buy you a drink before you go. We'll all miss you, Stella. Chicago doesn't know how lucky it is to get you back."

He gave her an awkward hug and then left the cabin. Stella watched him pull his old pickup out of the drive until she couldn't see it anymore.

When she turned to face the empty cabin, she felt strange and vulnerable. Usually if Eric was there, he showed himself. He wasn't even on the back deck, looking out over the river. She felt alone for the first time since she'd acknowledged that she was actually living with a ghost.

She jumped when the fire alarm went off from her emergency radio. There was no cell service on the mountain. Hero started jumping and barking as the call continued.

Stella was glad for the interruption in whatever was going on between her and Eric. She urged Hero to run down the mountain and left quickly on the Harley after him.

Eric watched her leave from the bedroom window. Lucky for him, Walt couldn't see his face. His old friend knew him too well for him to be able to hide his feelings for Stella.


"There's a structure fire at Fourth and Magnolia," Ricky yelled as he put on his bunker coat and boots.

Stella watched as other members of the fire brigade hurried into the parking lot at the firehouse, running from their cars and trucks to join the group.

As usual, she took out her clipboard and stopwatch. It was important to keep track of how long it took the group to respond to a call. Information had to be kept for state records as well as insurance companies that had policyholders in the Sweet Pepper area. Their speedy response to an incident was what kept insurance rates down.

Banyin Watts, the town librarian, came in the door first, huffing and puffing as she tried to catch her breath after her sprint from the car. She was taller than Stella but also carried a lot more weight. She'd managed to keep up with training but had put on a few extra pounds since the first of the year, making it harder for her.

JC Burris and his friend, Royce Pope, worked at the Sweet Pepper bottling factory. They were both black men in their thirties, mid-height, wiry, strong, and quick. They seemed to be everywhere at once during a fire.

Kimmie and David Spratt brought Hero's mother, Sylvia, with them as they always did. Both dogs had been rescued by the Spratts, who had later joined the fire brigade. The

Spratts were a little timid during training and fires, but they put their hearts into what they did.

"Where do you want me, Chief?" Patricia "Petey" Stanze was already in her gear, fire ax in hand.

Petey was Ricky's co-assistant fire chief. She was ninety pounds of tough determination, always out in front. She was a waitress at Scooter's Barbecue who worked hard to impress. Stella couldn't believe, at first, that she could keep up with men more than twice her size.

"You ride in the pumper. Kent will drive." Stella raised her voice so everyone could hear her over the sounds of getting their gear. "Everyone else, you know where you belong."

"Aye, Chief!" Kent Norris called out. He was an over-the-road trucker the fire brigade was fortunate to have as a volunteer. He was starting to get a little stomach from his wife's good cooking, but he was in good shape for a man in his forties.

"Where do you want me, Chief?" Tagger Reamis's rheumy brown eyes were hopeful that he was needed somewhere.

Tagger was a veteran of Eric's fire brigade. He was a little too old to actually train or go out on calls, probably in his mid to late seventies, but he knew the routines and he'd picked up on communications quickly.

Stella reminded herself that he was around the same age Eric would've been now if he'd survived.

"Monitor communications." Stella put on her gear. "Depending on where this is, we might need help from the forest service. I don't want to take a chance on starting another forest fire."

He saluted smartly. "You got it. Nothing will get by me."

Ricky Junior laughed as he and Stella headed out to the engine. "Chief, Fourth and Magnolia is nowhere near the forest."

"We have dangerous fire conditions," she explained. "All we need is a wind gust that carries burning ash to catch other trees on fire. We have to think ahead. The worst that will happen, if Tagger notifies the forest service, is that they'll be alerted for nothing."

She opened the engine door, passenger side, and that was all the invitation Hero needed. The young dog jumped into the cab and took his place on the seat between Ricky and Stella. He had begun to show his merit with the team, going into burning buildings to help check for anyone stranded inside.

Stella couldn't help but think that if Eric had a dog like Hero that night at the silo fire, he might have made it out alive. Maybe he realized it too, and that's why he'd grown so attached to the dog.

Thinking about Eric brought up a whole flurry of problems that she didn't want to deal with during the emergency. All of the volunteers needed their wits about them when they answered a call. It was their most important weapon.

To focus, she checked the time as the engine pulled out of the firehouse parking lot with the pumper/tanker and the Cherokee behind it.

"Good time," she remarked. "Looks like Bert couldn't make it."

Bert Wando was a high school senior, the star quarterback of the Sweet Pepper Cougars, and the son of Mayor Erskine Wando.

Even though he was a favorite of everyone local, he hadn't let it go to his head. He was a big help on the team too.

But he had developed an unfortunate problem of not showing up on time for training or for emergency calls. She hated to do it, but she was going to have to talk to him. They didn't have a large group of volunteers. If he couldn't make it, she'd have to recruit someone else.

Also missing from the group was Marty Lawrence, her

grandfather's stepson. There was no actual relationship between them, as he kept reminding Stella. He'd been trying to insinuate a romance between them—it wasn't happening for her.

She'd wondered many times if that was the only reason he'd joined the fire brigade, to get close to her. Many people had intimated that Marty wouldn't get anything when her grandfather died and he was cozying up to her for a share of the money.

Stella thought it was more likely that he'd planned to spy on them for her grandfather.

She felt bad thinking that about her own grandfather. A lot of it was due to people in the area always accusing Ben Carson of terrible things. She wasn't completely immune to their whispered accusations.

Whatever it was that had prompted Marty to join the fire brigade, he wasn't holding up his end of the bargain. Stella was going to have to put her foot down about him not showing up. She needed people like Petey and Ricky, Banyin and Kent, Royce and JC, who were dedicated and engaged. Even Tagger attended all the training and was there for calls.

The only other face missing from the group was police Captain John Trump. That was a whole other story. He was probably on duty at his real job, working as a Sweet Pepper police officer.

Ricky drove the 1976 fire engine like a race car, sliding along the curves and running too fast into town. She couldn't complain since he always got them there quickly and safely.

He'd blamed his fast driving on his grandfather, who he'd claimed was a moonshine runner. Stella wasn't sure about that history, but Ricky drove like a professional. He'd terrified her at first, but she trusted him now. He'd never gone off-road with the engine or hit anything. That was what mattered.

She saw John Trump climb out of his police car as they arrived at their destination.

"Hey there, Chief." He greeted her with careful politeness. "I called this in. You made good time."

"Thanks." She kept her gaze on the house, where she saw neither smoke nor flame. "What's going on?"

"That power pole over there snapped." He pointed to the dark brown pole that was very near the small white house. Sparks were flying around it where the lines had broken.

"Not sure what happened, but the lines are close to the house. I called the power company too, but they won't be out here for at least thirty minutes. They're coming from Sevierville. You know how that goes. It made me nervous, so I called in the alarm. Better safe than sorry, right?"

She nodded. "You did right. We should be here, just in case. We should probably take a look around, make sure everything is okay."

"Sorry I missed dressing out for the call. I knew you'd understand once you got here."

"I was wondering where you were," she admitted. "You never miss a call."

He smiled, but his gaze was guarded. "I'm here anyway. Maybe that will get me off of the no-show list I know you keep."

Stella knew she wouldn't miss these awkward conversations with John when she left Sweet Pepper. They'd dated for a while last year. It hadn't worked out. He blamed her grandfather—the whole Carson bloodline actually—for his father's death.

When she'd decided to stay in Sweet Pepper after her contract was up, John had been certain she was fulfilling his prophecy that she couldn't pass up the Carson money and power.

He'd called it quits. Stella had been relieved.

It was too much pressure trying to keep up with his off-again, on-again idea of romance. His intense hatred of a family she couldn't help but be part of was stupid. She needed someone fun, like Zane.

"Let's go up and take a look around," Stella said to Ricky and Petey.

She'd assigned each of them members of the group for their teams. It made it easier to know who was with whom when they were working and gave both her co-assistant chiefs experience being in charge.

Understanding their duties from long hours of training, the teams split up to assess the situation. Before anyone could move from their position at the street, Hero and Sylvia started frantically barking. They whined and pulled at their leashes, something they never did at a call.

Stella glanced up at the house and saw the first lick of red flame shoot out of the roof. "Never mind. Let's get the hoses."

# Chapter 5

~~~~~~~~

"**I** checked it out," John said. "There's no one in the house."

"Any pets?" Kimmie Spratt asked.

"Not that I saw."

"We'll have to get inside anyway," Stella said. "Why don't you and David take the dogs and check that out. Not everyone has pet stickers on their doors."

"Will do, Chief," Kimmie said.

Petey's team was connecting one of the smaller hoses to the fire hydrant. Ricky's team was using the thermal heat sensor to find hot spots in the house before they went inside.

"Watch out for those live wires," Stella yelled as Kent Norris got a little too close to the fallen power pole. "John, see if you can rush the power company. The situation has changed. We need those wires shut down now."

"I'll see what I can do." John got back in the car to call for help again.

"Those wires aren't even touching the house," Allen Wise said. He was a barber in town when he wasn't volunteering. "How could that cause a fire in the house?"

"The current builds back to the house," Stella explained. "The wires don't have to touch anything. Current can be carried through the ground or through the wires that are still connected to the house."

"Has anyone contacted the homeowners?" Petey asked. "Do we know who lives here?"

"Gerald Hatley and his wife live here," Allen replied. "I know them from church. They're probably down at the senior center. Want me to give them a call?"

"Do that," Stella agreed as she turned to John. "Anything from the power company?"

He shook his head. "They said someone's on the way. That's it."

Stella used her cell phone to call Tagger at the firehouse. "Find me an electrician. We need someone to take care of these lines before one of us gets hurt."

"I know just the person, Chief. I'll send him right out," Tagger promised.

"We found an old cat," David Spratt reported over the radio. "I think Kimmie has a carrier for her. We should be right out with her."

"Good news," Stella responded. "What about the fire?"

"The kitchen looks bad," David said.

"Copy that," Ricky said. "We're inside. The only room that seems to be engaged is the kitchen. Get the hose in here. We've got the windows out."

"Copy that," Petey added. "We're coming your way."

Everything seemed to be fine—until Royce and JC made it up the hill with the hose. As they turned on the water, there was a momentary loss of control. Water sprayed across the transformer, sending deadly sparks toward them.

Royce was yelling at Banyin for dropping her part of the hose. JC said to leave it alone and got his friend to focus on getting the hose into the kitchen window to put out the flame.

Stella watched as Banyin deserted her post, running back down the hill in tears from Royce's tirade. Petey picked up the hose that Banyin had dropped and called Kent in for support.

Kimmie and David walked down the hill with both dogs following. David was carrying a blue carrier with the cat inside.

"We think she's okay, Chief." Kimmie smiled at the gray cat. "She wasn't even near the fire and there wasn't much smoke yet. Should we have her checked out by a vet?"

"Wait until the owners get here," Stella said. "Leave her here with me. The two of you go back up and see if anyone needs you."

"The fire is out," Petey said over the radio. "Ricky is checking for hot spots but I think we got here in time and this was it."

The transformer was still sparking along with the downed wires. Smoke was coming from that direction and Stella pointed her firefighters that way. "Don't get too close. It looks like the pole could be on fire."

Elvis Vaughn chugged up in his old pickup that proclaimed him as an electrician but also added varmint removal as his secondary occupation.

"Chief Griffin." He always reminded Stella of the grizzled old prospectors who were killed for their claims in Western movies. "Looks like you got a problem out here."

"Can you help?" She cut to the chase. "I can't get the power company out here to do their job. We need the power cut to the pole and to the house."

He pushed his worn Sweet Pepper Festival ball cap back on his head. "Let me get my tools."

It only took Elvis a few minutes and the sparks were gone. Petey made sure the pole wasn't on fire, easier now since she didn't have to worry about being electrocuted.

The Hatleys came home, scared and devastated by the

mess they found. Betsy Hatley started crying when she saw that her cat, Miss Tibbit, had been saved. Gerald Hatley shook hands with everyone there, thanking them for their help.

"You'll need someplace to stay," Stella told them. "At least until you can get things cleaned up. Do you have someone who can help you out?"

Betsy wiped her eyes as she hugged the cat carrier to her chest. "Our daughter lives a few miles away. We'll stay with her. Thank you for asking, Chief Griffin. And bless you for saving our house."

"It's our job, ma'am." Stella always said the same thing, as though it was nothing that they risked their lives to be there. Still the Hatleys' words warmed her heart and told her she was in the right line of work.

"Let's get it cleaned up," Petey told her team. "We need that hose back down here on the truck."

"What happened to Banyin today?" Stella asked. "I can't believe she dropped the hose and ran. Do you think she got scared?"

Petey shrugged. "I don't know what's going on with her. The last two times we've gone out, she got all emotional. Not as bad as this. Do you want me to talk to her?"

"No, I will. Let's leave it for now and head back to the firehouse. Thanks, Petey."

Ricky came down the hill carrying a pike pole. "Nothing much to that. Just a kitchen. It was hardly worth coming out for."

Stella was glad the Hatleys were talking to John, too far away from where she was standing to hear his smart remark.

"Don't make me institute sensitivity training," she threatened. "It's a lot more than a kitchen for the victims."

"Sorry." He glanced toward the old couple. "I only meant—never mind."

"I've already forgotten it. Don't let me hear it again." Stella went to thank Elvis for his help.

He handed her a bill for turning off the power. "Glad to be of assistance, Chief. Any more trouble with snakes in the wiring up there at your cabin?"

Stella put the invoice in her pocket. Elvis had checked for problems with the wiring after Eric first started playing with the lights and TV when she'd arrived in Sweet Pepper. "No. Everything's been fine."

She'd thought at first, once she'd believed that the cabin was haunted, that Eric was trying to scare her away. Now she knew he'd wanted attention, someone to talk to.

They both watched as the truck from the power company finally made it to the scene—after it was all over.

Elvis laughed. "I guess old Eric likes having you there. Don't know what he'll do when you're gone. How long *are* you staying, Chief?"

"I don't really know yet. I'm sure there will be an announcement of some kind." She didn't want to make it public knowledge yet that she'd made her decision.

"I heard Bob Floyd the other day at the café telling Hugh Morton that the town is planning to burn the old cabin where you're staying, as soon as you're gone. They never had any luck renting it, you know. They couldn't sell it. Most people feel uncomfortable with a ghost around."

Bob Floyd was a member of the town council. Hugh Morton was the town attorney. It was probably a good bet that they knew what was going on.

Stella's heart fluttered a little to hear the news. She'd been wondering what would happen to Hero when she was gone and no one was at the cabin except Eric. What would happen to Eric if they burned the place down?

She kept her voice cool as she replied, "Maybe you should add ghosts to your list of varmints that you take out of houses."

"No, ma'am. Bad business there. I heard tell of a woman over in Frog Pond who fancied herself a witch. She took on that ghost at the old opera house in town here. She claimed she was gonna be on TV. That ghost ran her off, wouldn't leave her alone for a minute. They said she had to leave the state to get any peace. I'd rather tussle with bats, snakes, and rats than do anything like that."

She laughed at his tale—he always had one. But as soon as she'd said goodbye to him, she started worrying about what would happen if the town burned the cabin. They owned it. It was legal for them to do it.

Would Eric have to wander around the mountain at that point? Would he disappear forever because the cabin he loved so much was gone?

She wished the witch was still in Frog Pond. Maybe she'd have some answers for those questions. As far as she could tell, Eric didn't know what to expect from situations like that either. Death, like life, needed to come with a handbook.

Stella tried to comfort herself with a reminder that she didn't believe in witches. She used to be able to do that with ghosts too. She hadn't believed in ghosts either before she'd come to Sweet Pepper. Maybe there *were* witches in Frog Pond.

One thing she knew without a doubt—she couldn't spend the rest of her life protecting a man who was already dead.

Petey called her attention to something else at that moment and Stella put the issue on the back burner.

They talked about the problems with the hose when they got back to the firehouse.

"We're going to have to schedule some intense retraining on handling the hose over the next few days," Stella told her volunteers. "That slip-up today could've caused an injury, more damage to the house, or even loss of life."

"That was Banyin's fault for dropping the hose," Royce said. "It takes us all to hold it in place."

"When your teammate lets you down," Kent added, "there's not much you can do."

"I thought we did a good job picking up the slack," JC said.

"Well, you were all wrong." Petey stepped up front with Stella. It was her team that had fallen apart.

"First off, Banyin was wrong not to alert everyone else when she was having a problem. That's a lesson we should all learn. Then we need to be aware of that kind of situation. If she'd passed out or something, she could've dropped the hose and not had a chance to say anything. It could happen to any of us."

"I guess our job then would've been to step right over her to keep the water going into the house." Royce slapped JC's hand and they both laughed.

Petey didn't think it was funny. "We have a problem here, people. We need to shape up."

Royce, JC, and Kent started grumbling loudly.

Stella thanked Petey for her help but her words seemed to be making it worse.

"Let's leave it that we need some work." She didn't need a full-scale rebellion from her volunteers. "On the other hand, our time leaving the firehouse was the best we've ever had. Good job, everyone."

She looked at their tired, sooty faces and decided this wasn't the moment to tell them she was leaving Sweet Pepper. She felt like she owed them the first real notification. They'd become like a family to her. She'd relied on them to have her back in some bad situations during the last year. She didn't want them to find out from the town grapevine about the news. They needed to hear it from her.

But not now—later would be better—when she had more definite plans.

"Okay. Get cleaned up. Practice tomorrow is still at ten

a.m.," she reminded them. "If you have a conflict, let me know before practice, not after. Thanks for all your hard work. If you hadn't been there today, the Hatleys would have lost their home completely."

Her little band of firefighters seemed happier after that, even though they still had plenty of work to do cleaning all the equipment and getting everything ready for the next call. There was no time to waste looking for anything necessary when the alarm bell sounded. Chief Henry, back in Chicago, had drilled that into her from the beginning.

Bert Wando had finally arrived for the call. He'd remained at the firehouse with Tagger until they got back. He was anxious to talk to Stella about being late again.

He pushed his chin out and his brown eyes defiantly glared at her. He was young, tall, and strong. His brown hair was cut short to accommodate all the different sports helmets he wore during the school year. "Go ahead. Say it. I'm lazy and I need a twenty-four-hour alarm clock, is that it?"

Stella sighed. What was wrong with everyone today? There were a lot of raw emotions playing a part in what had happened. She looked at Banyin, who was waiting and crying in her office. She was going to have to deal with Bert first.

"No. You're the most responsible kid I've ever known. What I meant was that you have school and sports and I know it's hard for you to get to practice and calls on time."

"Oh." That deflated his anger balloon a little.

Stella wondered if his parents had been telling him he was lazy and irresponsible. If so, that might account for his flare-up. She'd never had children—although she hadn't given up on the idea—but she knew raising kids was hard. She felt sure the Wandos did the best they could. She knew they were proud of Bert.

"You have to understand that I need someone I can count on, or I have to find someone to take your place." She smiled to soften her words. "I like you, Bert. This is a sacrifice that not everyone is prepared to make. Notice how there aren't hundreds of volunteers? Everyone else on the team has lives and problems too. You can either work around them, or not."

He scuffed the toe of his expensive new tennis shoes on the blacktop, his hands in his pockets. "It may not always show, Chief, but I love this job. And my father will flip if I give it up. He expects me to volunteer at something. He says it's important to my character development. This is what I want to do."

"Bert—"

"I'm sorry. It won't happen again. If it does, I'll leave. You won't have to ask me." He smiled charmingly with all the charisma he would have someday as a man. "One more chance? What do you say?"

"One more," she agreed. "Practice is tomorrow at ten. Don't miss it."

"I won't." He enthusiastically hugged her. "Thanks, Chief."

Stella had agreed to one more chance for Bert, but she was fairly sure nothing would change for him. She didn't see how he could do it all, even without volunteering. What was the mayor thinking?

"Hey! Dad told me that it was conclusive that it was the old chief's bones we found here after the fire," Bert said. "That was strange, huh?"

"Finding anyone's bones in a wall is strange."

"Well, he said they're digging up the coffin from the cemetery this afternoon. I guess they want to find out who's buried in there now."

*That was fast.* Walt was right about some people being able to get fast results. "Did he say when?"

Bert glanced at his cell phone. "Right about now, I guess. Why?"

# Chapter 6

~~~~~~~~~

Stella didn't want to leave Banyin hanging, but she wanted to be there for the exhumation. She believed there were answers in that coffin.

She weighed her options. If she didn't leave right away, she'd miss it.

She'd have to talk to Banyin later.

"I'm sorry," she told the other woman. "I have to get over to the cemetery. The county is pulling out Chief Gamlyn's coffin. This could be the break I've been looking for in the investigation into his death."

"Sure, Chief." Banyin wiped her eyes and sniffled a little but wasn't actively crying. "I'll see you later."

"Are you working at the library this afternoon?"

"Yes. I'll be there until five-thirty."

"I'll catch up with you there."

Stella put Ricky and Petey in charge of getting everything cleaned up at the firehouse and then hopped on her Harley and headed toward the cemetery.

The Sweet Pepper Heavenly Peace Cemetery was located

on the other side of town, going out the main road. It was on a tall hill, with only a few trees growing there. The grass was green and abundant. There was a small chapel at the top of the hill. The graves, some from the early 1700s, spread down to the road.

It was easy to see where they were working. The coroner's van and a few cars from the Sweet Pepper Police Department were there along with several vehicles from the Fulton Mortuary, the local funeral home.

Stella drove her Harley up the steep gravel road until she reached the area where everyone was standing around. She parked the bike and went to join them.

The wind fiercely whipped around on the side of the hill, sharp and cold from the mountaintops. The constant force of it had caused the trees to grow stilted and slight, always bent to the north.

"Chief Rogers." She addressed the older man in the Sweet Pepper Police uniform.

She knew he'd be unhappy to see her there. He'd probably kept her out of the loop, despite her involvement in the case. Don Rogers had made no secret of his feelings toward her. She was a woman, and she wasn't from Sweet Pepper. Those were enough strikes against her for him.

"Ms. Griffin."

He'd never called Stella "chief" as many others did. She was sure it was his way of showing disrespect.

He looked to be in his mid-fifties, with his unbowed military bearing and his graying blond crew cut. "What brings you out? Is something on fire?"

Stella held her tongue. It was too easy to get into a name-calling match with him. "I heard you were exhuming Chief Gamlyn's remains."

"Not me." His pale blue eyes looked her over insolently from head to toe. "Is that making you nervous? Worried about *your* future?"

She laughed. "We all die, Chief. I don't worry about it. But when a firefighter dies in questionable circumstances, it's up to the rest of us to set it right."

If he was trying to make her uncomfortable, he'd have to try harder. She'd been the first woman recruit at her fire station back home. The pranks and taunts she'd received the first few months had been enough to hold her rock-steady when she was around men like Rogers.

"You didn't even *know* Chief Gamlyn." He said it like an accusation.

"You're right." *At least not while he was alive.* "But I'm still involved."

The usually jolly coroner ended the conversation as he reached them. "Hello, Chief Griffin. What brings you out today? Too many chiefs here, not enough work being done, huh?"

He laughed at his joke. When neither of the chiefs laughed back, he cleared his throat and tried again.

"There's not really anything either of you can do out here," he said. I appreciate you both stopping by, though."

"Just want to make sure things are done right, Judd." Chief Rogers's smile didn't reach his eyes. "And I can't imagine anyone digging up a body in *my* town and me not being there. No offense."

Judd Streeter didn't seem to take offense at much of anything. He was a round, gray-haired man who seemed more likely to play Santa in a department store than to examine dead bodies. Yet he'd been the county coroner for more than four decades. "And what about you, Chief Griffin?"

"I'm here because Chief Gamlyn was a firefighter and we take care of our own." She couldn't stop herself from darting an angry glance at Rogers. "What can you tell me about the bones found in the firehouse?"

"I can tell you it was an unusual place to find bones, don't you think?" Still not even a hint of a smile from the two chiefs.

He sobered and read from his clipboard. "I have established that the bones in the firehouse belonged to Chief Eric Gamlyn. He was shot in the head with a thirty-eight revolver at close range. I'm guessing it was around the same time as the silo fire, but we won't know for sure until we get those results back from the state. That could be another forty years."

"If you know that was Gamlyn, why are we out here? What are we trying to prove?" Rogers sounded a little irritated that the coroner had made him look bad in front of Stella who'd been asking for this moment since last year.

"I did the autopsy on the chief forty years ago when I was still wet behind the ears," Judd said. "Everyone thought the remains in the silo belonged to Eric. I guess I did too. I was wrong. I need to know who's buried in Chief Gamlyn's grave."

"It *should've* been done last year when we found Chief Gamlyn's bones," Stella said. "I'm glad you took the initiative."

"Let's get on with it." Chief Rogers stared down the hill where the team was using a backhoe to open the grave and retrieve the coffin.

"Excuse me." Judd was noticeably uncomfortable with the two, strong-willed people glaring at each other like they might get violent. "I think they need me down there."

After the coroner had walked down the hill, his short legs unsteady on the incline, Chief Rogers looked at Stella. "I guess you're feeling pretty confident now."

She watched the work being done on Eric's grave. Sometimes he seemed so alive to her that it was hard to imagine he was dead. Seeing his bones in the firehouse wall had made it painfully real. Coming out here to his grave was another strong reminder.

"I don't feel any way about it at all. I only want to know

what happened. Why are *you* so defensive about it? You weren't police chief back then. Were you involved in Chief Gamlyn's death?"

Chief Rogers drew a quick breath as though she'd slapped him. "Your *friend*, Walt Fenway, was chief. I was an officer. This makes us all look bad. If you were a man, I'd knock you on your backside for asking me that question."

She smiled at his arrogance. "Chief Gamlyn's burial was a mistake. Sometimes we see what we expect to see. His murder is different. I want to know who killed him and put him in the firehouse wall."

"Is that what's been holding you here? When are you going back to Chicago anyway? You've kind of overstayed your welcome, wouldn't you say?"

"I wouldn't say anything of the kind. The mayor asked me to stay on permanently a few days ago. I think some people are happy to have me here."

"Mayor Wando doesn't count as a *real* person, Ms. Griffin. I think if you talked to *real* people in Sweet Pepper, you'd find they want one of their own to run the fire brigade."

Stella turned back to stare at him again. She didn't care what his problem was with her. "Was there any *real* investigation done into Chief Gamlyn's death?"

"Honey, for being the fire chief, you sure don't know much about the nature of fire. Chief Gamlyn ran into the silo that night to help one of his men get out of that inferno. He was overcome by smoke and burned to death. There's not much investigating to be done in that scenario. How much do you think was left of him?"

"So, no?"

"You got it. But don't take my word for it. Talk to Walt. We all knew what we saw back then. There was no reason to think it was anything else. If there was an investigation, I'll be glad to have someone look up those files for you.

Maybe Captain Trump. Oh! *Maybe not*. I hear that plane has left the runway."

After amusing himself at her expense, Rogers ambled down the hillside to get a better view of the coffin being brought out of the rocky ground. At the mention of Walt's name, Stella wondered where he was. He'd said he was going to be there.

She sat down on one of the benches near the chapel and watched as the dirty coffin was hoisted to the back of a truck. She knew the coroner wouldn't open it there. He'd take it back to the lab to examine what he found inside.

Maybe Chief Rogers and Judd were right—she didn't need to be out there. It seemed like she should be. It felt like something someone would do for a friend. If nothing else, the spirit of Eric Gamlyn that inhabited her cabin was her friend. They had a lot in common.

No firefighter wanted to die in a fire, definitely not without questions being asked and answered. There was always something to learn that could save someone from the same fate in the future.

Stella got to her feet and climbed on her Harley, solemnly following the old truck bearing Eric's coffin down the hillside. She'd seen the coffin raised and taken away. She'd done her duty, as much as it saddened her to do so. There were other pressing issues that needed to be taken care of.

She decided she was better off doing those things.

She got to the Sweet Pepper library just before closing. Banyin was putting away some books that had been left out on shelves and tables.

Stella waited until she'd finished. The quiet of the small library was good for her troubled thoughts. She didn't know if she'd ever have answers to all the questions flitting around in her brain regarding Eric's death, especially since the rest of the world seemed to be tugging her away.

She meant to keep searching though, until the minute she got back on her Harley and headed for home.

Banyin came and sat at the table with her. They were alone. She smiled and played with the fringe on her pretty orange sweater.

"What's up?" Stella asked. "You're one of my best people. What happened today?"

"I don't know. I'm going through some issues right now, Chief. I don't want to give up the fire brigade, but I may have to."

"Why? Are you starting to get scared when we go out on a call?"

"I wish it were that easy." She rubbed her hand on her rounded belly.

Stella felt like an idiot. First the weight gain and then the emotional roller coaster. "When are you due?"

"Not until February." Banyin sighed. "I wanted to keep working and practicing. It's much harder now."

"Maybe that's because you're going to have a baby." Stella smiled at her. "I'm sorry I didn't see it before. You should've said something."

"I didn't want you to kick me out."

"I'm not going to kick you out. You're going to take a leave of absence until after the baby is born. You can't keep going this way. How does Jake feel about it?"

"He didn't want me to join up in the first place." She confided her husband's uncertainties about his wife being a firefighter. "But I love it, Chief. I like getting my hands dirty and really doing something for the community."

Stella wasn't sure what to do in this case. She'd never dealt with this situation back home—this would've been Chief Henry's domain. Maybe Banyin could stay on. She'd have to ask someone who had experience with this.

"Let's keep you away from the hoses and the heavy lifting for now," Stella compromised. "We'll decide what else we need to do. Congratulations! I know you and Jake have been trying to get pregnant for a long time."

Banyin hugged her, a little self-consciously, in her strong arms. "Thanks, Chief. I could talk to my doctor about it, if that would help."

"That would probably be a good idea." *Why hadn't she thought of it?* Maybe because she had no experience with the subject and had other things on her mind? "Let me know what she says and we'll work something out."

"That would probably shut Jake up about it too," Banyin said thoughtfully. "It seems like such a long time until February. If I totally stop now, I won't even remember how to hold a hose."

"Believe me, you won't forget." Stella got to her feet. "There will always be room for you."

"I hate to bring this up, but you can't know that. You're leaving, Chief. I wish you weren't, but we all know you don't plan to stay. The next chief might not feel like you do about it."

"You already know the next chiefs—Ricky Junior and Petey. I'm sure they'll understand."

Banyin played with an old hardback copy of *Gone with the Wind* that had been left on the table. "Some people think they won't be co-chiefs after you're gone. I've heard people say John Trump will take over the fire brigade."

Stella had heard that rumor before. She didn't agree with it, but there might be something to it. She couldn't discount it. "Even so, John would understand too. You don't have to worry about it. Volunteer fire departments are always short-staffed. It's hard to get good people to risk their lives for no money."

She wanted to ask Banyin who'd said that about John. He'd actually been her first pick to replace her because he had emergency experience and the maturity to carry off being chief.

Petey and Ricky were lacking in that sometimes. Stella believed her co-chiefs would gain that maturity as they went along. The two of them would bolster each other too.

Stella also knew that John loved his job with the police department and planned to be chief there someday when Rogers retired. That's why she hadn't tapped him for the position.

She didn't want it to get around town that she'd asked Banyin about it. Sometimes the walls seemed to have ears in Sweet Pepper, and news traveled faster than the Internet could deliver it.

"Whatever happens." Stella tried to regroup on her original thought. "You're a good firefighter, Banyin. You'll be fine. See your doctor. Let me know what she says. If nothing else, we'll put you on light duty. That way you'll still feel like part of the group."

"I will. Bless you, Chief."

Stella left Banyin putting books away and straightening up the library. She got on her bike and headed out to Scooter's Barbecue. The place was a little outside of town, on the main road from Sevierville and Pigeon Forge to Sweet Pepper, so it got plenty of traffic.

Sweet Pepper was famous for having the hottest, sweetest peppers in the world and the yearly pepper festival. Thousands of people visited for tours of the factory and other events. Tourists had begun coming in to ride the gentle whitewater on the Little Pigeon River too. Their kayaks and inner tubes had filled the roads over the summer.

Scooter's had once been a drive-in and it still retained the look, but without car delivery. It was popular with young and old from town. There were always plenty of people who waved to Stella when she went there to eat.

In this case, Zane was there with a few of his buddies from the forest service. They were sitting at a table with Allen, Kent, and Tagger from the fire brigade.

Stella smiled when she saw that Petey was their waitress.

Mayor Wando and his wife, Jill, were there sharing a table with Sandy Selvy, the town clerk, and Councilman Bob Floyd.

His parents' presence explained why Bert wasn't there. He and his father were obviously having difficulties right now. No doubt the younger Wando wouldn't want to be there with his parents looking over his shoulder.

"Chief Griffin!" Mayor Wando called her name loudly and waved at the same time.

Stella felt compelled to acknowledge him. She paid her respects to everyone at the table.

"We were just talking about you, Chief Griffin!" Bob Floyd's voice rang out through the diner.

He was a short, ambitious person who usually irritated Stella since he always seemed to be working some angle to benefit himself.

"I hope it was something good." She went along with the conversation.

"We were discussing what a good job you've done here." Jill Wando patted her perfect blond hair. "Take that fire you all put out today at the Hatleys. Why, they wouldn't have had two pennies to rub together if it wasn't for you, Chief Griffin."

"Not me, Mrs. Wando. The whole fire brigade. And thanks for the compliment."

"See, that's the thing." Mayor Wando collected himself and cleared his throat. "We want you to stay in Sweet Pepper, Stella. You've pulled all of this together for us, and frankly, there are many of us who worry that it will fall apart if you leave."

"If salary is the issue," Jill whispered, "we can find some extra money in the budget to give you a nice raise." She nudged her husband. "Can't we, Erskine?"

He jumped. "Of course we can. Of course we can."

"And if that old cabin isn't to your liking," Bob Floyd said, "we can find you something better right here in town."

Stella was actually friends with Sandy Selvy. She'd known Stella's mother when she lived here as a child. The town clerk had a sassy mouth and an irreverent way of looking at things that always made her laugh.

"I'm sure Stella enjoys being up at the cabin with the handsome ghost of Eric Gamlyn. How can town compete with that?" Sandy winked at Stella, patting her beehive hairdo.

Stella had told Sandy about Eric—about some of the things he'd done. "I like being at the cabin. Not so much because of the ghost. It's more because it's close to the firehouse. Eric had the right idea about building the two together."

Bob shook his head. "That cabin needs to come down. It's an eyesore and an embarrassment to the town. The sooner we get you out of there and let your fire brigade do a controlled burn up there, the better."

# Chapter 7

*So that's who wants to burn Eric's cabin down.*

Stella wondered what Bob Floyd would gain by that move. In her limited experience with the councilman, he never did anything unless there was something in it for him.

"I think that would be a mistake," Stella said. "Whether it's me, or someone else who is the long-term fire chief, the firehouse is easy to reach from there. Trying to get out there from town can take a lot longer, especially during heavy tourist traffic. The chief needs to be close."

Mayor Wando nodded.

Councilman Floyd frowned. "We'd like you to stay, Chief, don't get me wrong. But from what I've heard, you have no intention of being that long-term chief you're describing. John Trump, who would be our second choice to lead the fire brigade, has his own place already about a mile and a half from the firehouse. I don't see him giving up a place that has been in his family for several generations to spend time with the ghost of a man who was annoying and egotistical when he was alive."

*And that's where that rumor was coming from.* Stella smiled at the councilman. "I'm sure you're right. Excuse me. I'm late for dinner with my friends."

They all smiled and wished her well. She could feel their eyes on her as she walked across the crowded restaurant to sit with Zane and her friends.

"You know, Erskine." Bob didn't try to keep his voice down. "I think it's just as well she's leaving. No wonder she likes it up there at the cabin. She and Eric are two peas from the same pod."

Jill and Sandy disagreed with his statement. Mayor Wando tried to stay neutral in the debate.

Stella studied Bob Floyd after she'd ordered her dinner. Everyone else was talking about the kitchen fire today and Zane was telling them about the camper they'd finally found who'd made a campfire in the woods despite all the hazard signs posted.

She kept thinking about what Bob would stand to gain by getting rid of Eric's cabin. Both the firehouse and the cabin, along with the land they were on, had been left to the town when Eric died. No one had been able to live there so the town had maintained the cabin with nothing coming back to its coffers. Maybe that was it.

She'd known from the start that was why the town council had let her live there, rent free, while she was acting fire chief. No one else wanted to live there after Eric had scared so many people away.

She knew Bob would have to convince the mayor and the majority of the council to see things his way. It made sense to try to sell the place. Burning it down seemed a waste.

Stella finally forced herself to let it go. After all, it wasn't her fight. She had to stop trying to protect Eric's ghost from the rest of the world. She wouldn't be here much longer. It was the town's problem.

*And Eric's.*

She joined the conversation, telling stories about her experiences as a firefighter in the big city. It was as hard for her companions to imagine that life as it would have been for her to imagine life in Sweet Pepper before she came here.

The group went on to Beau's Bar and Grill a few miles away after dinner. Petey's shift was over at Scooter's and she went along with them. There was a live band there and Stella danced with Zane a few times while everyone clapped and generally acted crazy.

It was one of the rare times Stella had allowed herself the companionship of the fire brigade. At first she'd tried to keep herself separate from the group. She'd told herself it was because she had to be their boss and make life-and-death decisions for them.

It was Eric who'd pointed out the stupidity of that belief. He'd hung out all the time with the men he'd worked with (no women firefighters at that time). He'd convinced her that she needed more than her laptop and his ghostly company.

He'd been right. It was good to unwind with the people she counted on—new friends—even if she had to leave them behind when the time came.

Beau's was having two-for-one margarita night and the evening stretched into early morning as the bar closed. The bartender finally told them to go home.

Ricky had declared himself the designated driver. Most of them ended up in the back of his pickup, including Stella, who'd protested leaving her Harley at the bar. She knew she probably wasn't in fit shape to drive though, especially negotiating the sharp curves on Firehouse Road.

The porch light was on and the door was standing open, as it always was when she returned. Everyone shouted drunken goodbyes to Eric and told him they wished he could've been there. Zane kissed Stella as the others laughed and taunted Zane about being jealous that his girlfriend lived with a male ghost.

Stella told the raucous group goodnight and closed the cabin door behind her. There was a light on in the kitchen but the rest of the cabin was dark. She could see something had happened to the cakes, brownies, and other food that had been there. She hoped Walt didn't eat them all.

Eric was on the back deck. She could see him without any lights on. In the blackness, he had a faint glow about him. There were other times he appeared so real that she felt he could be mistaken for a living, breathing human.

Stella stumbled through the living room and tried to open the back door to the deck.

"It's already open," Eric said. "I think you've had a few too many."

She got through the opening and collapsed into one of the hardwood rocking chairs that he'd made when he was still alive. "It would've been a waste not to drink both margaritas since I got a free one with each one I paid for. It made good economic sense."

"Well, in the light of that economic discovery, I'm glad you didn't try to bring the Harley home."

"Me too." She sat back in the chair and listened to the noise from the river.

There was a steep drop-off from the cabin to the Little Pigeon River so that the structure seemed to hover over the water.

"It's so quiet here. I'm going to miss that. Back home, you can't sit outside for more than a few minutes without hearing people arguing or a siren going off. That's what happens when you live around a few million people."

Eric was in the rocking chair beside hers. "You don't have to go back. This is a good life here in Sweet Pepper. You have friends and an important job."

"I know." She closed her eyes. Her head was beginning to ache. Maybe those margaritas weren't such a good idea after all.

"But I don't belong here. Not really. I'm from Chicago. I have friends and an important job there too. Not to mention the extensive Griffin family. I can't stay here. Maybe I'd like to. But I can't."

"I guess you have to do what feels right to you."

"That's the problem." She stared at him. "I don't know what's right anymore. You've changed my life. Before, I only had to worry about me. Now I have to worry about you too. It was stupid of you to leave this land to the town. Bob Floyd wants to burn down the cabin. What are we supposed to do about that?"

He smiled. "I was expecting him to realize that this property joins his a long time ago. His father wanted to put a whitewater rafting access center here fifty years ago. I'm sure that's what he wants to do now. He wasn't particularly creative when he was a kid. I'm sure he's only following his father's game plan now."

"He wants to do it as much to get rid of your ghost as he does whatever else," she replied. "I don't think he likes you."

"It's a long story. He wanted to be a firefighter—he couldn't do the work. People grow up and get bitter about those things—and sometimes become the people who make the decisions."

Stella put her hand on his chest. There was a slight zing, like static electricity, but he was solid to the touch. "Why are you so calm about all of this? It really bothers me."

"As I've said, I'm dead. What else can they do to hurt me?"

"Burn down the only place you can be right now. You won't have *any* place to haunt. Don't you see? You'll be exercised."

He laughed at her. "You mean *exorcised*, I think. And no, I don't see that. I'll be able to wander around in the woods. I'll be a free spirit."

Stella leaned against him—she had this feeling that she was going to fall out of the rocking chair otherwise. The deck suddenly seemed to be tilting downward.

"You know I care about you, right? You saved my life. But it's more than that. I don't want anything to happen to you. I want you to live out your ghostly existence in your home. That's what I want."

"Don't worry about me. I'm from another time, another place. I'll be fine. I always have been. You have to live your life while you still have it. Get married. Have babies. Be happy. I had my chance to do that and I blew it. Don't make my mistakes."

One minute, Stella was listening to him—his blue eyes seemed too intense to be real. The next minute, she'd passed out on him. Lucky for her that he could be solid.

"Never mind," he whispered as he picked her up and carried her to the bedroom.

She let out a loud, snorting sound in response.

*No one could tell someone else how to live.* Eric put her in bed and pulled off her boots before he covered her with the comforter.

Friends, like Walt, had tried to tell him that he'd end up alone if he let the job consume his life. He never worried about it. There had been plenty of time ahead of him to find a wife, and father a family.

Then he'd woken up here after the fire, terrified and completely alone, and there was no time left for him at all.

He had forty years to think about everything he'd missed before Stella came into his life. Since then he'd thought many times about how wonderful they would have been together, if they were both alive.

That wasn't to be.

He watched her sleep for a long time, sitting on the bed beside her. Usually, if he tried something like that, she woke up and yelled at him, saying he was *"creeping her out."* She was out of it that night though. He could watch her as long as he wanted to.

Part of him hoped she would leave Sweet Pepper, for her own sake.

*His heart wanted her to stay.*

Maybe Bob Floyd would end that quandary by burning down the cabin. He was pretty sure that would mean the end of his half-life existence, even though he would never admit it to Stella.

Someone was knocking on the door.

Stella moaned as she put her head under the comforter.

Whoever it was kept knocking.

"Go away," she yelled. "Walt—that better not be you."

"Not Walt," Eric said. "It's two men and a woman. The woman must be related. She looks like you and Abigail."

"What?" Stella sat up quickly and then regretted it as a steel drum band started playing in her head. "It's my parents. Oh my God!"

"Is that your brother?" Eric looked out of the window space between the thick wood blinds.

Stella opened one eye and looked out. "It's Doug! What were they thinking? They brought *Doug*."

"Doug?"

"My ex-boyfriend." She was still dressed (*surprise!*). Her clothes smelled like smoke and margaritas. Her mouth tasted like something dead had curled up and died in there.

Oh well. She'd have to do.

"Shoes!" Eric reminded her. "Is that the man you found in bed with your friend?"

"Yes. Thanks." Stella recalled the first warning she got

about wearing shoes in the cabin to avoid being stung by a southern scorpion. "You know, I've never actually seen one of those in the cabin."

"I try to keep them and the snakes out," Eric replied.

"All of that and you bake too." She smiled at him. "What happened to all the cakes? You didn't float them down the mountain, right?"

"No, Walt took them to the cake event at the church."

"What about Hero?" She suddenly realized that she hadn't seen the dog last night and he wasn't barking at their visitors this morning.

"His mother came to get him yesterday, along with their two human friends."

Stella finished tying her shoes and pushed her thick red hair into a ponytail holder. "I hope there's at least one Coke left in the fridge."

"There is. Why would your parents bring your cheating ex-boyfriend to see you?"

"Your guess is as good as mine." She stalked out of the bedroom and answered the door.

# Chapter 8

~~~~~~~~~~

"**D**ad. Mom. What are you doing here?"

"Stella!" Her father grabbed her in a big bear hug. "You look terrible. Are you eating? You know how you forget sometimes and then eat something you shouldn't."

Sean Griffin was about six feet tall with a flat stomach and muscled chest. He had close-cropped bright red hair, blue eyes, and a heavily freckled face. He worked out religiously and ran a few miles every day. He was also a health food nut who had raised his daughter on wheat germ and fresh vegetables, as much as he could.

Barbara Griffin pushed her husband aside. "You're hogging up my daughter."

She wrapped her arms around Stella and held her close for several moments. "I've been so worried about you since you didn't come home in October. I think you have some explaining to do."

Barbara looked like an older version of Stella, but with brown hair, graying in places. They had the same brown eyes—one of the things that had reminded Stella of her when she'd first met her grandfather, Ben Carson.

"Come inside." They were still standing on the porch. Stella whispered as her mother moved away, "Why is Doug here?"

"Because he still loves you. He made a mistake. You've known each other your whole lives. I think you should at least talk."

Doug started up the stairs, a big, confident smile on his handsome face. "What? No hug for me? I'm hurt."

A cold breeze came from *inside* the cabin. It rushed between Stella and Doug, reaching him as he held out his arms to her. Nothing else moved, not even the wind chimes on the porch, but the breeze blew Doug right off the top stair. He hit the ground with a dull thud.

Barbara and Sean ran to help him up.

Stella looked at Eric, who was standing on the porch, laughing.

"That was nice." She had to school her face, torn between the urge to laugh and being upset with him.

Eric shrugged. "He deserved it."

"What in the world was that?" Barbara asked.

"Earthquake," Stella answered.

"Earthquake?" Her mother stared at her. "They never had earthquakes when I was growing up here."

Sean jumped in to support Stella's theory. "I've read that this area is on some kind of fault line. They get micro-quakes all the time."

Barbara didn't agree with that, but she helped Doug into the cabin.

Stella shut the door behind them. *This was going to be terrible.*

"This is quite the male retreat, isn't it?" Sean looked around. "Didn't you say it used to belong to the old fire chief?"

"Yes. That's right," Stella answered. "Would anyone like coffee?"

She grabbed the last Coke out of the refrigerator and chugged down half of it.

"Are you drinking coffee now?" Barbara looked at the coffeepot on the counter.

"Not really," Stella said. "But everyone else does around here, so I keep some handy. There aren't any coffeehouses around the block."

"You're still drinking those sodas loaded with caffeine and sugar." Her father frowned. "No wonder your color is bad. I'll bet there's not a carrot in that refrigerator."

*He'd win that bet.* "How about some breakfast?" she offered. Her father was a big believer in eating breakfast. It would also get them out of the cabin and give her a chance to collect her thoughts.

"That sounds great!" Doug's face perked up with the idea. "All we had were some crackers on the plane, and that was a long time ago."

Sean hugged his daughter. "You keep breakfast on hand. I'm so proud of you."

"If you consider Pop-Tarts a breakfast food," Eric added, unheard except by Stella, even though he was standing right in the middle of the excited family group.

"I don't exactly keep it on hand," Stella admitted. "But I frequently eat breakfast at the café in town."

"Is that still the old Sweet Pepper Café?" Her mother smiled. "Are Lucille and Ricky still there?"

"Yes. And their son, Ricky Junior, works there too. He's a member of the fire brigade, one of my co-assistant chiefs."

"Sounds good. I'm hungry. We don't have to eat grits, do we?" Her father put his arm around Stella's shoulders. "You'll have to tell me where you came up with your creative titles—co-assistant chief? Chief Henry would blow a gasket if he heard that one. So would your uncle!"

"Never mind," Stella said. "*You* try setting up a new fire department with old equipment and people who have never fought a fire. It makes you creative. And I think you should eat grits. You're in the South."

"Not me." Sean kissed his daughter. "You know I don't go in for politics. I put out the fires and then I go home. I'm not eating grits."

"Let's go," Barbara said. "It's only a few miles back into town from here, if I remember correctly."

Stella went to hop on her bike and realized it was still at Beau's. After explaining to her father that she'd left the Harley at the bar, she rode down with them in their rental car—in the backseat with Doug.

"I could ride with you on the Harley when we pick it up," Doug volunteered with the sweet smile that she remembered so well. "No reason for you to go alone."

Stella looked back at the three hopeful faces in the car as she got out when the car had stopped. "I don't think so."

Before Doug could insist—knowing her parents would be on his side—she cranked up the Harley and was gone. It only occurred to her a few minutes later that she'd forgotten her helmet. It was still strapped to the bike.

She stopped and put it on, wondering what could *possibly* make Doug think they should get back together. And why did her parents think it should happen? They'd been as angry as she was when he'd cheated on her.

Her mother had hinted earlier that she should be forgiving. Stella didn't know how to be forgiving when she was still as angry now as she had been then. A year wasn't enough time to forgive and forget seeing him in bed with her friend.

Maybe she just wasn't the forgiving kind.

Yes—she and Doug had grown up together. That made the broken trust between them even harder to bear.

Eric had been very clear about his feelings when Doug

had tried to come into the cabin. A smile tugged at her lips when she thought about it. She hoped she could keep Doug out of the way for however long they planned to stay.

*Had anyone mentioned how long that would be?*

Stella met her parents at the café and they went inside together. Ricky Senior and Lucille picked them out of the early morning crowd right away. They ran to hug Barbara and meet Sean, and then finally welcomed Doug and Stella.

Lucille sat them at a special table. She and Barbara cried as they talked about the past. Ricky Senior introduced his son and sent him for coffee, and what sounded like everything on the menu.

"Isn't there a fire somewhere, Chief?" Ricky Junior asked Stella.

She grimaced. "If there was, I wouldn't be *here*."

"That way is it?" He grinned at her. "It's not your parents, right? The problem is the ex, isn't it?"

"Don't you have food to get?" she asked.

"Yes, ma'am. I'll get as much as I can so you can take your time eating with *him*. No extra charge."

Stella rolled her eyes, sat back in her chair, and prepared to hang around for another hour until practice at the firehouse. Everyone in the café was staring at them. They were probably on their phones, spreading the information faster than Ricky got their breakfast.

How often did a local heiress come home after so many years?

She didn't mind her mother reminiscing about old times with Lucille. She very much minded sitting next to Doug. He kept trying to talk to her and was smiling at her.

He finally slipped his chair closer and bent his head near hers. "We could leave, you know? Just take off. Get out of here so we can be alone."

Stella glanced at her mother and father. They were actively involved in discussing Barbara's childhood.

She looked into Doug's blue eyes, which she'd once written a poem about when they were in sixth grade. "We aren't getting back together. I don't know what my mom said to you—it's not happening. You should've stayed home."

His confident expression faltered as he took in her words. "I told you I'm sorry, Stella. What more can I say? We all do things we regret. Like you punching me. What was that all about?"

Stella could hardly believe he'd even bring that up. "Punching you was about finding you in bed with my friend. How could you do something like that? We'd talked about getting married the day before."

"Like I said." His tone was reasonable. "We *all* do things we regret. I think it's time to forgive and forget, don't you? We've always been great together. You know that. We'll be stronger in the future because of this."

"I'll be stronger in the future because I won't be with you! I don't know how else to say it—without punching you again." Stella stared at him as she would have at a fire she was assessing. "You won't *ever* be part of my life again. You don't get a second chance. That's it."

She hoped she'd made herself clear. Maybe he'd head back to the airport now and leave without her parents.

Breakfast had begun to arrive when John Trump came in the café. He looked around until he spotted Stella.

He'd already heard that her family was in town, along with her ex-boyfriend from Chicago. He studied the lean, lanky man who sat beside her at the table, his thin face close to hers. *Was that him?*

"John." Stella latched onto his presence, hoping he had something important to tell her. She didn't care what it was. He was wearing his uniform and his grim face that usually meant he was unhappy about something.

Doug sized up the other police officer and got to his feet. He was taller than John. John was stockier, with broader shoulders. "I'm Officer Douglas Connelly from Chicago."

"Nice to meet you." John glanced at him and then turned to Stella. "I have some bad news."

"Not too bad, I hope." Stella felt guilty that she'd wished for it when he'd come to the table.

"Bad enough. Mace Chum is dead. The Highway Patrol found him off of the main road a few minutes ago. It looks like he lost control of his truck and camper. Chief Rogers wants the fire department on-site in case there's a problem getting the truck out."

"Oh no." She got to her feet and the pager in her pocket went off. She hadn't wanted *that* kind of distraction. "I spoke with him at the firehouse yesterday."

"I'm off duty. I'll suit up and help the fire brigade," John said. "You might need an experienced climber."

# Chapter 9

~~~~~~~~~

"What's going on?" Sean asked when he saw Stella's shocked face. "Are you in trouble?"

"This is Captain John Trump, Dad. Sweet Pepper police. John, this is my dad, Sean Griffin, Chicago firefighter."

The two men shook hands. Stella kept her voice down as she explained to her father what had happened.

"I'd like to come along," Sean said. "Maybe I could lend a hand."

"Me too," Doug added. "I'm a trained police officer. I could be useful too."

John shook Doug's hand as he sized up the other man. If this *was* the boyfriend who broke Stella's heart and sent her packing to Sweet Pepper, he was definitely *not* what John had been expecting.

"Sure," he said finally. "You can both ride along with me. I saw Stella's bike out front so I know how she's getting to the firehouse."

Barbara didn't mind being left with Lucille to catch up on everything that had happened since she'd left Sweet Pepper.

"Be careful, you guys. Mountains aren't the same as high-rises."

Stella was already at the firehouse when her father, John, and Doug arrived. Since Doug and her father were riding to the accident with the fire brigade, Stella had decided to drive the Cherokee to the scene. John would ride in the engine/ladder truck with Ricky Junior.

She didn't want Doug riding with anyone else and talking about how much he wished they'd get back together, especially John. She wanted her father with them to ensure she didn't get into any uncomfortable conversations with her ex.

"Wow!" Sean rubbed his hand on the fire chief's symbol and his daughter's name on the side of the vehicle. "I think they really like you, honey."

"It can be changed when I leave." She fastened her seat belt, but wasn't quick enough to prevent Doug from hopping up into the front seat with her, leaving her father to ride in the back. "Hold on. There are a lot of sharp turns on this road."

Ricky told her the engine was ready to go. She'd abbreviated the crew and left the pumper/tanker at the firehouse since they had assistance from the police department on this one. John also said county EMS had been dispatched to the scene.

The Cherokee took the lead with the engine and six members of the fire brigade following close behind. Traffic was light on the road, but the fog was rolling in. It would be difficult to see anything on the side of the mountain if it got any denser.

"I heard this was why they called them the Smokies." Sean held on to the door handle, a little nervous with the conditions and the sharp curves on the road. "They weren't kidding."

"It takes some getting used to." Stella kept both hands on the wheel. "Considering everything is flat back home, these mountains look really tall. They may not be the Rockies, but they're as much as I want to handle."

"I heard you've been having some forest fire issues this year," her father continued. "That must be another novelty for you. Is that one of the reasons you've stayed so long—all the new things to learn?"

"Not really." Stella kept her eyes on the dangerous turns, now disguised by the growing fog bank. "It's hard to explain, Dad. A lot has happened."

"Sometimes that's the way life is. I'm proud that you've been up to the challenge."

"Thanks." She smiled, but was mindful of Doug sitting next to her. She knew that look on his face. He was sulking after she'd told him they weren't getting back together.

*Too bad.* He should've thought about that before he climbed into bed with someone else.

Rain started falling fitfully as the fire brigade and EMS converged on the road about five miles outside of town. Sweet Pepper police and the county sheriff had blocked the bridge and the road going both ways from the accident site.

Stella put on her bunker coat and went to take a look, seeing the trees pushed down and other signs that a vehicle had gone off the road. She peered over the edge and could barely make out Chum's truck and camper. Both vehicles were on their side.

"Bad day for this." Don Rogers was waiting for her. "We've got two men down there, trying to get the body out. Once we knew he was dead, there wasn't much reason to rush."

"What do you want us to do?" Stella asked him. "I can send a few people down to assist your folks."

Chief Rogers chuckled when John joined Stella. "You mean *one* of mine, right? You can put him in a fire brigade uniform, but he's still Sweet Pepper police. Howdy, John."

"Chief." John nodded. "I'm off duty. I thought the fire brigade might need me."

"Always happy to have you—whatever the uniform," Rogers said. "I'm not so worried about bringing poor old Chum up. Time doesn't mean anything to him now. What's bothering me is that his truck might catch fire. I called the forest service and they're standing by in case we need the helicopter or Big Bertha. I don't want to start a fire, but I thought if we do, we can catch it right away with your people, Ms. Griffin."

Stella agreed. "We'll be ready with the tank on the engine."

Big Bertha was an old plane that was fitted to be a water tanker. It carried thousands of gallons of water or chemicals that could be dispersed very rapidly. The helicopter could carry water too, but it was more likely Chief Rogers would use it to help get people off the ground, if necessary.

Sean ended up going down with Stella and John. Ricky and Petey complained because they didn't get to go down the mountain, even though Stella had explained it was only a threat assessment.

"Be ready up here in case we need help," she told them. "Don't be afraid to use one of the big hoses if you have to. The four of you can handle it. If you only need the two-inch, Royce, you and JC take it."

Going down the mountain didn't seem as though it would be that hard. The angle and slope lent itself to moving downward. The trick, apparently, was not going down *too* fast.

Stella had done some training on rappelling during the first few months she'd been in Sweet Pepper. She'd never had to use it before—all of their fires had been on mostly flat surfaces.

Her father was fast. Stella came down a little more slowly with John.

"What's the matter?" Sean grinned when she'd reached him. "Scared of a little mountain?"

It looked as though some large boulders, two the size of

houses, had stopped Chum's downward plunge. The front end of the truck he was driving was smashed in. The vehicle had flipped on its side and caught between the boulder and a pine tree. The trailer was hanging, suspended, over the side of the mountain. It was still attached to the truck.

The first two rescue workers were trying to get Chum out of the crushed cab. Stella offered her help when she saw the daunting task. Grimly, the five of them managed to cut the truck door open to free the deputy's body.

Carefully, they laid the mangled man on a stretcher basket that had been rigged with ropes to pull back to the road.

Before one of the EMS workers could cover Chum's face, Stella stopped him. There was a large ugly wound on the left side of his head that wasn't caused by falling down the mountain.

"I don't think this man died of a heart attack," Sean whispered to her. "He was shot."

"I know." She stood aside as the body was readied for transport. "Let's take a look at the truck."

The truck had come down quickly, going through the smaller trees and scrub bushes like a hot knife through butter. "He must've been shot while he was driving." Stella examined the truck's engine and gas line to see if they were intact. "He came down fast. Deputy Chum was driving way over the forty-five-mile-per-hour limit, I think."

"That's what I was thinking too," Sean said. "Someone had to drive up close to make that shot. It wasn't easy going that fast. The killer was either an expert or got lucky."

The rain was falling harder as they got under the truck. It seemed as though it would be all right to have a tow truck pull the vehicle out. Neither father nor daughter saw anything that appeared to be a fire hazard.

"Maybe we should disconnect this trailer." John joined them once Chum's body was headed up the mountain. "It's going to be a drag on the truck. We can haul it up after the truck for the crime scene people to look at."

Sean agreed. "We better make sure there's not bottled gas or anything that could ignite, in case it falls."

Before Stella could make a decision on who was going down to take a look, Sean had already climbed down to a spot where he could see inside the trailer. She watched him go, not liking the possible danger involved—both because he was her father as well as someone who wasn't a member of her team.

"Your dad is a real go-getter," John said. "You're a lot like him."

"A little." She kept her eyes on her father, about ten feet below them. "Don't climb inside that thing," she yelled down to him. "If you can't see from the outside, we'll find another way."

Sean saluted to show he understood, not using his radio. He moved in closer, his hands resting on the side of the trailer.

"If he falls, my mother is going to kill me," Stella said.

"What about the truck?" John answered his radio. "Chief Rogers wants to know if he can call for a tow."

"It looks secure," she told him. "We'll have to keep an eye on it as it goes up but from here, it looks safe."

He nodded and answered Chief Rogers. By that time, Sean had already climbed back up to where John and Stella were standing.

"There's no gas or connections that I can see, at least in the front," he said. "I couldn't see the back of the trailer, but there were some pots and pans. There might at least be Sterno, or some other chemical heating device. We should probably take some hazmat containers down there and clean it out before you try and move it."

"They're going to pull the truck out first," Stella said.

"We'll go from there. Thanks, Dad. Don't *ever* do that again."

Sean laughed. "You're just jealous because *you* didn't get to do it."

Stella, Sean, and John waited on the side of the mountain so that the tow truck driver didn't have to come down to hook up the vehicle. The rain was coming down harder, soaking them and the mountainside.

While Sean and John were talking, Stella inspected Chum's truck. Rain from the broken windshield was making the bobblehead dog on his dashboard move. There was blood everywhere.

*Poor old guy.* Stella thought about how scared Chum had been when he'd talked to her. It seemed a little too coincidental not to think that his retirement had something to do with his death. Had he been killed because someone had seen him talking to her at the firehouse?

There was a long dent and a scratch of black paint on the driver's side of the blue truck. It could've been from the killer, trying to get up close enough to get a good shot. If so, the killer also had a big blue streak on his or her black vehicle. She used her cell phone camera to get a shot of it in case no one else had.

Maybe it was enough to arrest someone for this. She hoped Chief Rogers would be able to catch the person who did it. It was possible, if Chum was killed for imparting information about Eric's death, that it could even tie in with that investigation.

The tow truck finally arrived and the driver lowered the big hook and heavy cable. Stella connected it to the back of the truck. She'd done it so many times in her career that she thought she could do it in her sleep.

She radioed Ricky to let her volunteers know to keep alert as the vehicle was raised. The plan was for John, Sean, and Stella to hold their positions to make sure everything was secure as it started up.

The tow truck began to haul the truck up to the road. Stella and her crew stayed well away from the path of the vehicle. Everything seemed to be going fine as the heavy steel cable dragged the truck away from the spot where it had come to rest against the rock.

Staying in place was getting harder for the three firefighters. The new torrent of rain had made the loose rock and mud slippery underfoot. All of them were connected by ropes in case they lost their footing. Stella slipped once as she made way for the truck, slowly inching toward it. She skinned her knee before she could right herself, but it was only a scratch. She signaled that she was okay.

The truck was hanging above the ledge where they waited, swinging like a big, rusty pendulum. Something squealed at the top and the ascent abruptly stopped. The truck swayed sickeningly against the mountain, making noises that caused Stella's stomach to churn.

"It's not gonna hold," Ricky yelled into Stella's radio. "Get out of the way!"

An instant later, there was a loud snapping sound. The tow truck driver yelled out a warning right before the line broke and the truck went crashing down the mountain.

# Chapter 10

~~~~~~~~~~

John and Sean huddled together with their arms around Stella as the old truck slipped close by them. It hit the trailer and both vehicles bounced hundreds of feet into the foggy valley below them.

There was a small explosion and a shaft of fire shot into the foggy air. The heavy rain put it out before Chief Rogers had time to call the forest service.

"We didn't need the engine after all," Sean said with a smile. "I hope the bars are open. I need a drink."

Sean, Stella, and John climbed back to the top again. Their feet and hands slipped at nearly every movement up the face of the mountain. They were covered with rain and mud by the time they reached the top, but the important thing was that they made it.

Their hands were scraped and scratched from the climb and Stella's leg was bleeding. Regulations said they had to let the paramedics treat them at the scene in case they needed to be transported. After cleaning and a few bandages, they were released.

There was a lot of handshaking and backslapping. The fire brigade put away its equipment and the tow truck got ready to leave. The ambulance had to wait at the site for another vehicle to transport Chum's body to the morgue at the coroner's office. They weren't allowed to pick up a dead body and take it anywhere.

Chief Rogers congratulated Stella and thanked her for her help. "Thought you might be a goner down there for a minute. I'm glad you're okay." He stopped short of smiling at her. "I'd like to see you in my office as soon as you get back and get cleaned up."

"What's the problem, Chief?" Sean got between them. He didn't like the way the other man was looking at his daughter. "You got a beef with my daughter?"

"There's no problem," Rogers assured him. "We got some new information about Deputy Chum's death that I want to follow through on. Your daughter had a talk with him right before he left Sweet Pepper. Whatever he might've said to her could be important. I promise not to keep her away for too long, Mr. Griffin."

"I'll go with you." Sean possessively took her arm. "I'll be right there with you, Stella. Don't worry."

"I can handle this on my own, Dad." She nodded to Chief Rogers. "I'll be there as soon as I can."

They didn't talk much on the way back to the firehouse. Stella was used to it. Mostly, firefighters weren't as talkative as Ricky. It was a little better when they saved a life. In this case, they had dropped the only evidence that might have helped find Chum's killer and he was dead to start with.

Stella got back to the firehouse, showered, and changed clothes. She was still cold, despite the warm shower and the heavy sweater she took out of her locker. She wished she was going back to the cabin to curl up in front of a nice fire that Eric had made. It would have to wait.

Her father had borrowed some warm, clean clothing from

JC. They were around the same size. There was almost a full crew at the firehouse, waiting to hear what had happened after they were told to stay home from the call. After everything was cleaned up and put away, Stella thanked everyone for their hard work and shared a minimalized account of what had happened.

It looked as though many of her volunteers were going to hang around the coffeepot and talk, as they frequently did. Stella had to get back to town. She started toward the Cherokee, the rain still falling.

John intercepted her before her father and Doug could join her. "So that's the ex? I expected more."

"Me too."

He swallowed the remark that he might have made about Doug. It sounded too much like jealousy. He certainly *wasn't* jealous. "Your parents seem nice."

"My dad is," she shot back, still stinging from his rejection of her because she was part of the Carson family.

"What about your mother?" *He walked right into that one.*

"She's a Carson." Stella shrugged. "You know how *they* are."

John opened the driver's side door of the Cherokee for her. "I'm sorry, Stella. It's just that—"

"Save it. Thanks for your help. Did you notice the black paint on the side of the truck? I'd say someone got up close for that. I got a picture of it before the truck went down."

His mouth tightened. She could make him angrier than any woman alive, though he'd die before he admitted it. "I saw it. The chief will want that. I'll see you back in town."

Stella ignored him as he slammed the door and stalked off.

She took her father and Doug back to the Sweet Pepper Café. Ricky Senior got her a hot cup of coffee to go—Ricky Junior had made it back before her and told him what was going on.

"I'll be back to get you guys in a little while," she told her parents.

"Stella, are you in trouble?" Barbara looked concerned.

"No. Chief Rogers has a few questions. That's all."

"I offered to go with her," Sean complained. "She turned me down."

"Stella—"

Stella grabbed some sugar for her coffee. "I'll see you in a few minutes."

Town hall was on Main Street near the single stoplight going in and out of town. It was both the home of Sweet Pepper's daily functions and the police station. Given her relationship with Chief Rogers, Stella was glad there was a separate firehouse and it was a few miles away.

Rogers was waiting for her in the conference room. He had a satisfied look on his weather-beaten face—like a cat that has a mouse under his paw and is thinking about what fun he's going to have next.

"Ms. Griffin."

"Chief Rogers."

Stella took a seat at the long shiny table. It was only her, Chief Rogers, and John. They didn't really need a whole conference room. Why hadn't they gone into his office? Was he trying to intimidate her?

"I suppose Captain Trump already filled you in about everything since he is the liaison between our departments."

"Only at the barest level," she replied. "What happened to Deputy Chum?"

"He was murdered. Someone shot him in the side of the head and he lost control of his vehicle before he drove off the side of a mountain."

Stella shook her head in frustration. "I could see that for myself. Do you have any suspects?"

Rogers was noncommittal. "He was a good man. He

served the community all of his life. He deserved a better ending."

"And you think I'm involved somehow?" It was in his tone and the way he looked at her. "Is that why I'm here?"

"I never said anything like that."

"You know about my meeting with Chum. I might have been the last person to see him alive. He told me he was leaving Sweet Pepper right away. He was afraid for his life—with good reason, I guess."

She didn't trust Chief Rogers, despite Walt telling her he was a good man. He was Walt's protégé, the man he'd chosen to take his place when he retired. She didn't care.

He wasn't too young to know what had really happened to Eric. He could be working for one of those people Chum had warned her about, the people he was afraid of.

Rogers looked up from the piece of paper he was writing on and smirked at her. "He wasn't a firefighter, Ms. Griffin. And, as far as I can tell, the two of you weren't exactly friends. What did you talk about that was so important? Why was he afraid for his life?"

John seemed to be listening intently, but hadn't spoken or even glanced at her. She knew he was careful around his superior. He rarely did anything that would upset Chief Rogers and jeopardize his future plans to run the police department.

Stella wondered who'd told Rogers that Chum was at the firehouse. She hoped, if she strung him along a little, she might get more details. "I didn't say it was important."

"Don't play games with me! You may be right about being the last person to see him alive. That could make you a person of interest in his murder."

It was Stella's turn to smirk. "That's a stretch, even for you."

Her brain was running through the list of everyone at the

firehouse who knew she was there with Chum. There was only Tagger and Ricky.

She didn't think Ricky would say anything to Chief Rogers. On the other hand, Rogers and Tagger were friends. She wouldn't put it past the police chief to use that friendship to his advantage.

"Maybe. It all depends on what he told you." The chief tapped his pen on the desk.

"Okay." She sat back in her chair and fought the urge to get up and walk out. "I'll play. Chum and I weren't exactly friends. He told me he was leaving town and we talked about my grandmother, Abigail Carson. I'm assuming you know all about the first time Deputy Chum and I met."

His pale blue eyes were almost hidden beneath his mostly closed eyelids as he listened to her. "Why don't you tell us about it?"

Stella described her first meeting with Chum, when he'd thought she was the ghost of her dead grandmother. "He never gave me that speeding ticket. He took off like something was after him. I didn't know why, until he told me later."

"And that was?"

"It seems Abigail's death was his first homicide investigation—the first time he'd ever seen a dead person outside a coffin, as he put it. That's what we talked about, Chief Rogers. What was it that you *thought* he said to me?"

Even though he still seemed angry, Rogers's posture relaxed a little.

*There was something there that he didn't want her to know.*

Did it have to do with the body, maybe Eric's body, being carried out of the silo fire forty years ago when no one was watching? Had Chum been killed for telling about it, as he'd feared?

She had stumbled on the motive for Eric's death—thirty million dollars. Now she had to figure out who killed him. Had they killed Eric while he was still in the silo, or later in the car before they took him to the firehouse?

"I guess you're free to go," Chief Rogers said. "Sorry to have bothered you."

"Not a problem." She got to her feet, sorry that she didn't get anything more from the conversation. "I hope you have better suspects than me in mind."

"Chief Griffin has a picture of a long, black paint scratch on the side of Deputy Chum's truck," John told Rogers. "Would you like her to email that to you?"

"She can send it to you, John," Chief Rogers answered, going through his paperwork as though she was already gone.

It took her a second to find the pictures she'd taken and send them to John's phone. "Done. See you later."

Stella left the room but didn't close the door. She waited, pretending she was looking up something on her phone. She figured she could always claim that she thought there might be another photo she hadn't sent.

"Did you really think she was involved in this?" John asked.

"Nah. I like to rattle her cage now and again. I don't suppose you know what's keeping her here?"

"Not me. Not anymore."

There was a small pause. Stella was about to walk away when Chief Rogers spoke. "See if you can find anyone who was traveling along that stretch of road yesterday about the time Chum left town, huh? Maybe we'll get lucky and someone saw what happened."

"Sure thing. I don't know if you heard or not yet, Stella's parents are both in town."

"Barbara Carson? After all these years? Well, ain't that a kick in the teeth. Looks like Marty has some competition besides Stella for the old man's money. If Barbara comes back to Sweet Pepper to stay, he's gonna find himself out in the cold."

Stella moved quickly away from the door when she heard the sounds of a chair moving. She ducked into a small, empty office as John walked out of the room and left the building.


Stella's parents had left the café with Doug in the rental car. Ricky Junior said they were headed back toward the cabin.

Saying a little prayer that Eric wouldn't open the door for them and then find other tricks to play on her ex-boy-friend, Stella took the Cherokee and quickly followed them.

She only had a few minutes to get to the firehouse before practice at ten. She hoped it was enough time to convince Doug that it would be better to stay somewhere else. Maybe he could stay in Sevierville. There were nice hotels there.

She was relieved to see the rental car at the firehouse on the corner before she turned to go to the cabin. She let out a sigh of relief.

It wasn't so much that she cared if *Doug* got scared and left Sweet Pepper—she didn't want her parents to get upset about her living with a ghost. She also didn't want any new ghost stories about the cabin getting around now that she knew how Bob felt about Eric.

The rain had slacked off to a fine drizzle. Sean was busy talking to the volunteers already assembled for practice in front of the firehouse. He was in his element—talking about his life's work, and his daughter.

Scheduled practices went on no matter what the weather. The volunteers would have to fight fires and be a part of search and rescue no matter how wet, cold, hot, or dry it was. Besides, with volunteers trying to find time for practice between their jobs and families, they had to stay on schedule.

Barbara had been given a lawn chair in the open garage bay beside Tagger to watch the practice. They'd be dry there.

Stella didn't see her ex anywhere. She parked the Cherokee in the back of the firehouse and walked through the kitchen. He wasn't there either. "Where's Doug?"

Her fears of Eric doing something terrible to him shot to the forefront of her mind again.

"I'm not sure." Barbara smiled at Tagger. "Excuse us, Mr. Tagger."

She took her daughter's arm in a firm grip and walked behind the engine with her. "Stella, you could at least treat Doug with some respect. There's no reason to be mean to him."

"Mom—" She stopped and shook her head. "I don't even know what to say. How could you bring him down here with you? I thought you knew how I felt."

"I thought you might want to see him again. It's been a year. I can't believe you're going to let *one* stupid mistake mess things up between you. I should never have encouraged you to come down here."

"I don't think this has anything to do with coming to Sweet Pepper."

"Of course it does! Out of sight is out of mind. If you'd stayed in Chicago, the two of you would've already patched things up. Doug's parents are devastated too, you know. We always planned for the two of you to marry someday."

"Mom—"

"I think you still love him, but you can be as stubborn as your father."

"I don't love him anymore, Mom. I know you and Dad are good friends with Doug's parents. I know we grew up together. But we aren't ever going to be together again. I'll never trust him. I'll never love him again."

Stella hadn't realized that she'd spoken so loudly. Everyone was in the bay, watching and listening. She looked around, uncomfortably, for a moment and then addressed the situation.

"Okay. Everyone knows about my love life now. Let's see if we can get some practice in with the hoses, shall we?"

There were a few giggles and some whispering, but everyone started taking out the hoses and getting ready for practice.

Sean joined right in, giving pointers to the volunteers from his thirty-plus years of experience with the Chicago Fire Department.

Stella let him have at it. He certainly knew more about what he was doing than she did. She laughed as he goofed around with all the people she'd come to know and envied his ease of handling situations where he didn't know anyone. Her father was one of those people who had never met a stranger.

It would've been much easier for her when she'd come down here if she'd been less reserved. She was more like her mother.

Maybe John was right about Carson blood.

Ricky came late. He'd warned her that the electric dishwasher at the café was broken and they were washing dishes by hand. Banyin came in with a note from her doctor that said she could do normal practice with the group, but shouldn't go out on any fire calls.

"I can still do communications," Banyin said cheerfully. "I can help clean up and lots of other things."

"Okay." Stella smiled at her and garnered another hug. "Go ahead and change clothes."

Barbara was impressed. "I never really thought of you as being a fire chief. You were always so against the politics. Yet here you are, handling everything like you were born to it. I think this experience has changed you, honey."

"I think so too," Stella agreed.

She pointed out Bert who was working with her father

and JC on a two-inch hose that was connected to the old pumper truck. "He's the mayor's son. Still in high school and a star athlete. He's also a great volunteer—when he makes it in."

"This is quite a band you've assembled here." Sean left the volunteers to practice on their own and joined his wife and daughter. "You've done a great job."

"Thanks, Dad. It's been a lot of work."

"I know it's been tough. You were here alone, the only one with any real-life experience. I can't imagine what it must've been like. Back home, we depend on the new kids learning from the old guys."

Tagger coughed to get their attention. "I was a volunteer with the first Sweet Pepper Brigade when I got back from Vietnam. I was glad to help out."

Stella glanced at Tagger, wondering again if he was the one who told Chief Rogers about Chum coming to see her. She wanted to ask him but decided to wait until a time they were alone. She didn't want to embarrass him. It could have been Ricky who didn't realize what he was telling Chief Rogers.

Bert had made practice, but Marty, her erstwhile Carson relative, wasn't there. She'd left him voice mail and texts about practice but he still hadn't shown up. The only thing she could do was take him off the books and look for someone else.

*Speaking of the Carson family.*

A big, black Lincoln pulled into the parking lot. It looked as though someone had already told Ben Carson that his daughter was in town.

# Chapter 11

~~~~~~~~~~~~~

"**B**arbara!"

Ben Carson didn't even wait for his chauffeur to come around and open the back door for him. He climbed out of the car, his shoulders stooped a little, gray hair thinning. He was a tall man, made spindly by old age.

That didn't stop him from loping to his daughter's side. Forty years, and too much that needed explanation, were between them. While they had spoken recently, they hadn't seen each other for more than forty years.

Everyone stopped to stare at the millionaire and land baron who some said ran Sweet Pepper. No one had ever seen him approach another person this way. Not many had seen him with tears streaming down his face.

He reached his daughter and clutched her to him. "I can't tell you what it means to see you back home. I wasn't sure if I'd live to see the day."

Stella couldn't help noticing that her mother was not as enthusiastic in her embrace of the old man. Barbara tried to keep her distance—all but impossible with her father holding her so tightly.

Sean shook hands with the father-in-law he'd only recently learned about. Barbara had kept her Sweet Pepper roots and family a secret their entire married life. While this had caused some recent consternation between them, they'd gotten through it.

Ben looked at Barbara, wiping tears from his eyes. "My whole family, here together. How long are you staying? I had the housekeeper make up your old room. It will be like old times."

His daughter had other ideas. "I'm sorry, Dad. But Sean wanted to stay in Pigeon Forge so we could see some sights while we were down here. He's never been to Tennessee."

"Oh. Okay. That's fine," Ben said. "He can do that from the mansion too, you know. Please, Barbara, don't deny me this small thing. I'd like to see you under my roof again."

Stella knew from talking to her mother on the phone that Barbara didn't feel like she could stay in the house where her mother had died. She couldn't face the bottom of the long staircase where she'd found her mother's body.

Barbara didn't believe her father had killed her mother—at least not anymore. She'd retreated from that accusation. She blamed it on her youth, and the terrible aftermath of her mother's death. That had been the only way she'd been able to talk to her father again and think about returning to Sweet Pepper.

"Mom, you know you said you wanted to stay with me." This wasn't what Stella had wanted at all—unless Doug could be convinced to stay elsewhere. She doubted that since he'd been confident enough to come and see her. "I have plenty of room."

"Of course." Ben backed off at once. "If you'd rather stay with Stella, I completely understand. I've tried my best to get her to move in with me and Vivian, but she's stubborn and independent. I wonder where she gets that from?"

Barbara looked relieved. "I want to spend time with you while we're here, Dad. I need time with Stella too. I hope you understand."

He hugged her again. "Of course I do. But come for dinner tonight. We can at least eat dinner together, can't we?"

Stella watched her mother's face. Barbara smiled in a resolved way that Stella knew so well from her childhood. It meant she'd made up her mind about something she didn't want to do. Sometimes it took her a while, but once she was set, it was hard to budge her.

"Dinner would be fine, Dad. We'll be there."

Ben didn't leave Barbara's side again while he was at the firehouse. He held her hand and looked at her like she was something more precious than gold.

"He doesn't seem so bad," Sean said to Stella as they joined in the practice session. "From the things your mother said, I was expecting some evil dictator millionaire. He seems like a normal millionaire, with a mansion. How bad can that be? I always wished my dad would turn into an evil millionaire with a mansion."

Stella smiled. Being around her father was like a breath of fresh air.

"He's been okay with me while I've been here. There are some terrible stories that people tell about him. I think he may have been evil in the past. I don't know. He's definitely the big cheese around here. What he says goes, in a lot of cases. I think he got me this job to lure mom back down here."

"Maybe he did." Sean put his arm around her shoulders. "But you ran with it, my darlin'. You pulled all this together. They're lucky to have you. At least they *were* lucky. It's time for you to come home."

"I guessed this little impromptu visit was all about bringing me back home."

"Right you are. I always said you were a smarty-pants. I think you've shared enough of your time and talent with these people. We miss you. Sweet Pepper can't have you forever."

Stella paired Petey and Ricky on hose practice together. That was a mistake. She was trying to get everyone used to handing off a hose in case the need arose again, as it had with Banyin. She didn't think it would matter who the pairs were, and different people would learn to work together.

Ricky and Petey both wanted to take charge. They jerked the hose and lost control of it. The pressurized water sprayed across everyone in the parking lot—until Banyin turned off the water from the pumper.

"Okay. What was that all about?" Stella asked.

"He was trying to snatch it away from me," Petey complained.

"Whatever," Ricky groaned. "It's always got to be about *her*."

Stella had no sympathy for them. "Never mind all that. This is about working *together* as a team. Let's try again. No one has to lead. This isn't dancing."

She had Royce and JC hand off the hose again to Petey and Ricky—with the same results.

"Isn't this a waste of time, Chief, since Ricky and I are on different teams all the time?" Petey demanded after the hose was turned off again.

Stella wiped the water from her face. "Humor me!"

Royce and JC glared at the co-assistant chiefs. They were both soaking wet for the second time.

The two men picked up the hose again. Banyin turned on the water. Royce and JC handed the hose to Petey and Ricky. This time it went more smoothly, but there were still some issues that had to be faced.

"He keeps grabbing it," Petey complained, glaring at Ricky.

"Well, it feels like she's gonna drop it," Ricky countered.

"Maybe it would be better if she stuck to bossing people around and let the rest of us handle the *real* work."

"I think we need a little trust work here," Sean said with a grin.

"Trust work?" Petey questioned.

Stella looked on as her father set Ricky and Petey up to learn to trust each other. He had Ricky wear a blindfold while Petey guided his hands to take the hose from Royce and JC.

The water was on. It wasn't easy. Again and again, Ricky groped around blindly, fighting her, until he finally trusted that Petey was putting his hands in the right place.

"That's what we're looking for," Sean said. "You have to trust the person you're with."

It was Petey's turn next. She wasn't happy about the idea. "I don't think I can do this. I'm sorry, Chief. He's just—you know."

Stella finally convinced her to put on the blindfold. Petey tried to cheat by looking under it as Ricky tried to guide her hands on the hose.

"None of that." Sean tapped the side of her head. "Cheaters never win."

Finally, Petey gave in and accepted the inevitable. She was going to have to trust Ricky. The rest of the group applauded and cheered as the hose was handed off again, and this time there was no hesitation.

"I've been a firefighter most of my life," Sean said to all of them. "I've saved some of my partners' lives, and they've saved mine. You have to trust your partner. All of you have to learn to completely trust each other during practice or you can't work together. You have to know that this man, and that woman, have your back during emergencies. That's the only way a team can be safe."

Tagger was sniffling as he wiped tears from his eyes. "That was beautiful. Trust is a beautiful thing."

All of the fire brigade members were paired up with different people for the next hour and a half until everyone had worked with everyone else, blindfolded, handing off the two-inch hose in what became a seamless ballet.

"Yes!" Sean yelled. "You've got it. And it looks like lunchtime to me. I'm buying beers for anyone who wants them at wherever the local pub is."

He looked at Stella. "Sorry. Just enthusiastic." He gave her a quick salute. "If the Chief says it's time to quit."

Stella laughed. "That works for me. Good practice, people. Let's get cleaned up and head to Beau's before my dad changes his mind."

There was a lot of enthusiasm and excitement as the group cleaned up and stored everything where it belonged—much more than the usual practice. Stella knew it was her father's attitude. Maybe there was some way she could capture some of that in her own training sessions.

She reminded herself that there weren't many of those left, if she was going home. It surprised her that she felt a little depressed at the idea that there was no future for her here with these people. She'd thought it was only Eric who was keeping her in Sweet Pepper. Maybe she was wrong.

Petey had finished cleaning up and had closed her locker door. Ricky performed the same task, at the same moment.

"That was good today." Petey smiled at her competitor. "Kind of weird wearing a blindfold."

Ricky agreed. "We got through it, though. I know we've had our differences—"

"You mean like it was unfair for the chief to make *both* of us assistant chiefs."

"Like that. When clearly, I should've been named chief."

"Yeah." Petey stood close to Ricky, really seeing him for the first time. He was good-looking. She really liked his eyes.

"It's okay." Ricky noticed how cute Petey was when she wrinkled up her little nose. "I kind of like it."

"Yeah." Petey's smile kept getting bigger—and suddenly they were in each other's arms. Her back against the lockers—Ricky's lips pressed against hers.

Stella cleared her throat as she walked by the pair who only a few hours ago couldn't work together. Trust was indeed a beautiful thing.

"Sorry, Chief." They both quickly moved apart and blurted out.

"That's okay. Just wanted to tell you I'm leaving. Banyin is taking calls. Lock up when you're done."

Stella smiled as she got on the Harley to head for Beau's for that free beer. Ricky and Petey were an unlikely couple. She was fairly sure they both had someone else they were dating. Maybe they didn't need all that enthusiasm at practice after all.

Her mother and father had already left in the rental car. She texted, reminding Stella that they still hadn't seen Doug since they'd left the café. Stella had forgotten. She didn't want to go and look for Doug. She also didn't want a ghostly incident.

She took a left from the parking lot, up Firehouse Road, and to the cabin.

Doug didn't have a car and was in a place he didn't know. It made sense that he might have walked the mile or so back to the cabin. She hoped it wasn't a mistake for him. She prayed Eric hadn't let him inside.

There was no sign of him when she parked her bike in front of the cabin. The door was open—Hero ran out to greet her. She rubbed the puppy's neck and they walked up the stairs to the porch together.

Kimmie and David had taken both dogs to rescue practice out of town today and been excused from the regular session in Sweet Pepper. Most of the time their practices were scheduled so they could manage to do both. Stella was excited at the progress the dogs were making, though, and was happy to accommodate them.

"Doug?" Stella called when she was in the kitchen.

"He's on the deck." Eric appeared unexpectedly.

"You startled me." She watched as Hero ran, barking, out on the back deck. "I don't see him out there."

"He's in the hot tub," Eric added.

"Did you do anything to him?"

"No. He's fine. I didn't hurt him."

Stella ran across the living area to the back deck. Hero was barking frantically at Doug, who was in the hot tub, fully clothed.

"I can't get out." Doug's voice was high-pitched and scared. "I'm not sure how I got here in the first place, and now I can't get out."

He demonstrated by trying to push himself out of the warm, bubbly water. He couldn't move. "I don't know what it is. I think you should call an ambulance. I may be having a stroke or something."

Eric lounged back in one of the rocking chairs, a smile playing across his lips. Hero stopped barking as Stella shushed him. The dog went to lay close to Eric's feet with an unsatisfied whine.

"Let him up." Stella turned her back to Doug.

"I think you should call an ambulance," Eric agreed with Doug.

"*Just let him up*," she hissed. "He's not sick."

Eric shrugged and suddenly, Doug was able to move. Stella got him a towel as he climbed out of the hot tub on shaky legs.

"How long have you been in there?" She looked at his wrinkled hands.

"I don't know." He moved away from the hot tub. "I think

I fainted or something. I don't know how it happened. I was walking into the cabin and then I was out here."

Stella gave Doug her long pink robe—he had no dry clothes with him—and put a blanket around him. She sat him by the fireplace with a glass of brandy. The fire crackled merrily as he took a few sips.

"You'll be fine," she said. "Sit here and take it easy for a while."

Doug looked up at her, his eyes pleading with hers. "What happened to us, Stella? I know you think it started when you caught me—found me—but it was before then. She was just the-uh-*manifestation* of the problem."

Stella hadn't realized he'd thought there was a problem between them. "I don't know, Doug. When did you stop loving me?"

"Never!" He denied it vehemently and took a big sip of brandy for courage. "I *never* stopped loving you! I thought you didn't love *me* anymore. You were always gone, always working. I know both of our jobs are demanding, but it was more than that."

She shook her head. "It's kind of late now. I'm sorry you thought I didn't love you. I didn't know anything was wrong with us, until the '*manifestation*' of seeing you naked with my friend."

He grabbed her hand. "She meant *nothing* to me. I was just trying to show both of us that there was a problem, I think. I guess I went too far."

"I haven't hurt him—*yet*—can I do it now?" Eric was standing behind her.

"You know this would be easier without an audience," she said to him.

Doug jumped up. "Is someone else here?"

"No," Stella reassured him. "It's only us."

"Like hell it is," Eric said. "What did you ever see in him?"

"Leave him alone," Stella whispered. "This is none of your business."

"Are you going home to marry him?" Eric demanded.

"No! I'm not marrying him."

"Stella, give me—give *us*, a second chance," Doug pleaded. "Let me make it up to you."

"I could hang him under the deck," Eric offered. "I don't think anyone would miss him."

"Go away!" she yelled.

Doug's expression was tragic. "If that's how you feel."

"Not *you*," she amended. "I was talking to that annoying fly that keeps buzzing around."

"I didn't notice a fly." Doug glanced around the room.

"Unfortunately, I can't go far enough away not to hear this," Eric said. "Maybe you two should leave. I don't like soap operas."

There was a knock at the door. Before Stella could answer it, Eric identified the caller as Walt Fenway and opened the door for him.

"Thanks, buddy." Walt smiled and looked around the cabin. His arms were full of files. "Stella, I've been down at the department of motor vehicles. I got records for all the Impalas I could find listed to owners in Sweet Pepper for the last forty years. It's a mess of them. Have you had lunch yet?"

# Chapter 12

~~~~~~

Walt saw Doug. "Oh, you have company. Sorry. Let me drop these off. We'll start looking through them later."

"All the Impalas for forty years, huh?" Stella grinned when she saw the mountain of paperwork. "That's a lot of Impalas."

Walt agreed. "You said Chum saw Eric's body being shoved into the trunk of a Chevy Impala. I figured it must have belonged to someone in Sweet Pepper. I started thinking about it. Maybe we'll get lucky and whoever the owner is kept the car. It would be a classic now."

As soon as Walt had put the papers on the table, he crossed the room and offered his hand to Doug. "Walt Fenway. You must be a friend of Stella's."

Doug shook his hand, careful to keep the brown blanket pulled up over Stella's robe. "Doug Connelly, sir. I was once, *almost*, her fiancé. Back in Chicago."

Walt glanced at Stella. "Oh. Stella's mentioned you a time or two. You're a police officer, right?"

"That's right." Doug smiled at Stella. "I've been on the job for ten years."

"I'm Sweet Pepper's retired police chief. Looks like we've got something in common."

Lunch was inevitable. Stella scrounged together what she could. It was mostly bread, cheese, and eggs. There was bottled spring water to wash it down. The three of them split the last of Eric's baking frenzy, the custard.

When Doug told Walt about his experience in the hot tub, Walt looked around the room—silently acknowledging what he thought must be Eric's hand in that event. He didn't speak to Eric again, as he usually did. He understood what the problem was between the two men. *Stella.*

"So what are you looking for with these Impalas?" Doug asked. "Was there an Impala fire or something? How did the retired Sweet Pepper police chief and the temporary fire chief meet?"

Stella didn't want to talk about Eric. She hoped Walt would feel the same. Doug wouldn't understand, and worse, they'd have to discuss how anything like that was possible. Despite Doug's hot tub time, it was unlikely that he would suddenly become a believer in the supernatural.

Walt briefly explained how he and Stella had met. Then he told Doug he was helping her look for the former fire chief's killer.

Doug smiled. "Stella, you didn't tell me you became a police detective while you were here. Do your parents know you're searching for someone's killer?"

"I've mentioned it to them." She felt forced to tell Doug about finding Eric's bones at the firehouse. "We've got a few leads, and they finally dug up the fire chief's coffin. We're hoping there might be more answers there."

"Let me help you take a look at it while I'm here," Doug volunteered. "Maybe some fresh eyes might help. Eight months is a long time with no real leads. Forty years is a cold case that's gone arctic."

Within a few minutes they were talking over possible angles and ideas. Stella told Walt about the large black scratch on the side of Chum's truck.

"I think he was definitely shot at close range," she said. "Probably while the car was right up next to him. The momentum from the truck suggests Chum never had a chance to slow down when he hit the side of the road. Chief Rogers talked to me about Chum's death, supposedly because I was the last one to see him alive."

"He was shaking a few trees to see what came down," Walt told her. "Poor old Chum."

"So this is still an active investigation?" Doug realized with excitement. "If you think Deputy Chum was killed because he gave you information about the old fire chief's death, the killer must still be alive and living in Sweet Pepper. Now we're talking!"

"That's what I was thinking too," Stella agreed with less enthusiasm.

A sudden gust of wind from within the cabin blew all of the loose papers off the table, scattering them across the room. Walt and Doug scrambled to pick them up.

Doug glanced around to see what had caused it. Walt nodded with a smile.

Stella knew what had happened. She saw Eric wave his arm across the table as he said, "It's bad enough you two are doing this. I won't have this meathead helping out."

"Someone's having a bad day," Stella told Walt.

"Can't blame him," Walt said. "It's gotta be hard on a man when other people are talking about him being dead."

"Who's talking about being dead?" Doug asked. "It would've been better if this was all on a computer."

"If it would've been, I don't think the DMV would've let

me take the computer home," Walt chuckled. "Besides that kind of thing doesn't go back that far here."

"Maybe we should work somewhere else," Stella suggested.

"You might be right." Walt grinned at what he hoped was Eric's ghost close by them. "I guess I better get going. Let me know what you want to do."

Hero started barking again and Stella looked out the window. "I guess you might as well stay and meet my parents."

"I'd like that." Walt turned his head from side-to-side. "If you think *he* won't mind."

"I live here too. He's going to have to deal with it for now."

Sean and Barbara came in and met Walt. Doug helped Sean bring in their suitcases, tossing off Stella's pink robe. He didn't try to explain what had happened in the hot tub.

Stella made coffee and everyone sat around the fire drinking it. The rain and fog had made the day chilly. Stella didn't turn on the furnace. It was still summer, even though it sometimes felt like fall on days like this.

She realized she was going to have to go to the store. Between people showing up, and Eric baking, her cupboards were bare. Even worse, she was nursing her last warm can of emergency Coke.

The conversation went quickly from Sean's amazement that his daughter could build a real fire—to the reason Stella had stayed on in Sweet Pepper after her contract with the town was up.

Doug didn't hold anything back that he'd learned about her investigation, mostly from Walt. Barbara and Sean were both shocked and horrified that Stella was involved in an active murder investigation.

"You're a firefighter, for God's sake," Sean reminded her. "Not a police detective."

Stella wasn't surprised by his attitude. Didn't she have similar conversations with Eric all the time?

"I didn't realize this was what you meant when you said you were trying to figure out what happened to the old fire chief," Barbara said. "You said it happened forty years ago. I thought it was some historical project."

"Look, I know I'm not a cop," Stella explained. "Walt is a retired cop, and I have a friend who's on the job in Sweet Pepper right now who helps out when I need him. I'm not trying to do this alone. Someone needs to do it though, and I guess that's me."

"Why you?" Barbara asked. "Why not the police or the FBI or something?"

"Because no one else is interested," Walt said. "It's been a long time, and forgive me for saying so, Mrs. Griffin, but you know how things work. Once they're dead and buried, we tend to forget about them."

"When we found Chief Gamlyn's remains behind the fake wall in the old firehouse, it was obvious he hadn't died like everyone thought," Stella continued. "All this time, the town mourned a lost hero who'd died doing his job, protecting the community. Instead, it appears that someone took him out of that burning silo, shot him in the head, and stuck him in the firehouse. I'd hope someone would come along and do this for me, if that was my fate."

Stella's words were passionate and heartfelt. No one, including Eric, could doubt her sincerity. He stood close to her as she was surrounded by her family and felt ashamed that he'd argued with her about this, that he'd felt so much anger at what had happened to him.

She wasn't to blame. She was only trying to help. He had to let go of the bitterness and anger that had consumed him from the moment he saw what was left of him in the ruins of the old firehouse he'd built.

He had to try to remember what had happened to him. He had to find a way to help her so she could go home with her family. In the time he'd known her, he had learned how stubborn and determined she could be. He had no doubt that she wouldn't leave Sweet Pepper until she found out what had happened to him.

"I can see how serious you are about this," Barbara said. "But if someone killed that poor man on the road to keep the answer hidden, this might be too dangerous for you, Stella. Who's going to protect *you* if you discover what your dead friend knew?"

Sean added, "I hope you're not depending on that Chief Rogers for help. I don't think he likes you, honey. Maybe that other one—what's his name—Trump? I think he likes you a lot. Sorry, Doug."

"That's okay." Doug said. "My only concern about this civilian investigation is that Stella doesn't have the rest of her life to figure this out. It's already been forty years and, obviously, local law enforcement hasn't been able to find any answers. No disrespect meant, Walt."

"None taken, son. It's not an investigation my office ever undertook. There was no sign of foul play when Eric died. He ran into the burning silo after realizing one of his fire-fighters was still inside. The roof collapsed after that man was safe. Eric didn't come out."

Walt shook his head and sadly gazed around the room. "We only realized that it wasn't an accidental death after we found Chief Gamlyn's bones in the old firehouse. Who-ever put my friend behind that wall after they killed him never expected him to be found."

Stella got more wood for the fire and realized Eric was listening to them talk from behind the big brown leather sofa. She wished she could say something to him, but there was no way to disguise that conversation. They'd have to talk later.

Walt explained that several important breakthroughs had happened in the case. "I know Stella is on a deadline now. I don't want her to lose her job back in Chicago. I'm hoping we can crack this nut in a short time—or at least find enough information to get law enforcement seriously involved."

Stella put more wood in the fireplace. Sparks flew up around the dried pieces of oak. Hero barked a few times, and then seemed surprised by the sound. They all laughed at the dog.

"I guess we'd better think about getting ready for dinner at Dad's," Barbara said. "Anyone got a Valium handy? It might be the only way I'll make it through this."

Walt said his goodbyes and Stella took Doug upstairs to the second floor of the cabin. She'd only been up there a few times. It was filled with things that had belonged to Eric—wood carving projects, his fire chief helmet, and other personal effects.

There was also a bed and chest of drawers up there. She hoped Eric would behave and not throw Doug down the wood stairs in the middle of the night.

Stella ran her hand over the smooth surface of a small baby cradle that Eric had carved. She always looked at it when she came up here. It made her feel all weepy to see it and realize that Eric had plans for the future and a family when he'd died.

It was a beautiful piece of furniture. She could imagine him carving it while he sat on the back deck and watched the river go by.

Eric had told her once that he missed carving wood almost more than anything else. He said it took a lot of concentration to do anything with solid objects as a ghost. It wasn't too hard to do something fast, like throwing papers on the floor. Anything that took more time than that was a strain.

"You should be comfortable up here," she told Doug. "I

don't think any other strange things, like the hot tub incident, will happen." *I hope not anyway.*

"Thanks." Doug put his duffel bag on the bed. "You know, I really thought you'd want to see me again when I came down here with your parents. I wouldn't have come otherwise. We've had our disagreements, but we always made up."

"I know."

"I can see, now that I'm down here, that you don't need me anymore. You've kind of outgrown us, haven't you?"

"I don't know if that's the word I'd use, but yes, I've changed."

"This place, being fire chief—you're different. It's okay. Maybe I can help you find your dead fire chief's killer, and the trip won't have been a waste."

"That would be great. We could use all the help we can get, even if it's only for a few days."

"You know, your mom and dad are real serious about you coming back with them. Your dad already bought a packing crate for the Harley so you could ship it."

"Thanks for the heads-up."

"I appreciate you letting me stay here. I'll try not to make it more awkward than it has to be. I'm sorry it happened this way."

"Not a problem." She smiled and started to go back downstairs.

"Do you think Barbara's father meant for me to come to dinner too?"

"I think so. It's a big place. I'm sure they can squeeze you in."

"Thanks."

Stella had decided her parents could take her bedroom and she'd sleep on the sofa. She'd slept out there plenty of times for less reason. It was comfortable.

The bedroom door was closed when she got downstairs.

She figured her parents were showering and changing. She should've warned them about the limited hot water supply. *Oh well.* They'd find out soon enough.

While she was waiting to change, she noticed Eric on the back deck. Putting on a sweater, she joined him. She hoped her parents wouldn't see two rocking chairs moving. She supposed she could always blame the wind.

"I hope you're over Doug now." She settled into a chair.

"I hope you are too."

"Technically, that's none of your business. I'm sure Doug and I are over, but I suppose something unexpected could happen to change that."

"Like he sweeps you off your feet and asks you to marry him?"

"No. And this isn't a fair conversation. You don't have any girlfriends for me to razz you about."

"Yeah. They seem to be in limited supply here."

"Eric—"

"No. Don't say anything until I apologize." He rocked in the chair for a few minutes, his eyes unfocused as he gazed out at the mountains that surrounded them. "I'm sorry I took it out on you, Stella. I know you're only trying to help. I feel like such a fool. I can't even remember how I died. That seems stupid to me."

"I suppose it was fairly traumatic." She tried to empathize. "It's hard to remember anything that happens around an accident or injury. Your mind kind of goes blank. I can't imagine what it must be like dealing with understanding your own death."

"That being said, I know your parents want you back. I don't blame them. I can't tell you how much I hate the idea of losing you. I understand that you have to go. I appreciate whatever time and effort you can give me to help Walt figure out what happened."

"I'll do the best I can, Eric. I hate the idea of leaving you too. I wish I could bring you home in my suitcase. I suppose you probably wouldn't be very happy haunting my apartment anyway. No mountains or river to look at."

He grinned. "I don't think it works that way."

"I know we've been over this before, but would you consider thinking back to that night that you died? Knowing that someone brought you out of the silo might jog something in your memory."

His face was grim. "No promises, but I'll try."

# Chapter 13

The wind sighed as it blew through the eaves around the deck. The rain danced lightly on the roof above them, but didn't reach the chairs.

"We knew the silo fire would be bad," Eric recounted. "I called the county for help. I don't know if they ever got there. The fire was burning so hot—there was no way the structure was going to stand for long. I called everyone to make sure they got out before the roof collapsed."

"And you were standing at the front of the building when that happened?" She tried to visualize the situation.

"Yes. Tagger was Ricky Hutchins's partner. He ran out and told me he'd lost contact with Ricky. I tried to get Ricky on the radio but there was no reply. Everyone else was out of the building. I had to go inside and find him."

"How many fire brigade members were at the silo fire?" Stella asked.

"The whole crew—probably about twenty-one. I got them all on the hoses, put on my face mask, and ran back inside. The smoke was like a wall surrounding me. I could barely make out anything. Even with the hoses going full force, the heat was unbearable. I knew Ricky wouldn't last long like that. Me either, for that matter."

"Okay. So you found Ricky. He was almost overcome by smoke. He told me you gave him your face mask. He put it on and ran out the front where you'd come in, right?"

"Yes."

"So why weren't you running out right behind him? You knew you couldn't do anything else in there. You knew the roof was about to collapse. What made you stand there for that extra time?"

"It sounds crazy, but it was a shadow." Eric thought back. "I saw a shadow move to the left of me. I thought there might be someone else trapped inside. I moved toward it."

Stella waited a minute and then nudged him when he didn't continue. "You went farther in to see if anyone else was still there, didn't you? Then what happened?"

"I don't know." He looked at her blankly. "It's like one minute I was standing there, looking for one of my men—who else would be in the silo? The next, I was here. There was nothing else. I always assumed I was overwhelmed by the heat and smoke. Or the roof collapsed on me."

"You didn't see the roof collapsing? It sounds more like heat and smoke."

"It sounds that way."

"You think someone else was really in there with you? Or was the smoke playing tricks on you?"

"I don't know," he admitted. "That's all I remember."

"I think, given what we know now, we can assume if there was someone in the silo with you, it was probably your killer."

"Does Ricky remember seeing anyone before he ran out?" Eric asked.

"Only you, I think. But it can't hurt to ask him again."

"Stella?" Barbara opened the door to the deck and looked

around. "Who are you talking to? I thought you said cell phones didn't work up here. It's freezing. You should come in and get ready for dinner."

"I'm coming right now." *Once a mother*, Stella thought with a smile.

She waited until her mother had gone back inside. "Don't worry," she said to Eric. "We'll figure this out."

"Thanks. That means a lot to me."

"I hope someone would do the same for me too. See you later."

"Who were you talking to?" Barbara repeated as Stella went inside and shut the door behind her.

"No one. Just mumbling to myself. I spend too much time alone, I guess."

Her mother paced the open wood floor. "I'm a nervous wreck about this whole dinner thing. It's not like I didn't expect to see Dad while I was here. It's been a long time. I wanted to thank you for coming to my rescue about staying with him. I don't think I'm ready to sleep in my old room. I hope I'm ready to eat at the mansion. I don't want to alarm your father. You know how he can be."

"Feisty?" Stella grinned. "I know."

"I don't know how we avoided talking about it on the way down here. Probably because Doug was there and we were discussing our strategy on how to get you on a plane with us going home."

Stella shook her head. "Mom—"

"I know. I know." Barbara paced some more, this time right through Eric as he came in from the deck. She shivered violently but kept walking. "I haven't been to the mansion since I was a kid. I was so young when I left home." She laughed self-consciously. "I suppose it's hard to imagine all that drama, huh?"

"It definitely doesn't seem like you. If Dad had told me *he* was from a rich family he'd never mentioned, I wouldn't be surprised." She studied her mother's face. "Why didn't you tell me?"

Barbara sat down on the worn leather sofa. Stella sat beside her, their hands joined. Eric was in the large, easy-chair by the fireplace. If he could tolerate her digging into his past, she supposed she'd have to tolerate him listening to her family secrets.

"I know you must think I'm the worst mother in the world," Barbara said. "What kind of mother let's her daughter walk into something like this and doesn't say anything?"

"I've wondered that a few times, especially after you told me you thought Ben—sorry I can't think of him as my grandfather yet—might have killed your mother."

"That was silly kid stuff. I realized a long time ago that those suspicions were part of the trauma of finding my mother dead at the bottom of the staircase. When Dad contacted me after you broke up with Doug, I realized that I'd been wrong about him. My whole life had been built around a lie."

Barbara continued, with tears in her eyes. "How was I going to tell you and your father, or anyone else, that I was a wealthy heiress from Sweet Pepper, Tennessee? It sounded crazy, even to me."

"That's exactly what you are," Stella reminded her. "Ben never had another child. You're it. Me taking this job and coming down here, surely that was the best lead-in you were ever going to get."

"It was. I thought about it, believe me. Your grandfather was so worried about how my story would affect you that he asked me not to say anything. He wanted to be the one to tell you, after you got to know him a little. I hadn't done such a great job of handling the whole thing with my past. I kept quiet a little longer."

Barbara twisted her plain gold wedding band on her finger. "Now here we are, in Sweet Pepper, about to have dinner with my father. When I left here, I called him a murderer. I reported him to the police and almost caused him to go to jail."

She looked up at Stella. "I never thought I'd come back. I wrote off this life and never thought about it again after I met your father."

"Knowing all that," said Sean as he joined them, freshly changed into a gray suit and red tie with the Chicago Fire Department emblem on it, "you still didn't give us a heads-up. It scares me now, thinking what other secrets you're hiding."

Barbara stood up and kissed him, smoothing a stray strand of his hair that had a tendency to stand up. "The rest of my life is an open book. Outside of my father being a millionaire and living down here in his own little kingdom, that's it."

"And sure you could've mentioned that you were a princess in disguise during some of those times when we barely had beans on the plate for dinner, my darlin'. Your daddy could have thrown a million or two our way."

"I'm glad we made it on our own," Barbara said. "I wouldn't have wanted it any other way. I'm glad Stella wasn't raised in the rarified environment that I was raised in where nothing was ever good enough for me. It may sound silly, but it's hard being the only rich girl in a small town."

Stella glanced at her father and they both broke out laughing.

"It sounds tough to me." Sean hugged his wife.

"Never mind. I knew you wouldn't understand." Barbara sighed. "I'm glad both of you will be there tonight anyway. I couldn't have done this alone."

Stella uncurled herself from the sofa and hugged both her parents. "It's okay, Mom. I don't think you're the world's worst mother. How could I? You're an heiress. I'd like to make my birthday request now. I'm thinking about a new

Harley. I know someone who could really customize it for me too. Not more than fifty thousand dollars. You can handle that, right?"

Eric was laughing as Stella winked at him and then went in to take a cold shower and get dressed.

She'd never seen her mother this way. She was normally the calmest and most composed person she'd ever known. On the other hand, she could understand her nervousness after meeting the Carsons. She wondered how Barbara would feel about Vivian—Ben's current wife—and her son, Marty.

Stella had been in the mansion, in her mother's old bedroom. It was still like she'd left it, complete with her clothes and toys. There was bound to be more Carson drama there tonight.

She dressed carefully in a soft-as-butter black knit skirt and a matching sweater, both handmade in Sweet Pepper. It was one of her many purchases that was going to add up to a lot of extra baggage going home.

Eric appeared next to her on the bed as she put on her knee-length black boots.

"You know you're not supposed to be in here when I'm dressing." She reminded him of their pact as she zipped up one of her boots.

"You were already dressed."

"That implies that you knew I *wasn't* dressed. We aren't married, you know—just housemates."

"You could watch me change clothes anytime—if that ever happened." He grinned. "What's that new term I've heard on TV? 'Friends with benefits'?"

*"Eric—"*

"Sorry. I remembered something. I wanted to tell you before I lost it again."

"Okay." She finished putting on her boots and started brushing her hair. "What's up?"

"I heard something."

"At the silo that night?"

"Yes. When I saw the shadow move, I heard something."

Stella had been in a burning building plenty of times. There were all kinds of strange sounds as wood popped and splintered in the heat and glass shattered.

"What did it sound like?"

"Music."

Stella stopped brushing her hair and looked at him standing behind her in the bathroom mirror. Only a ghost could have fit in the tiny bathroom with her.

"Chum said he heard music when he saw the men taking the body out of the silo that night. He said that's what caught his attention in all the chaos."

He frowned. "What could that mean?"

"Was it like someone was singing or whistling?"

"No. I don't think so. More like the radio, maybe."

She put on some lipstick, trying to work that piece into the puzzle. The man who killed Eric was listening to the radio in the middle of an inferno? It seemed unlikely, but she couldn't afford to overlook one of the last things he remembered that went along with what Chum had told her.

"I have to go," she said. "We'll talk about this later. I'm sure it means something."

"All right." Eric moved into the bedroom. "Have a good time. Be careful. You know Ben doesn't want you, or your mother, to leave Sweet Pepper again. We don't know how far he'd be willing to go to accomplish that."

"We'll be fine." She grabbed her handbag. "I'll eat very carefully, in case the food is drugged."

It was always there—the undercurrent of fear and anger about the "old man," as many people referred to Ben Carson. People blamed him for everything bad that had ever happened in their lives.

If he was as evil as John and Eric considered him, she

felt fairly sure he wouldn't have been able to go the last year without doing something to cement his reputation. She'd even provoked him, giving the pepper processing plant a safety citation and making him clean up his act. A few people thought he would have killed anyone else for defying him.

Stella thought it was a lot of nonsense—and possibly some darker deeds on his part in the past. Her mother wasn't the only one who'd thought Ben had killed Abigail. Chum had hinted that he'd thought so too.

Ben had an alibi, though. He'd been working at the pepper plant. Chum had told her that there was a brief investigation before it was concluded that Abigail had missed a stair and tumbled down to her death.

John had peppered that information by telling her that nothing bad had ever stuck to the Carson name.

They drove to the estate, which was a few miles away, in the rental car. The rain and persistent fog made the trip longer.

Stella felt more comfortable in the car with Doug this time. He seemed to be okay with the fact that their relationship wasn't going further than friendship. They talked the whole way about Eric's death and the murder investigation.

"I wish you'd put that behind you, sweetheart," her mother said. "It's not your place to look into this. Let the police do their job."

"Listen to your mother," Sean added. "Put your brain on moving plans. Have your stuff sent home so you can fly back with us. You've been on vacation long enough. It's time to get back to work."

Stella didn't have time to restate her position on finding Eric's killer. They had pulled into the grounds of the Carson mansion with its wide drive, gated entrance, and tiny guardhouse.

Sean rolled down his window to address the older man who waited there.

"Good to see you, Miss Stella." Bernard removed his cap for a moment in respect when he saw her in the car. "You must be her father. Mr. Carson is expecting you. Welcome home, Miss Barbara."

Barbara smiled at him. He had been a very young man when she'd left Sweet Pepper. She was surprised to find herself tearing up when she realized who he was. "Thank you, Bernard. It's good to see you."

The big iron gates swung open and Sean whistled as he steered the car up the steep hill to the house. There were lights everywhere, outlining the stone wall along the drive and illuminating the trees.

"This is nice," he said. "This is *very* nice. Maybe Stella has room for me on the fire brigade and we could move down here and claim your birthright."

"Don't even joke about that," Barbara and Stella said at almost the same time.

"Why not?" Sean asked. "This is the good life. Why wouldn't you want to be part of it?"

"Because you're only joking," Barbara said. "You wouldn't leave your family or your job to come down here. My father would take those words very seriously. Don't even *hint* that we could stay."

Sean laughed as he rounded the circle drive in front of the large house, equally well lighted. "You make him sound like an ogre. Are we walking into a trap—or a lavish dinner for a runaway heiress? I hope the latter. I left my sword at home."

Barbara didn't find his attitude funny. "Don't be your normal self tonight, please. The Carsons aren't like the Griffins. There won't be any friendly banter or ghost stories. My father is different than what you're used to."

"I'm sorry, darlin'." Sean stroked her arm. "I wasn't taking it seriously. I'll be good. I promise. No jokes."

Doug seemed too awestruck by his surroundings to even speak—and he wasn't in the house yet. Stella smiled at him when they got out of the car and were met by the housekeeper, Felicity.

"Welcome to Carson Manor," she said as they started up the walkway. "If you need anything while you're here, please don't hesitate to ask."

"Are you okay?" Stella asked Doug, taking his hand.

"I wasn't expecting anything like this." He stared at the mansion as though he might never get over it.

"It's just a big house," she said. "I'm sure you've seen other mansions."

"Sure. Driving by. I never ate dinner in one. And I never knew people who lived there."

Stella decided there was nothing more she could say to him about it. He'd have to get through it on his own.

Several young housemaids met them at the door that opened into the beautiful foyer and the breathtaking staircase that dominated it. The huge chandelier dropped dramatically from the ceiling, crystal teardrops reflected across the rooms.

Stella saw her mother grab her father's hand and squeeze hard. It was the only outward sign of the emotional part of her homecoming. Ben and Vivian came in immediately, and the moment passed.

Ben did the introductions. Vivian was dressed to kill in what looked like a green designer gown with fabulous diamonds around her neck and in her ears. The light from the chandelier gleamed in her blond hair as she smiled at her husband's only child.

When they married, it was too late for her to conceive an heir to take the place of Ben's reluctant daughter. For a long time, Vivian had pushed her son, Marty, into trying to be Ben's son, at least in affection. That had never worked out.

There was no doubt in Vivian's mind that this plain Jane, who looked so much like the long-dead Abigail, would be Ben's heir. Barbara would get it all—unless she didn't want it—and in that case, it would go to Stella.

Vivian and Marty had no claim on the Carson money— *at least not yet.*

# Chapter 14

~~~~~~~~~~

They all went into the library for drinks before dinner. The huge painting of Abigail in her youth dominated the elegant room filled with antiques and first editions.

Seeing her mother there with the portrait made Stella realize how similar the three of them looked. *What was Abigail like?* she wondered, staring up at her portrait.

She saw Vivian looking at the portrait too. She was probably wondering if there was any way she could get Barbara to go back home and forget that this was all hers when something happened to Ben.

Vivian had made her position very clear to Stella. She hadn't given up so much of her life to Ben not to get anything in return—despite the prenup she'd signed when they were married.

"This is a beautiful place." Sean admired the antique globe on a stand near a large wood desk. He was drinking a local red wine in a crystal glass. "I like this wine."

"This is made from the muscadine grape right here in Sweet Pepper," Ben said. "I've been cultivating grapes for the last twenty years. We've got a few producing vineyards now that are beginning to show a profit. You never know when the pepper business might dry up."

Vivian's laugh tinkled delicately around the room. "You shouldn't joke about things like that. People might decide they don't like peppers anymore."

Ben finished his wine and poured himself another. "We've been growing the hottest, sweetest peppers in the world right here for the last hundred years or so. If anything, business has never been better. Sean, you and Doug will have to let me take you on a tour of the factory and the farms. Stella is learning about the business. She's going to be a tour guide at the festival this year."

"That's still in October, isn't it?" Barbara frowned at her daughter.

"That's right." Ben didn't realize he was adding to the debate between Stella and her mother. "It's a pleasure knowing there's another Carson generation helping out. Remember when your mother took part in the festival? She always made that pepper and cheese pie. People couldn't believe how good it was. Won ribbons every year—never had another like it."

Barbara didn't say anything else about the festival, but Stella recognized that look on her face. She was going to have plenty to say about it later. Maybe she'd been wrong to agree to another festival.

Stella listened as Ben described the whole pepper festival in great detail.

She wasn't happy thinking she might never attend another festival. She liked the Sweet Pepper Festival, despite all the primping and ostentation. She wanted to be part of it again.

The festival people had been so happy when she'd agreed to be a tour guide. She'd enjoyed learning about the peppers and how they grew. What harm could it do to stay a little longer, if she could talk Chief Henry into holding her job until then.

She knew her parents were hoping she'd leave right away. But what did *she* want? Was her investigation into Eric's death the *only* thing keeping her here? If so, maybe she could leave with an easy conscience since the police seemed to finally be interested.

The timetable for her leaving Sweet Pepper didn't seem to matter as much to her as to everyone else. She was letting other people rush her into making a decision she wasn't ready to make yet.

She knew she was also being influenced by her earlier conversation with Eric. Now that he had acknowledged that he needed her help, that changed everything again.

"Wouldn't you say so, Stella?" her father asked.

Everyone was looking at her. She'd been so lost in her thoughts that she had no idea what they were talking about.

Fortunately for her, Marty blew into the room. His sun-bleached blond hair looked as though he'd been riding in his convertible with the top down. His white linen jacket was wrinkled and had grass stains on it.

"Sorry I'm late, Vivian." He casually kissed his mother's cheek. "Time got away from me."

He introduced himself to Sean and Barbara as he grabbed a glass of wine. He smirked when he shook hands with Doug. Everyone in town knew about Stella's cheating ex-boyfriend.

With his entrance, everyone forgot what the conversation had been about. Marty didn't have much of anything else going on for him, but he had smooth social skills. He took over the conversation, making everyone laugh with his jokes about where he'd been that day.

Stella and Marty were about the same age, but there the resemblance ended. He was flashy and had trouble committing to anything. Stella couldn't say his mother had spoiled him, she didn't know either of them that well.

Ben's dislike for his stepson was clearly written on his face. He didn't say anything—just stood to one side, frowning at Marty.

"Dinner is served," Felicity told them with a gracious smile.

"Let's head down then. Don't want the food to get cold," Ben joked.

They all walked down the large, sweeping staircase, Ben and Vivian in the lead.

Stella saw her mother falter as she came to the bottom step.

There was nothing visible there, certainly nothing left from Abigail's death forty years before. Everything was polished to perfection. Not even a hint of dust.

Barbara still stopped abruptly, unable to proceed. Her pretty face was a mask of fear and terror.

Sean and Stella hurried to her side and each grabbed one of her hands. They helped her down the rest of the stairs and into the dining room.

"Is there a problem?" Ben looked back and asked.

"No." Sean smiled. "I was admiring the scenery. This is a beautiful house you have here, sir."

Ben smiled and his face got a little pink with pride and pleasure. "I built it for Abigail and Barbara. It's been lonely here, not having family to share it."

Stella looked at Vivian. The elegant woman's eyes opened wider for a moment, as though the careless remark from her husband took her by surprise. Then her icy blue gaze narrowed as she turned and walked the rest of the way to the dining room by herself.

Sean walked with Barbara. Doug was still caught up admiring everything from the chandelier to the expensive furnishings.

"I see why you dumped him." Marty slid up next to Stella and took her arm. "He's kind of a lump, isn't he?"

"You haven't answered calls or been to practice recently." Stella wasn't discussing her feelings about Doug with Marty. "I'm going to have to kick you off the fire brigade if you don't participate."

"I'm family. Doesn't that deserve some consideration?"

"No. I'd kick anyone off who doesn't pull their weight. And we aren't family, as you've reminded me many times."

He smiled in a seductive way that Stella felt sure worked with many women, from what she'd heard of his reputation.

"We *could* be." His finger trailed lazily up her arm. "You've never really given me a chance to get close to you."

Stella moved his hand from her arm. "It's not going to happen now either. Show up for the next call and practice, or you're out."

Marty shivered. "There's a distinct chill to the air tonight. I wonder if it could be Abigail Carson's ghost wandering around. She does sometimes, you know. The servants have complained about it from time to time. Is that why your mother had a hard time going down the stairs?"

The sheer audacity of him making jokes about her dead grandmother—especially since he knew her mother had left Sweet Pepper because of her death—almost took Stella's breath away.

She shouldn't have been surprised. Nothing was too low or sleazy for Marty. She'd learned that during the limited time they'd spent together. Stella glanced into his eyes and realized that he knew this was a hot button for her. She forced herself to relax and let it go.

The dining room was beautiful with candlelight and fresh flowers. The crystal goblets and real silver shone on the white linen tablecloth. The china pattern was reserved and elegant, like Vivian who presided over the meal at one end

of the table. Ben sat at the other end. Wine flowed as plenti-
fully as the conversation.

"So I hear you're going home soon, Stella," Vivian said.

"I'm not sure yet." Stella wondered why the other woman
had singled her out to pick on. "I'm trying to tie up some
loose strings before I go."

"That's right." Vivian smiled. "You've been looking for
the former fire chief's killer, haven't you? How is that
going?"

"We're still picking up clues as to what happened the
night Eric died."

"Eric? Was that his name? You sound very intimate with
a man who's been dead since before you were born."

"I suppose reading about him and looking at all the old
records has made him seem very real," Stella replied.

"I've heard he haunts your little cabin. Have you ever
seen his ghost?"

Stella laughed. "People from Sweet Pepper see a lot of
ghosts, don't they? It might be the peppers."

"I've heard that you're going to finish off your investigation before you leave town." Vivian smiled at Ben. "I hope
you're not *too* disappointed if you don't find the answers
you're looking for. There may be ghosts here, but their
secrets seem to stay dead and buried."

Ben changed the subject. The conversation swirled
around Barbara again for a few minutes. Stella's parents
were describing their lives in Chicago. Barbara worked as
an accountant for a small firm downtown. She liked and
understood numbers.

Stella watched Vivian roll her eyes and hide a bored yawn
behind one beautifully manicured hand that sported a large
diamond ring.

"I can't believe it!" Ben said with a laugh. "You always
*hated* math when you were in school. Remember how you

wanted to join the Peace Corps when you graduated? You know, I could use a good accountant around here, if you decided to stay."

Barbara didn't respond. She smiled and sipped her wine.

Sean rushed into the conversation to talk about the fire brigade and how proud he was of his daughter putting it all together.

Stella felt confident her mother didn't plan to stay in Sweet Pepper since Barbara had been urging her to go home. Ben was grasping at straws. Of course he wanted his daughter to stay. But Barbara's and Sean's lives were in Chicago, just like Stella's. It wasn't going to happen.

Her mother seemed more relaxed, waiting for dessert after the great meal. Maybe it was the wine. The servers kept their glasses topped off.

Stella couldn't imagine what it had been like for her, leaving her father, her home, and everything she'd ever known. All those years she'd tried to stay hidden, afraid for her life because she believed Ben had killed her mother.

Even more amazing was that she'd kept the secret for so long. It always seemed to Stella that her mother could hardly keep Christmas presents secret while she was growing up.

Knowing that Barbara had kept this huge secret gave her a different look at the woman, not the mother she'd always known. She could see where her father really could wonder what else Barbara had kept from him.

Marty was practically lying back in his chair, not taking part in the conversation, and drinking more than he ate. Ben must have insisted he had to be there. He didn't seem too happy about it.

Stella's pager went off, startling her. It was a fire call. She was glad she'd only had one glass of wine. She'd been lucky there hadn't been a call after margarita night at Beau's. It was unacceptable to be the chief and be less than what was needed.

"Oh good." Marty looked at his cell phone. "I guess this means we'll be leaving now. Thank God."

Stella got up. "I think you've had a little too much to drink to go out on a call."

"I'm not driving," Marty argued. "I can still hold a fire hose."

Sean stood up. "I'd like to come too. I agree with Marty. You drive us there, darlin', and we can handle the rest."

Stella could hardly argue with that. "All right. Let's go."

She wasn't sure about leaving her mother at the mansion. She'd handled most of the experience well, so far. Did she want to stay there for what might be hours?

Barbara took care of the problem. "I'll drive all of you to the firehouse and go on to the cabin. Stella, I'm sure you can get your father home after the call."

"No," Ben protested. "Stay with me a while longer, Barbara. I'll have someone take you back to the cabin when you're ready."

"I appreciate that, Dad, but I'm exhausted." Barbara smiled. "I want to get some sleep. I'll see you tomorrow."

Ben kept trying to talk her into staying, but Barbara walked out the door with Sean, Doug, Marty, and Stella. Marty saluted them as he went to get his own car.

Doug had enjoyed the muscadine wine a little too much. He was leaning heavily on Sean as they got out to the car.

"I guess I'll tuck Doug in too," Barbara said. "It's probably the mountain air. You have to learn to breathe differently."

Sean laughed. "I'm sure that's it. That, and a bottle or two of wine."

"It's not nice to make fun of a man who can't defend himself," his wife reminded him.

She dropped two of her passengers off in the firehouse parking lot. All of the lights were on, cars and trucks swerving into the lot to discharge other members of the fire brigade.

"Be careful." Barbara kissed her husband.

"I always am," he replied.

Stella smiled at the ritual goodbye that had always happened between them for as long as she could remember. She didn't linger, though, walking into the firehouse to find out what was going on.

"What are you doing here? You didn't get my text?" Ricky was already in gear. "The fire is up at *your* cabin."

# Chapter 15

~~~~~~~~~~~~~~

"**M**y cabin?" Stella demanded.

"Yes."

"Then let's go!"

She got her gear on and raced for the engine with Hero right beside her. She was glad the dog wasn't at the cabin with Eric. Even if it was a small fire, Hero could be injured. Eric could take care of himself.

She wished she could call her mother to tell her that they were on their way. It would be no help to her that Doug was drunk and sleeping in the backseat of the car. She hoped her mother would stay outside and not try to go in. Surely as the wife and mother—not to mention aunt and godmother—of a family of firefighters she'd know better.

As Ricky pulled out of the parking lot in the lead, Stella's mind raced ahead. If Eric could keep snakes and scorpions out of the cabin, surely he could keep the fire to a minimum.

She couldn't help but consider that Bob Floyd had been threatening at Scooter's to burn the cabin—and now there was a fire there. If she saw any sign that the fire wasn't completely natural, they'd have words.

Fortunately it was a short drive to the top of the mountain, even in the big vehicles. Smoke was in the air, filling the trees around the cabin when they got close. Stella didn't see fire, but the smoke had to come from somewhere.

Barbara had parked the rental car well away from the cabin and was still inside of it, waiting, as she knew she should. Sean went to check on her.

"It's a small place," Stella said to Ricky. "Let's see what's going on."

Petey and JC joined them. They went below the deck and checked under there for any sign of fire while Ricky and Stella went inside.

It smelled like smoke inside the cabin but not more than if a puff had come out of the fireplace. They each checked all the rooms and the back deck carefully, but there was no sign of fire.

Stella told Ricky to go and help outside, in case there was a fire in the trees. She needed to talk to Eric if she really wanted to know what had happened.

Eric appeared as soon as Ricky was gone. "There was someone in the woods. He started a fire out there. None of it touched the cabin, but the trees might still be burning. I can't believe anyone could be that stupid with these dry conditions."

"Probably not stupid. Bob wants to burn the cabin, remember?"

"I take it back then. He might be that stupid. I couldn't tell who it was. He was dressed in black and wearing a black ski mask that covered his whole face."

"I'll check outside," she said. "Then I'll have a conversation with Bob about playing with matches."

"Stella, don't worry about the cabin. I can take care of it."

"He needs to know that I realize he could be involved in this."

"First and foremost, you should be safe. Bob isn't a nice person."

She didn't respond, running back outside to check on the progress being made. She used the radio to alert the forest service that they were out at the scene. If this was a fire in the woods, they needed to know.

"Anything out there?" She asked for reports from her volunteers who were fanned out through the smoke-filled area.

There were several immediate responses—no fire, just smoke. The group continued to tromp through the leaves and underbrush, down to the river, but it seemed that the fire had gone out.

Petey came to find Stella. "Obviously, something was going on out there, Chief. Where there's smoke, there's fire, right?"

Sean joined them after working his way back up the embankment. "It's bone-dry out there. It's hard to believe there was a fire and it went out on its own."

Ricky reported in on the radio. "There's nothing out here, Chief. My group is headed back up from the river."

Stella listened to the reports. No sign of fire was good, but she couldn't afford to take any chances. "Let's hose it down anyway. I don't want to miss something and have to come back later."

She reported her actions to the forest service. They offered to help, but she thought the fire brigade could handle the situation. If it looked like something more, she promised to call back.

As the firefighters began to hook up the two-inch hose to the pumper/tanker, a Sweet Pepper police department vehicle pulled in with its lights flashing. It was Officer Richardson, checking out the situation. The police department was automatically notified of any fire emergency.

"Looks like someone was careless up here as they were going down to the river," he remarked to Stella.

"This isn't a river access," she reminded him. "No one should've been out here building a fire near the cabin."

He chuckled. "What's right, and what happens, are two different things. Looks like you've got it under control anyway, Chief Griffin. Let us know if you need anything."

Stella was a little irritated by his offhand manner. She wondered if he'd have the same attitude if his own home had been on fire.

When the hose was connected to the pumper, JC and Petey took it to the edge of the embankment and began to spray water through the trees.

The pumper/tanker was old, a leftover from the original fire brigade in the 1970s. It held 750 gallons of water that sprayed out under pressure.

They turned emergency lights on the area. It was hard to see anything in the darkness that surrounded them. Stella wanted to be careful not to wash too much of the soil and rocks away from the side of the embankment. The water would flow down to the river, hopefully hitting any hot spots that might have been missed.

"Hey Chief!" Ricky yelled to get her attention.

Stella watched as JC and Petey handed off the hose to Ricky and Royce. She held her thumbs up as the event went smoothly.

By the time they had finished, most of the smoke had dissipated. The group took one more look around the base of the cabin and into the nearby woods. There was no sign of sparks or flame.

"Are we going home sometime tonight?" Marty, wet and covered with leaves and mud, came up from a last recon.

"You are." Stella called the pumper/tanker crew back.

"Let's get the pumper back to the firehouse and get cleaned up. Don't forget your reports."

"Thanks." Marty saluted her.

"For saving you from dinner?"

"You have to admit it was worse than a bad movie. I actually expected the old man to bend over and kiss your mother's feet."

"I agree. I'm glad I could save you from that." Stella smiled at him. "But this is the last call you're taking without practice, Marty. I can't afford to have you get hurt."

"Funny. I thought you needed all the help you could beg for."

"I never need help from inexperienced people. If practice is too much trouble, so are fire calls."

"Whatever you say, Chief Stella. I can take a hint." He went to join the rest of the pumper crew.

Stella wasn't sure what he meant by that, but she was serious about him not going out on calls without practice. It looked bad for the rest of the group who put themselves out to come to practice, and it was dangerous. She probably shouldn't have let him come tonight.

"Insubordination?" Sean joined her. "You seem to have handled that well. Is he always that way?"

She grinned. "There's one in every unit. You told me that the first time I complained about someone not coming to practice, remember?"

"I do indeed. And it's true. Not everyone takes it seriously. It seems like you'd have even more of a problem here because they don't get paid. It's more like a hobby than a vocation."

"I think you can see that most of them take it very seriously. Marty is my only problem child. John doesn't always show up, but he's on duty so much that I can't expect that from him."

"How about the chief?" he asked. "How serious is she about leading this band? You know you'll never make chief back home. It's political, and there are too many others who want the position ahead of you."

"I can't say I haven't thought about that," she honestly admitted. "I like being chief. It's going to be hard to go back to being captain back home. But I'll manage."

Once the pumper was out of the driveway, Stella called the rest of the group back. They packed up the engine/ladder truck and Hero jumped in the front seat. Sean decided to stay at the cabin so he could shower and go to bed.

"I'll let you break protocol this one time," she said with a smile. "Don't ask for favors again."

He laughed and waved her on. Barbara took that as a cue to help Doug into the cabin. "I guess everything is okay?" she asked.

"I believe it is," Sean said. "The chief is very thorough. She's good at this, honey. I don't know if she should come back home. She'll be wasted there."

"Don't be silly. She has an important job there too. You can't want her to stay here, Sean. We'd hardly ever get to see her."

He put his arm around her shoulders as they walked into the cabin. "I guess we'll see what happens."

It took Barbara and Sean to help Doug get up the stairs and into bed. They went into the bedroom downstairs afterward, but Eric sat by Doug's bed and studied him.

He knew briefly about Stella's relationship with this man. He knew they'd grown up together and was sure Doug had broken Stella's heart.

He wanted to do more than hold him prisoner in a hot tub for a few hours. Out of respect for Stella's request not to hurt him, Eric satisfied himself with throwing all the blankets, sheets and pillows on the floor.

Maybe another way to express his dislike of Doug, without injury, would inspire him later.

Stella didn't get back to the cabin until after midnight—

again. It was becoming a habit. Tonight it was because of cleanup and paperwork. It wasn't as much fun as being with Zane and drinking margaritas.

Exhausted, she closed the door behind her quietly. Hero looked up but didn't bark. She slid down on the sofa, glad a small fire was still going in the hearth.

Weather forecasts were calling for the temperatures to rise again tomorrow. She was looking forward to it, much as she hated the hot weather. It wasn't so much the cold here that bothered her, but the damp, misty weather.

Stella wasn't sure if she was going to be able to sleep that night. Without knowing what had happened, she felt edgy and uncertain. What if Bob *had* come out and started a fire to destroy the cabin?

There was nothing keeping him from trying again. She wouldn't know where or what had happened until morning when she could get a good look around. Until then, she was nervous.

It wasn't just her welfare or the cabin she was worried about. Her parents were asleep in the next room. She had to worry about them too.

"I don't think Bob would be brave enough to come out here by himself and start a fire." Eric was perched at the end of the sofa. He sounded as though they'd been discussing the matter for the last hour. "He's not made that way."

"So who then?"

"I don't know. I suppose Bob could have hired someone who didn't mind sneaking around in the woods at night and taking a chance on getting caught in the fire he started."

"That doesn't make me feel any better."

"How was dinner at the mansion?"

She frowned when he changed the subject. "It was all right, except for a few problems. Ben wants Mom and me to stay here now. Vivian wants us both out of the way."

"I imagine she does. With both of you alive and in the old man's will, that makes it hard for her and her son."

"I suppose so. I wish there was some way to reassure her that neither one of us wants the pepper business." Stella put her feet up and stared into the fire. "My dad said something tonight about me staying here so long because I like being chief."

"And?"

"And I didn't realize I thought that much about it. He may be right." She explained briefly why she wouldn't reach that rank at home. "Maybe I like being the boss."

Eric smiled. "Are you looking for reasons to stay—or to go?"

"Maybe both." She smiled back at him and yawned at the same time. "I think I'm confused. Everything seemed so clear in my life before I got here. Now it's kind of hazy."

"It's not unusual to want to advance your career," he said. "Give yourself a break, Stella. You're a good chief. Your people like and respect you."

"Maybe." She yawned again and pulled the blanket that was folded on the sofa around her. "I don't know. I thought staying was only about helping you figure things out, but maybe that was an excuse. My ego might be totally out of control."

She snuggled down into the comfortable sofa and closed her eyes. "I guess I can sleep for a while knowing you're here to take first watch. Goodnight, Eric."

"Goodnight, Stella."

The cabin was quiet around him except for the sounds of people sleeping. This was what he missed the most—being around other humans. It was what Stella had brought here with her. It was more than his emotional feelings for her that made him hate to see her go. She was going to take his life with her when she was gone.

Stella was up as the sun peeked over the top of the mountains. It was foggy again, but quickly dissipating in the drier weather.

She put on boots and gloves, took Hero for a short walk, and then went out to search for the point of origin for last night's fire. It had to be somewhere around the base of the cabin.

The early morning sunshine cut through what was left of the fog, leaving only the smell of smoke lingering in the trees. Birds sang from the branches and the river gurgled as it moved across the rocks.

Eric watched from the deck as Stella moved slowly through the trees, turning over branches and checking around the bases of tree trunks. He knew she'd found something when she looked up and nodded at him. He had to wait, impatiently, until she came back with a full report.

Stella had been a few hundred feet from the cabin when she'd found a black, charred area at the base of a tree. It had started very hot—probably with some accelerant—but had burned out without going very far.

She looked up. If the tree had ignited, the top branches would have dropped sparks and probably fallen onto the roof and deck of the cabin as the tree had burned.

It was clever, really. No one could be blamed for burning the cabin if it was just a careless person in the woods who started a fire. That happened all the time, as Zane could testify.

If the cabin itself had been set on fire, it would be arson and would attract a lot more attention.

"Is this it?" Sean found her looking at the spot outside and taking samples of the charred wood.

"Yep. Good location for burning the cabin."

Sean's eyes followed the same path hers had. "Is that what you think happened?"

Stella told him about the threat from Bob Floyd.

"I'm sure the councilman didn't mean while you were still occupying it," Sean said. "Even if he wants this land, most people aren't willing to do something that drastic. He only has to wait until you leave, if I understand the situation with the town owning the property."

Stella couldn't disagree with his logic. Yet, here they were, looking at a good spot to get rid of the cabin without anyone taking the blame for it.

"I wonder what stopped it," Sean said. "You can see how hot it was." He put his head down at the blackened tree bark and sniffed. "Definitely gasoline. Why didn't it burn right up?"

"Maybe the rain and fog yesterday was enough to keep it from taking off." Stella suggested the idea because it could make sense. She didn't believe it, but it was a rational answer.

She really believed that the tree might have been close enough to the cabin for Eric to influence the fire. He had a fifty-foot proximity outside the cabin. It was how he kept out scorpions and snakes and kept Hero from running away. She didn't know how that worked but supposed it was possible that he could keep a tree close to the cabin from burning.

"Maybe." Sean looked around them at the large old trees and the river. "If you're right about someone starting this fire to burn the cabin, it's going to be a big surprise when they realize it didn't happen."

"I guess we should go back inside so I can scrounge up breakfast, if that's possible."

"Don't worry about it," Sean said. "Your mother already tried. She can't figure out how you're surviving up here with no food in the kitchen. She went down to a convenience store she remembered seeing on the way into town yesterday."

They walked together through the crunchy leaves underfoot as they climbed the embankment back to the cabin. They were talking about going home and the fire brigade, with a few comments about Ben Carson thrown in.

As they reached the bottom step of the porch, Doug came running out, still in his underwear, a look of fear on his face.

"Stella, this house is haunted! Don't go inside. We could all be killed."

# Chapter 16

〰〰〰〰〰〰

**"S** low down, Doug," Sean cautioned. "You should take a deep breath and go put some pants on."

Eric was standing on the porch, obviously amused.

Stella glared at him and then turned to Doug. "What happened that makes you think the cabin is haunted?"

"Well, first it was the bedclothes all out on the floor. I didn't put them there. Then, I was coming downstairs and happened to glance toward the deck. The door opened and something closed it back. Then a chair moved at the table. I saw the fireplace screen move too. I'm telling you, there's a ghost in there—just like they have on those reality TV shows."

Sean glanced up at the cabin, his eyes narrowing as they focused on the porch, exactly where Eric was standing.

Stella wondered for a moment if he could see Eric standing there too. There had been all those childhood stories about people with "the sight." Maybe that's why she could see Eric.

But either Sean didn't trust his eyes or he was looking at something else. He shook his head and berated Doug. "Get hold of yourself, son. This is not the way to win Stella back. She's been living here for months. Don't you think she'd have noticed if there was a ghost about the cabin?"

Doug shivered. "I know what I saw. Something *weird* is going on in there."

Barbara pulled up at that moment. "I'm glad all of you are out here—though I think Doug needs some clothes. You can help me carry in the groceries." She opened the trunk, revealing dozens of bags full of food.

"What did you do?" Sean laughed. "Is this the way a pepper heiress buys food? We're only staying a few days. An army couldn't eat this much in a week."

"Just take it inside," Barbara said. "And Doug, get dressed."

"There's a ghost inside," he argued.

"I know. The ghost of the dead fire chief." She smiled at him. "I told you not to listen to those stories at Beau's. People told Stella the same thing when she first got here."

Barbara looked at her daughter. "Has anything scary happened since you moved in?"

*Since you put it that way*—"Not a thing. I've never been afraid of living here."

Stella probably would have lied if her mother had asked her if she'd seen a ghost. This way, she didn't have to.

Doug stared at the cabin with dread etched on his face. "I won't go in alone."

Barbara took two bags of groceries and walked into the cabin. "You're not alone. Now go upstairs and get dressed. I'm making pancakes."

Eric took a step out of the way for Barbara to walk inside. He wasn't as kind to Doug and made the man walk right through him.

Stella knew from experience that it was a disconcerting feeling to walk through a ghost. It was like an electric current running through you—from the inside out.

They talked about what Stella and Sean had found outside that was left from the fire. Sean felt like Stella should report it, whether she believed a town official was involved or not.

Doug agreed with him. "How can you expect the police to do their job if you don't tell them everything? You should tell them about this whole investigation into the fire chief's death too. It isn't your job to investigate murders."

"It is my job to investigate arson," Stella said. "We don't technically have an arson investigator."

"Is anyone going to think a small fire in the woods is arson?" Sean asked.

"I do." Stella shrugged. "I guess that's what matters."

"So what's next then?" Barbara wondered. "Do you have any suspects?"

Stella explained about Bob Floyd. "I'm going to talk to him today. At least he'll know I'm not stupid enough to think it was some random act. I don't expect him to confess, just be aware that I'm watching him."

"I'll come with you," Doug offered. "It never hurts to have backup."

"I'll come too," Sean said. "Do you want to add your muscle to the group, Barbara?"

"Me? No, I don't think so. I'm meeting up with Sandy Selvy, an old friend of mine. She's the town clerk now." She smiled at Stella. "Sandy tells me you two talk all the time."

"We do," Stella agreed. "I guess you could drop the three of us off at the firehouse and I'll pick up the Cherokee. I'm not sure where we'll find Bob. We might have to look around for him."

Barbara wasn't happy with what she was wearing or what the damp weather had done to her hair while she was out. She went back in the bedroom to change clothes while Sean took Doug to look at the burned spot on the tree.

Stella had said she needed to take care of something and didn't join them in the woods. Instead, she went out on the deck to talk to Eric. He was leaning against the rail watching them.

"So you think it was set on purpose," he said without turning around.

"There's no doubt. We could smell the gasoline. I think even Bob won't be too surprised when I come looking for him today. If it had worked out, I don't know if anyone would've noticed that small area where the fire was started. It would've taken out the cabin."

"I told you—I won't let that happen."

Stella didn't want to bring up the fact that the old firehouse he'd built had also been under his protection when it had burned.

Instead she said, "You're not Superman, Eric. You can't stop everything bad from happening. If the woods caught on fire, you probably couldn't protect the cabin."

"So what stopped the fire from spreading if someone put gasoline on the tree?"

"You've got me on that one. I don't have to tell you how it should've gone. The fire died out, from what I can tell. It may be that it was close enough to the cabin and you protected it."

"I can't protect much outside the cabin."

"I don't have any other explanation for it. The woods are dry. There wasn't that much rain after the fire was set. You fill in the blanks."

"I don't know." Eric looked out at the trees that surrounded them like sentinels. "He'll try again. He won't give up that easy."

"We'll have to keep that from happening."

Eric glanced at her. "I'm sorry I scared Doug this morning. I knew your parents were outside. I forgot he was upstairs."

"Yeah. Right."

"He's not that bad—for a cheating, womanizing cop."

Stella laughed. "You like him that much, huh?"

"John Trump isn't any better. You have to do something about your bad taste in men if you ever hope to get married and settle down someday."

"I'm glad you don't get to make decisions about my love life." She turned to go inside. "I'm going into town to find Bob and, hopefully, scare him off."

"Bring him home for lunch." Eric grinned maliciously. "I'll scare him off."

"I don't think he'd come here. He *believes* you haunt the cabin. That's probably why he wants to burn the place rather than use it as part of his whitewater rafting access."

"Too bad." He stood beside her. "Be careful. I'm glad your father and Doug are going with you. I wish I could lend a hand too."

Stella left him on the deck as Doug and Sean came back into the cabin. Barbara had changed clothes and was ready to go. They all got into the rental car, with Hero, and drove down Firehouse Road.

Tagger had been on duty with communications. He was finishing up his shift and logging out as Allen Wise, the barber, came in to take his place.

Stella saw Tagger yawning and stretching, talking to Allen about how quiet the night had been after their busy day. She thought this might be a perfect opportunity to talk to him about how Chief Rogers had known Chum was at the firehouse before his death.

Sean and Doug waited in the Cherokee for her. Stella caught Tagger before he went outside to meet his ride. The older man didn't drive anymore and had to depend on people bringing him to the firehouse. But he'd never missed a practice, or his time to monitor communications.

He sometimes went out on calls with them, only in a supportive role. Usually he preferred to sit in his chair and give instructions to the volunteers at the firehouse, between stories about the Vietnam War and the old fire brigade.

"Tagger? Could I have a minute?"

"Sure, Chief." He smiled broadly. "What can I do for you?"

"I think someone told Chief Rogers that Deputy Chum was here talking to me before he died."

His grin got bigger. "That was me." He pulled at the Sweet Pepper Cougars ball cap he was wearing. "I told him all about it."

Stella was surprised by his admission, maybe more so by his enthusiasm to admit it. "Why did you tell him?"

"He asked me. I couldn't lie to him—he's the police chief. I wouldn't lie to you either. You're the fire chief."

Stella frowned. "So in other words, he already knew Chum had been here. He wanted you to confirm it."

"I guess so. You know, the police have to do an investigation into what happened to Deputy Chum because he died suspiciously." Tagger leaned toward her, enough for her to notice that he'd been drinking a little again. "Between you and me, Chief, I think Chum may have been murdered."

She realized that Tagger didn't know anything else about the subject. She was going to have to look elsewhere for the informant who'd seen Chum at the station and then told Chief Rogers.

Tagger could be a source for another subject, though. "What about Chief Gamlyn? Was he murdered?"

Tagger's face twisted and went pale. "I've heard people say that. Eric was a hero. You know that, Chief. He saved our lives when the firehouse burned. He watches over all of us. Who'd murder a man like that?"

"I've heard that he was shot during the silo fire and two men brought his body here and hid it behind the wall." Stella pushed a little further. "Have you ever heard that?"

Tagger's ride, waiting in the parking lot in his old green pickup, honked his horn. "I gotta go, Chief. Bear don't like waiting."

"This is important." She stopped him with a hand on his arm. "Do you think that could've happened that night? You were at the silo fire, right?"

He was squirming, beads of perspiration forming on his forehead and upper lip. His eyes were never able to focus on one thing for long, a result, everyone said, of Agent Orange from his time in Vietnam. They were roaming now, everywhere but her face.

"Tagger?" Stella was determined to get an answer. It was obvious that he knew something.

Finally his eyes focused on hers. "I've heard that story. I don't believe it. No one would want to kill the chief and put his body in that old Impala. I gotta go."

She watched him walk away as quickly as his arthritic legs would take him. He'd definitely heard the story before. Chum had said he'd never told anyone else about seeing the Impala.

Did that mean that Chum was lying, or that Tagger had seen Eric taken out of the silo too?

Stella spoke with Allen briefly, making sure he was monitoring the forest service calls too.

The fifty-something barber, who worked for Bob Floyd, pulled his fingers through the thick head of tobacco-colored hair he took such pride in. "You got it, Chief! Glad to hear that old cabin is okay after the fire last night."

"Me too. Thanks, Allen. See you later." Stella left him and went back to the Cherokee for the ride into town.

The town of Sweet Pepper had about five thousand residents. It was still a Main Street kind of place with small shops up and down the two-lane shopping district.

The Sweet Pepper Café was next to town hall. Potter's Hardware was next to the Daily Grind Coffee and Tea Shop. A little farther down, the Smittys ran the *Sweet Pepper Gazette* weekly newspaper. There were a few hair and nail salons along Main Street, with a computer store and a souvenir shop for the tourists.

Baker Lockwood ran the pharmacy and loved to lean on the counter, gossiping with his customers. There was a sporting goods store and a tiny bookstore next to the town attorney's office.

The VFW Park and picnic area was a short walk away, close to Flo's bed-and-breakfast. Following the road, the older houses with quaint names and gingerbread charm kept watch with their hundred-year-old oaks standing guard beside them.

Going north, the historic old mill that had helped build the town still stood. The town was trying to do repairs on that property and open it for visitors.

The Sweet Pepper bottling factory was on a high hill, looking down at the town it supported. Most of the people who didn't own businesses worked there in the dozens of metal buildings where the peppers were processed, canned, and sent to market.

Stella pulled the Cherokee into a space in front of town hall. Bob Floyd's barbershop was a short walk. She felt confident that Bob would either be at the barbershop or town hall. If not, there was always the café, where people liked to hang out.

She saw John getting ready to go out on patrol and flagged him down. He waited for her and she smiled at him, thinking again that he was a handsome man with his dark brown hair, square jaw, and one dimple.

There was more than that to him though. He was steady and able to handle any crisis with calm assurance. Stella liked that about him.

"Good morning." She used her hand to shield her eyes from the sun streaming across the mountain. "Working days?"

"I wish. I've been on duty since last night. Now the chief is sending me out to serve a warrant." He smiled back at her, wishing there weren't so many roadblocks to being with her. "I heard you had some excitement out at the cabin last night. I don't know why people don't understand that they can't burn anything when it's this dry."

"This wasn't carelessness, John." She explained about the tree that had been set on fire. "It was leaning toward the cabin and there was gasoline used."

His brown eyes narrowed. "Who'd do something like that?"

"I was thinking someone who wants to burn the cabin."

"*Bob?* Stella, you gotta know that was only talk. The town owns that property. He wouldn't set it on fire. If he really wanted to get rid of it, he could talk the rest of the council into putting the whole thing up for sale again. They tried to sell it a few years ago. Why would he go to those lengths?"

"I don't know, but he's been talking to everyone about burning the cabin after I leave. I guess I'll go ask him why he can't wait until I'm gone."

John put his hand on her arm. "Don't mess with him. He can be a dangerous man to have as an enemy. Let me ask around and see what I can find out. Are you going to report the fire as arson?"

"I guess it all depends what Bob has to say."

"You're not going to leave it alone, are you?"

"Probably not. My parents are staying there, John. Suppose we'd all been in the cabin, asleep, when Bob decided to torch the woods. I think he and I need to have a little talk."

# Chapter 17

~~~~~~~~~~~~~~~~

"**I**'d like to go with you—"

"My father and Doug are going with me. I think we can handle this."

"All right." His mouth hardened into a narrow line. "Anything else?"

"I was wondering how Chief Rogers knew to ask Tagger if Chum was at the firehouse before he died. Tagger said Don told him he needed to *verify* the information."

"I'm not sure. I think Don said someone called in about it and said he saw Chum at the firehouse before the accident. Why?"

"Is that person on the suspect list for killing Chum?"

"I don't know, Stella. Maybe you should talk to Don."

In other words, he wasn't going to tell her.

"Any sign of the black vehicle that rubbed up against Chum's truck?"

"So far, there's nothing. No one saw what happened. The sheriff's department is talking about offering a reward for information. That might bring someone out."

"Okay. Thanks. I'll see you later."

"Be careful, huh? Eric Gamlyn's ghost might be able to protect that old cabin, but I don't think he can protect *you*."

"You might be surprised."

Stella could feel John's gaze on her as she walked back to the bright red Cherokee that bore her name. She wondered if he felt anything but anger when he looked at her.

"Any good information from that source?" Sean asked when she reached him.

"Not really." She watched John drive away to deliver the warrant. *Why were there always thorns between them?* She wished she could read his mind.

"You two used to be a couple, right?"

"Sort of." She smiled at her father. "Not for long."

"Just as well," Doug chimed in. "There are a lot of miles between here and Chicago."

Stella glared at him. He had no right to say anything about her life anymore.

"We're on our own with this," she told them. "I guess we'll go and find Bob Floyd now."

It wasn't hard to do. Bob was sitting in his old barber chair, the one he'd inherited from his father, according to the stories Stella had heard about him. Technically, he was retired. He had hired Allen and another man to run the business.

Allen had told her that Bob reluctantly gave him time off to train for the fire brigade. The mayor had convinced him that it would look good when it came time to run for reelection.

"Mr. Floyd," Stella addressed him as she walked into the quiet barbershop. "Kind of slow this morning, huh?"

He nodded, but didn't get up. "It's a good morning for Allen to be off. Do you have any notion of how many hours you expect from your volunteers, Chief Griffin? Even without fire calls, you have them practicing or monitoring calls out there at all times of the day and night. I might have to hire an extra barber so he can work with you all."

"You're right. It takes a lot of practice to keep people on their toes when we head out the door for an emergency. Firefighters get hurt a lot. We want to do everything we can to keep ours safe."

He smiled in an edgy manner. "Why, you sound like you're one of us, Chief. Is Sweet Pepper growing on you? I haven't heard anything about you wanting a new contract."

"I'm not leaving yet," Stella said. "In fact, that's what I came to talk to you about. I suppose you've heard about the fire out at the cabin last night."

"Yes. Oh yes." His head bobbed up and down like a bird. "That was a close call. I'm glad you and your parents were safe. I assume this is your father."

The two men shook hands and exchanged names. Doug shook Bob's hand too, mentioning that he was Stella's friend from Chicago.

"So I hear." Bob sized him up, knowing exactly who he was. "Well, I'm glad none of you were hurt. Fire can be bad when it gets dry."

"It's especially bad when someone uses gasoline to start a fire less than a hundred feet from the cabin." Stella stepped closer to him. "I know you want to get rid of the cabin. You've been crazy enough to tell everyone your plans. Don't go near it again or you'll be sorry."

"You need to watch what you're saying, Chief," Bob growled in a low tone. "You're coming mighty close to *slander*."

Sean moved up behind Stella, not liking the look on the other man's face. Doug took his cue from him and did the same, scowling at the man in the barber chair.

"I could call fifty other people in here right now who'd swear they heard you say you want to burn the cabin. Scooter's was full the other night," she said.

"You have no proof that *I* did anything. Fires start sometimes when the woods are dry. There are *accidents* and careless people."

Stella smiled at him. "Actually, I have remains from the fire that any lab would find gasoline residue on. And I have something even better. I know that wasn't *you* out there. It was someone you sent out to do the job. Know how I know?"

"I know you're full of hot air."

"*Eric* saw your arsonist last night. Why do you think the fire didn't work?"

All the color left Bob's face. He started trembling. "No. That isn't true."

"He told me it wasn't you," Stella continued. "He said you were too much of a coward to be in the fire brigade when he was chief. He doesn't believe you've developed any more of a spine since then."

Bob put his shaking hands up to his face. "How could you *know* that?"

"How do you *think*? Everyone says the cabin is haunted. Who do you *think* is haunting it?"

"That's just talk. He's not really there."

"Yes, he is. And he has a message for you."

"What-what is it?"

"He says leave the cabin alone or he'll have to find somewhere else to live. That might be with *you*, Bob. I'd think about it, if I were you."

Stella knew she had terrified him. She hoped it was enough to keep the cabin safe, not only now but after she was gone. The town remembered Eric as being larger than life. Most people believed he haunted the cabin. Why not use the two together to help him keep his home?

She left the barbershop without looking back. Sean and Doug kept up with her.

"The cabin really *is* haunted," Doug said. "I *knew* it. I'm not crazy."

"Don't be silly. She was only using the man's fear to get him to back off." Sean smiled at his daughter. "I still think you should take the residue to the lab and report the arson."

"I intend to," she agreed. "I don't think much will come of it. There are no fingerprints, or any other evidence besides the residue. The forest service deals with a dozen cases of carelessness in the woods every day."

"I think you handled it well," Sean said. "You put the fear of the Lord in the man anyway. Do people *really* believe the old fire chief is haunting that cabin?"

"Absolutely. Like they believe the sun is going to rise and set today. There are plenty of local ghosts in the area. Eric's reputation has gotten stronger since he'd died. I hope it helps save the cabin."

"I hope so too," Sean said. "How about some coffee at the café? I'm sure your mother won't be done with her gab session for hours yet."

They sat down in a booth at the Sweet Pepper Café. Lucille brought out coffee for Doug and Sean, and Coke for Stella.

Ricky Senior brought out two-inch-high slices of blueberry pie. "This was made fresh this morning." He grinned, his iron-gray flattop, muscular arms, and deep chest making him look more like an older Marine than a café owner. "On the house."

He and Lucille stood together, smiling at them. They were a perfect representation of Lucy and Ricky on late night TV. They even dressed the part on Halloween.

Lucille had the same bright red hair that she wore up on the back of her head. It was emphasized by her constant green apron, which Stella had never seen her without. Ricky Senior even did a mean Cuban impression of Ricky Ricardo.

"We're paying if we eat this pie," Stella said. "I thought we settled that."

For the first few months Stella was in Sweet Pepper, no one would let her pay for anything. She thought it was a nice way to welcome her, but she'd insisted on paying as time went by. The town was paying her to be the fire chief.

"Your money isn't good here," Lucille said. "It's a pleasure having you come in, Chief Griffin. Thank you for bringing your family with you."

Sean, who'd had experience with this, smiled at her. "I hope my money is good then. Back home, the only people who ask us not to pay are people who want special favors."

Ricky frowned. "No. That's not it. We want to do this for her. We don't want anything in return."

Lucille put her hand on her husband's arm. "If it makes you feel better, you can pay for the pie—but not the coffee. Okay?"

Stella shrugged. It was a good compromise. There were many times when she'd argued with Ricky Senior and Lucille but had finally given up.

Ricky Senior shook hands with Sean and Doug. He put in his earbuds and adjusted his iPod as he started back toward the kitchen.

*Music!* Stella remembered Chum and Eric hearing music during the silo fire.

"Hold on a minute!" She got up to talk to Ricky. "I'll be right back, Dad."

Ricky Senior took Stella into his tiny office in the back of the kitchen. There were invoices, pictures taken at the café, and recipes for new dishes posted all over the walls and flooding the desk.

They sat down opposite each other. Ricky asked several times if Stella needed something to eat or drink.

"I'm fine," she assured him with a smile. "I talked to you before about Eric Gamlyn's death. Now that the state has confirmed that those were his bones in the firehouse, I thought I'd come back again and see if you've remembered anything else."

As before when they'd talked, Ricky's dark eyes welled with tears. "I've thought about it a lot since you asked me. I've gone over and over it in my mind. It was a terrible night. Maybe I've forgotten most of it because I want to."

"I understand." Fires were traumatic enough without feeling responsible for someone's death. "I had a conversation with Deputy Chum before he died."

Ricky crossed himself and closed his eyes. "God rest his soul. He was a good man."

"He told me he saw two men carry Eric's body out of the silo *before* the roof collapsed."

"No way." Ricky's expression was comical in his disbelief. "Are you saying he wasn't dead at the silo?"

"We don't know that. Obviously, he didn't die like everyone thought. He may have been shot first and then carried out and put in the firehouse wall. Or he may have been overcome by smoke and then taken out and shot."

"That's even worse. Eric had a big heart. He did a lot of good for this community. I can't stand that someone killed him. It was bad enough when I thought he died for me."

"Chum also mentioned hearing music. He said that was what made him look in the direction where the men were taking out the body."

Ricky looked down at his iPod, which he'd put on the desk when he sat down. "What are you saying?"

"Ricky Junior told me that you're never without it. He said it was better now because you have earbuds."

Stella really liked this man and hated to ask these questions that could sound like he was part of what had happened to Eric. She had no choice. "Could that have been your music Chum heard that night at the silo?"

# Chapter 18

~~~~~~~~~

"I guess it's possible. I was in the silo. I don't know how Chum could've heard it outside. There was a terrible roar from the fire and all those other noises—popping and breaking. I don't know if I had my transistor radio with me. I probably did—in my pocket. I don't know how he could've heard it."

Ricky Senior painfully searched his memories of that night.

Stella wished she could tell him that Eric had heard it too. Using a ghost to threaten Bob was enough of that for one day. She needed this information to be real, not part of someone's imagination.

"Did you see anything—anyone—before you ran out of the silo? Were you and Eric the only two men inside when he found you?"

Ricky closed his eyes again. He muttered words under his breath that made Stella think he was trying to relive the moment. As she listened, she realized that he was praying.

"Forty years ago, I was afraid. I knew people were waiting for what I had to say. I didn't want them to judge me harshly. I was afraid for my family too. But not anymore." He opened his eyes. "There *was* someone else in the silo that night. I remember it as clearly as if it happened yesterday."

Ricky went on to explain how it had all gone down. "The fire was called in late. The silo was already fully involved when we got there. Someone said there were still workers inside who'd been sent in to get as much of the grain out as they could. Baskets and barrels, everything they could use, to bring out the grain."

"Eric sent me in with Tagger while the other men started hosing down the building. We were trying to hold off the inevitable until we could get those workers out."

"Did you rescue anyone?"

"No. That was one of the odd things. It looked like they'd been bringing grain out, but Tagger and I didn't see anyone in there working and no one ran out. Our two-way radios weren't working right. We couldn't let Eric know what was going on. Tagger went outside to give him the all clear while I did a last sweep of the place."

"I guess Eric got worried about you," Stella said.

Ricky grinned. "He was like an old mother hen where his team was concerned. I was surprised that night that he didn't go in with us at the beginning. That's what he usually did. He was a big, strong man. I once saw him carry two people out of a house fire at the same time! It seemed like there wasn't anything he couldn't do."

"You were having trouble breathing inside during the last sweep, weren't you?"

"That's the way it worked sometimes. It was like one minute you were fine, and the next you couldn't breathe. It was so hot, and the smoke was so thick. I think I panicked a little. I looked up and there was Eric."

"Then what happened?"

"He was afraid my mask wasn't working right so he put his mask on me and told me to get out of there. I said, 'You're coming out too, Chief, right?' He nodded. It was the last thing I ever said to him."

Ricky was tearing up again, wiping the drops that slid down his cheeks with an impatient hand.

"You said you saw someone else in there. Was it a worker?"

"No. It was someone who shouldn't have been there at all—*Shu Carriker.*"

"The old plant manager?" She remembered hearing the name used in conjunction with her grandmother's death. He'd been her grandfather's alibi for Abigail's death. That was before the silo fire.

Shu Carriker had been the manager of the pepper plant at one time. He'd sworn that Ben Carson was with him when Abigail had died. Then he'd disappeared.

A lot of people thought he'd been killed to protect Ben's secret. That was yet another dirty deed laid at her grandfather's feet.

"Yes. It was so weird," Ricky continued. "He was standing there in the middle of the burning building. I thought I was hallucinating! He was never a member of the fire brigade. He didn't work at the silo either. I couldn't figure out why he was there. I thought he was a ghost at first because we all figured he was dead."

Stella was confused. "Did he come out of the building?"

"I don't know. I didn't see him come out. It was chaos, Stella. He was standing about ten feet away from me. I ran for the front door and got out of there."

"What happened next?"

He swallowed hard. "Once the roof collapsed and we knew Eric was trapped inside, our world was crashed in too. Everyone was yelling and crying. We couldn't believe it. A few of us even thought about trying to go back in and get him. Thank God they held us back."

She could imagine the scene. She'd been on calls where they'd lost firefighters, some were friends of hers. It was exactly as he described it.

"Did anyone look for Shu afterward?"

Ricky shook his head as he looked down at the floor. "I never told anyone until right now. I was scared of what might happen."

What he was saying sounded so much like what Chum had said. Stella didn't understand what had made both men too scared to say anything about what they'd seen.

"It was a different time." He finally looked up at her. "You're not going to like what I have to tell you, but I think it's time someone said it. Your grandfather ran this town with an iron hand. No one defied him; except for Eric, who did it on a regular basis. The old man wanted the county to take over the fire service. He wanted to get rid of the fire brigade."

This didn't come as any surprise to Stella. She'd heard this story before. "So you're saying my grandfather killed Eric."

Ricky nodded. "Not him *exactly*—Shu did it. Shu was his go-to man. Any loose ends, he took care of them. Eric had gone to the legislature and made a lot of friends up there. There was even some talk of him running for a seat. Eric was popular, and your grandfather hated it."

"Okay." Stella tried to get a handle on what he was saying. "So you thought all of this time that Shu had killed Eric and you didn't say anything because you were afraid of what my grandfather might do to you."

"That's it in a nutshell. After that night, Shu disappeared again. I kept my secret to protect little Ricky and Lucille. I guess I hoped I was wrong. I hoped Eric really died in the fire. Now I know different—and I know what happened. I'd be willing to testify in court, if need be."

Stella wasn't sure what to think. All of it had happened so long ago. It was easy to blame it on her grandfather. Ricky and Chum probably both thought they knew what had happened.

But were they right? The answer had stayed hidden in the firehouse wall for forty years. With all of this secrecy, was it possible to really figure it out? Every time she thought she had a handle on it, something new popped up.

"Thanks for being honest with me," she said.

The part about the radio still bothered her. How loud would that have been turned up to hear *inside* the burning silo? Chum had said it was that sound that caught his attention *outside*.

Stella didn't think the deputy had heard Ricky's radio inside the silo. Yet Eric heard it too, right before he died.

Could Ricky have been one of the two men Chum saw putting Eric into the trunk? It would account for Eric hearing the radio playing in Ricky Senior's pocket at one point, and Chum hearing it later when Eric was carried out of the silo.

*Was Ricky still lying to her? If so, what was he covering up?*

"I'm sorry. I should've spoken up before. I'm going to go right over and tell Chief Rogers about what happened. I hope it helps him find Eric's killer."

Stella thanked him again and then went to rejoin her father and Doug.

She liked Ricky and didn't want to see him get into trouble. Something was still off about his account of what had happened the night of Eric's death. She was going to have to go on with the investigation if she was going to figure it out. She hoped Ricky Senior and his family weren't hurt by it.

Barbara and Sandy had decided to come down and get Lucille to look through old high school yearbooks with them.

Stella smiled when she saw big spoonfuls of homemade vanilla ice cream on top of their blueberry pie. The three women were giggling like the schoolgirls they once were as she passed their table.

Sean was staring at them. "She wouldn't even sit here with us. I guess we're not good enough for her anymore. The pepper heiress rears her ugly head."

Stella thought for a minute that he was serious and was ready to defend her mother's girlfriend time.

Then he winked at her and drank the last of his coffee. "I think I need to run a little after all that pie. Maybe I should do a few laps around the firehouse."

"That's fine with me." She looked at her watch. "I have to go and continue my study on how peppers are made."

"You don't need that if you aren't staying," Doug said.

"I'd like a tour of the place anyway, if that's okay with you," she shot back. "I made Ben spend some money on upgrades to keep the filters from catching on fire. I'd like to make sure those are working properly as well."

"Well, count me in on the pepper tour," Sean said. "I've always wondered how they get those tops on so tight. Doug, what about you?"

Of course, Doug also wanted to go along. Stella took a deep breath and acted like she didn't mind being shadowed everywhere she went. It was only for a few days.

She wasn't sure yet what was coming after that. She was trying not to think that far ahead.

"*Shh!*" Pat Smith from the *Gazette* turned up the volume on the television. "Look. It's about Sweet Pepper."

Stella turned and saw something she'd never expected to see—Eric—alive and dressed in a dark suit and a tie with the Sweet Pepper Fire Brigade emblem on it. He was addressing a crowd of reporters on the steps of the Tennessee legislature building.

He was handsome and intense, his blond hair neatly combed back. He was fighting to keep the county from destroying everything he'd worked for.

"Even with the money the state has proposed, the county fire service won't be able to handle the calls from Sweet Pepper and other non-incorporated areas. Response will be slow and inadequate without a full-time, firefighting organization located in my town."

A man with short, dark hair came on the screen. Eric's face was frozen in a small square on the side of the picture.

"That was the scene forty years ago when Sweet Pepper's fire chief, Eric Gamlyn, came to persuade state legislators to leave the firefighting system in his town alone. Some say he would have persuaded them, but Gamlyn was killed in a tragic fire that ended the debate."

The news anchor showed more footage of Eric talking to state representatives, shaking hands with the governor, smiling and waving.

"Recently a horrific discovery was made at the Sweet Pepper firehouse. Chief Gamlyn wasn't killed in a silo fire after all, according to county coroner, Judd Streeter. Gamlyn's remains show that he was shot once in the head and then sealed in a wall. He was found, ironically, after a fire claimed most of the firehouse."

The news anchor related the story with a blank expression.

"I haven't seen Eric's face since I was a kid," Lucinda Waxman said with a smile. "He was as handsome as I remember. Why do the good ones always die young?"

"All you have to do is go out to his cabin late one night and maybe he'll give you a dance." Tommy Potter from Potter's Hardware laughed.

The news report finished up with showing Chief Rogers

and his pledge to find the person or persons responsible for Eric's death.

"Of course," Tommy Potter said. "He's running for reelection soon. He's gotta make sure we feel *safe.*"

Tears stung Stella's eyes. It was one thing to live with Eric's ghost. It was another to see him alive on TV. He had so much of his life taken away from him. Lucinda was right—he died too young. Maybe he would have run for the state legislature. Maybe he would've been governor.

No one would ever know because someone hadn't liked him fighting for his fire brigade and had killed him. The unfairness of it struck her like a blow to the chest.

Her feelings were even stronger after the news broadcast. She had to find his killer—whether it was Ricky Senior or her grandfather. Eric needed justice for the life taken from him. She was going to see that he got it, no matter how long it took.

It was all she could do to drive to the pepper plant and spend time touring it. She wanted to go straight home and reassure herself that the part of Eric that had survived was still there. She couldn't free him from his half-life, trapped in the cabin, but she wanted to make sure that he was *real.*

It was probably just as well that she didn't go straight back, she realized as she drove to the plant. She would've ended up blubbering all over Eric and making them both feel worse.

Instead she was almost finished sniffling and wiping her eyes when plant manager Greg Lambert met them at the main office.

The original structure of the first pepper bottling plant was still intact from the 1800s. It was used as the office and administration building. The whole facility and distribution center covered more than ten acres and employed hundreds of workers.

"Good to see you, Chief Griffin," Greg said.

He was probably in his sixties yet still maintained some of his youthful good looks. Life had been a disappointment to him and it showed in his face. No amount of time spent in a tanning bed could make his chiseled face less cold and hard or put warmth into his eyes.

Stella introduced Sean and Doug. Greg acted as though he was thrilled to have them there. She knew better. He wasn't that friendly. They got in one of the visitor golf carts and Greg took them to one of the large metal buildings.

"Sweet Pepper was founded by the Carson family in the 1800s when they discovered the unique combination of soil and weather that grew the best peppers." Greg gave his tour speech as they walked through the plant. "Of course, I don't need to tell you that, Chief Griffin. It's your family history."

Stella smiled at his attempt at humor. She was glad to see the new ductwork was doing just fine. There had been no regular calls for the small fires that used to occur here.

About a hundred people were involved in getting the peppers ready for canning. The bright red, orange, and green peppers ran down from a conveyor belt into fresh water for washing and then were sorted by quality, color, and size.

"Each of the buildings handles a different process," Greg explained. "This is the first step after local farmers drop off their peppers. It ends with the bottled peppers being readied for shipping. There has been constant growth here since the first building became inadequate for the needs of the business. Probably the biggest growth spurt happened in the late 1970s and early 1980s, when four buildings and two, ten-truck loading sites, were added."

He went on to explain that those new facilities had sped up production like never before. "Today our peppers are shipped to twenty-six countries and every state in the U.S. Everyone loves the sweetest, hottest peppers in the world."

Stella considered the time frame he was talking about. In

other words, a large amount of money was spent on the new facilities—right after Eric had died and thirty million dollars went missing.

Could it be that obvious? Did Ben have his hit man, Shu Carriker, kill Eric during the silo fire so he could get his hands on the state money to improve his pepper-packing plant?

# Chapter 19

Stella followed her father and Doug through the building as they listened to Greg describe how the peppers were processed and packed. She feigned an interest she didn't feel. Maybe she needed to know this stuff, but her mind was on one thing—figuring out how she would prove who killed Eric.

If her grandfather was involved in Eric's death, he certainly wouldn't admit it. No one knew what had happened to Shu Carriker. Chum was dead.

It was hard to believe Ricky Senior would have killed Eric, despite the radio music Chum and Eric had heard that night. It was easier to think that Ben Carson was as evil as people in Sweet Pepper painted him, even though he had been nothing like that with her.

In her opinion—wealthy, powerful men didn't get that way by following the rules.

Doug was right. There had to be a connection to someone who was still alive and trying to cover things up. Otherwise,

Chum would be living it up in retirement instead of on a slab in the coroner's office.

But how did she even begin to follow the clues she had? Nothing seemed to go together.

The tour was over. Greg gave them each a tiny bottle of peppers to take home. Stella wanted to give it back—she had several of them at the cabin. She wasn't much of a pepper eater.

Greg wouldn't hear of it, so she thanked him and took the bottle with her.

She looked around at the "newer" buildings that might have been built with blood money. There was probably a record of that money being spent—how much and when— if not where it came from.

Stella realized she needed the police.

Maybe it was time to come clean with Chief Rogers. He was really the only one who could investigate the trail of money. She could claim her right to be part of that investigation since it had all started with the fire at the silo and Eric's death. She was the fire chief, even if she didn't have that role forty years ago. There was no statute of limitations on murder.

She had to take her chances with Don Rogers. She didn't trust him, but not working with him on this might mean never finding answers.

Stella found her perfect opportunity to talk to Chief Rogers when her mother called and suggested they all spend the rest of the day in Pigeon Forge. Stella told them she had paperwork to do and waved to Doug and her parents as they left Sweet Pepper to go sightseeing.

Before she lost her nerve, Stella marched right into the police station and asked to see Don. His assistant told her he was in the conference room. Stella thanked her and went to find him.

To her surprise, Walt Fenway and Judd Streeter were already seated at the big table with John Trump and Chief Rogers. There were two other men she didn't recognize, although she was betting on the man in the dark suit being from outside the area.

"Come right on in," Chief Rogers said to her. "You've been part of the investigation, even if it's only been an annoying, *small* part. You're probably going to want to hear whatever Doc Streeter has to say."

He introduced the two men she didn't recognize as Brad Whitman—the man in the suit—who was from the Tennessee Bureau of Investigation. Jerry Ryan, the younger man, was Judd's assistant.

They all shook hands and Stella sat down. She noticed Judd had a file folder in front of him. She hoped it contained good news.

"Doc, why don't you tell us your findings and we'll go from there," Rogers invited.

"Thanks, Chief." Judd lumbered to his feet. It was easy to see he was uncomfortable talking to people. He laughed and pulled at his beard. "I'm afraid my news isn't very helpful. We were able to make a determination about the remains found in what should have been Eric Gamlyn's coffin. The remains belong to Shu Carriker."

Everyone, except Don Rogers, seemed surprised by Judd's statement. They all knew who Shu Carriker was. They just didn't expect to find him in Eric's coffin.

Judd sat down, his face a little red. "This is my mistake. I take full responsibility. I don't know how it happened, but there it is."

Jerry Ryan got up. His black hair stood straight up on his head, no doubt with some help from a hair care product. His T-shirt had the image of a man crawling out of a grave on it.

"We were able—well, *I* was able to quickly learn the identity of the remains in the coffin. There was a metal rod in the right femur that had a number on it. Tracking it was simple. The subject seems to have died from a serious head injury that smashed in his skull."

"I think that was why I made the mistake," Judd explained. "The bones were charred and the skull damage would have been consistent with a heavy object, like the roof of the silo, hitting the victim. I expected it to be Chief Gamlyn, like everyone else. I should have done a more thorough examination."

Judd's hands were shaky as he sipped his coffee. His pale face wasn't at all jolly. He looked like a man whose longtime career could be over because of a mistake he'd made in his distant past.

"So there we have it." Chief Rogers took a deep breath. "I think we can assume from this evidence alone that Shu Carriker probably snuck into the burning silo and shot Eric Gamlyn, for reason or reasons unknown. No doubt someone paid for that job. Carriker wasn't able to get out of the silo after the job was done, and perished in the building."

"Then how did Gamlyn's remains end up in the fire-house?" Brad Whitman questioned. "Was there another assailant who took the body out and made his escape from the collapsing roof?"

"Who do we like for hiring Carriker to kill Gamlyn?" John stared at Stella.

She knew what he was thinking. It was, no doubt, what everyone at the table was thinking.

"Anyone have a thought on that?" Rogers asked.

Stella knew she had to share her information. It wasn't easy. "Deputy Chum told me something about the night Eric Gamlyn died."

All eyes shifted to her. Walt looked a little anxious.

"He told me he saw two men take Eric's body out of the silo *before* the roof collapsed. He said they put him into the trunk of a Chevy Impala."

"A Chevy Impala?" Chief Rogers tapped his manicured fingernails on the table in irritation. "Any idea why he didn't come forth earlier with that information? Or did he say something, Walt, and you didn't bother telling anyone forty years ago?"

"Deputy Chum—or anyone else—never said anything to me about this," Walt denied. "We would have investigated. All of us knew, or we *thought* we knew, what had happened to my friend, Eric. We ignored it, and concentrated on him dying a hero so as not to upset the balance of this town. But we all know who Shu Carriker worked for. This wasn't the only time he took care of Ben Carson's dirty work."

It was out on the table. Brad Whitman furiously scribbled in his notepad.

"Any ideas why Deputy Chum didn't come to *me* with this information instead of *you*, Ms. Griffin?" Chief Rogers asked her.

"He said he kept quiet all these years because he was afraid for his life," she answered. "He only told me because he was leaving town and I'd been looking into Eric's death since we found his bones at the firehouse."

"You think he was alluding to the fact that Ben Carson was responsible for the fire chief's death and would kill Deputy Chum as well?" Brad Whitman sat forward and waited for Stella's response, pen poised.

"He never mentioned Ben Carson's name," Stella said.

"In all fairness, Agent Whitman," John added, "Chief Griffin is Ben Carson's granddaughter."

Whitman's eyes narrowed and then he wrote that information in his notebook. "I'm sure I don't need to remind you, Chief Griffin, that this *is* privileged information that is part of a murder investigation."

"Yes, sir." She knew a warning when she heard one.

"That's bull anyway, about Chum." Chief Rogers shoved

aside his empty cup of coffee. "I knew him all my life. We worked together plenty of times. He could've told me what he suspected and I would've protected him."

"Maybe he didn't trust you, Don," Walt observed. "Maybe he told Stella his secret because he knew she'd actually try to *do* something about it—whether Ben is her grandpa or not."

Chief Rogers didn't like that at all. Stella thought for a minute that he might jump across the table and strangle Walt.

Instead, he smiled. "I think we might need to conduct an investigation into our *former* police chief too. How did things like this happen and everybody turned a blind eye?"

Agent Whitman took over the conversation. "First of all, Chief Rogers, I'm here to find out who killed Chief Gamlyn and why. If Mr. Fenway becomes part of that investigation, we'll deal with that too. In the meantime, Deputy Chum's murder seems to be part of what happened to Gamlyn forty years ago. We'll include that in our investigation."

"I understand, Agent Whitman." Chief Rogers gazed at Stella. "I'll need a statement from you before you leave today, Ms. Griffin. And I want to know *why* you didn't come forward with this information right away. You're a public official. You have to be held to a higher standard and not go sneaking around behind my back trying to solve *my* crimes."

"Excuse me, Chief Rogers," Whitman smoothly intervened. "We'll be taking over this investigation from here on. Since there is some idea of local corruption that could be involved, it would be better for preparing our court case, and so that your citizens have a feeling of security. I believe that's it. Thank you all for coming."

Stella would have laughed at the expression on Rogers's face but she was afraid he might explode. He turned and walked out of the conference room, slamming the door on his way out.

"Nice going," John murmured as he reached her. "Now the state has the investigation. We don't need help from *them*."

"I don't know how this is *my* fault, but it sounds to me like someone needs to look for some answers that no one has bothered with in forty years. If I did that, I'm okay with it. And thanks for pointing the finger at me about Ben."

He shrugged. "Just trying to be *fair*. I don't think you can be objective about this case. Think of how it will affect your mother if Ben is guilty of having Eric killed."

"I think you were trying to make your point about me being part of the Carson family, like you always do."

Before John could say anything else, Agent Whitman asked Stella to join him in his temporary office to give her statement.

John gave her a mock salute and left the room. Stella ground her teeth, wondering what she'd ever seen in him.

The town had given Agent Whitman a small "office" while he was there. It was all the two of them could do to get into the closet-sized room and sit down.

"We don't get special treatment in cases like this." He apologized to Stella as they sat at the small foldout table. "You can imagine that local law enforcement doesn't like us intervening in their work. They feel like we're taking over their private turf and that it says something about the quality of their work."

"And does it?"

"No. Not at all. Usually it means there are bigger fish to go into the fire. In this case, we're actually investigating a link we discovered between your dead fire chief and thirty million dollars missing from the state accountant's office."

"Forty years later?"

"The mills of the gods grind slowly, Chief Griffin. And it helps when there is a murder investigation we can link with it. You see, we think that money ended up here, in

Sweet Pepper. We think Gamlyn was murdered because he'd volunteered to help the TBI take care of this problem."

"What? Why him?"

"He had friends in high places. He didn't want that money allocated to the county. He was willing to work with us as a confidential informant on the case the state was trying to make. The TBI had heard rumors about what was going down long before the money went missing. We were waiting to see where it ended up. Then Gamlyn was dead. What does that tell you?"

"He was in the wrong place at a bad time. How could you know about the money before it was stolen, and why didn't you follow up after it was gone?"

"Funding the county to take over municipal and volunteer fire departments was a long-term project of a legislator from this area—Barney Falk."

"Sorry. Not from here. Never heard of him."

"Yes. I know." He smiled at her. "I've done my research on you or we wouldn't be talking. Falk was a powerful man at the time. Some people say he still is, but more behind-the-scenes now. He's retired and lives here in Sweet Pepper. We think he was doing a last solid for a friend—your grandfather—before he left office. Gamlyn stood in his way. It's even possible he became aware that he was working with us."

"So they killed him." Stella's heart ached for all she had to tell Eric about the circumstances of his death. She thought things like this only went on in places like Chicago where everyone knew there was corruption.

"I'm afraid so." Agent Whitman shuffled through some papers on the table. "We've always had doubts about Gamlyn's death being a part of his job. But there seemed to be no link between what happened and his position with us. When you all found that he'd been murdered, we felt it was justified to open the old investigation as well."

Stella took a deep breath. "What do you want from me?"

Agent Whitman was an average-looking man with gray-ing brown hair and the face of a schoolteacher. He had a pleasant smile. Stella once had an insurance agent who looked a lot like him.

"Right now, I want your statement about what Deputy Mace Chum said to you. I'm not going to lie to you—we think you might be our best link to Ben Carson and his involvement in this. I want to know what you know about Gamlyn's murder and the death of Deputy Chum. Then I'd like your help figuring out how all of it fits together."

# Chapter 20

～～～～～

Stella didn't know what to say. If the TBI was investigating all of this, Eric stood a better chance of getting real answers. Was she willing to spy on her grandfather as he was making peace with her mother?

Agent Whitman was admitting he didn't know for sure if Ben was involved in Eric's death. She gave him credit for that since almost every other person in Sweet Pepper would lay Eric's death at Ben's feet.

If asked, they couldn't tell you *how* they knew, or any pertinent information. But if something bad had happened, one of the Carsons had to be involved.

"I'll be glad to tell you what I know. It isn't much. Besides rumors, I don't have any information that Ben was involved in Eric's death. As far as I know, he doesn't have an Impala."

Agent Whitman sorted through some papers. "You tell me what you know so far and let me see what I can find out about it. I understand Walt Fenway, the ex-police chief, got a listing of all the Impalas in the area during that time."

"Yes. He's been looking through it. I've been working on other angles."

Stella told him about what Ricky Senior had said, including the questions she had about the music playing the night of the silo fire. "That's not much after all this time. I noticed that there was a large group of improvements done at the pepper factory around the same time. I wondered about that, after I heard about the missing money."

"We've looked at that too. As you say, it's been a while. All of the records at the pepper plant from the late 1970s and early 1980s were destroyed by a fire."

"That's convenient."

"Exactly. All of it seems to fit together, but finding out that Gamlyn was murdered was the first solid clue we've had. Everything else might make sense with that—if we can prove it."

"So what do you want me to do?"

"Would you be willing to ask your grandfather some questions?"

"Sure. He knows I've been looking for answers. Asking him about Shu Carriker, now that we know, would fit in."

"Would you be willing to wear a wire?"

Stella was uneasy about that request.

She wanted her grandfather to be punished if he'd sent Shu to kill Eric so he could confiscate thirty million dollars, but did she want to be that heavily involved in taking him down? She wasn't sure how her mother would feel about it either.

"If you know about my background, you know this is my mother's first time back to Sweet Pepper since before I was born. I'm not sure how either of us would feel about entrapping her father."

"Okay. I can respect that. You're related to Ben Carson. Why don't you think about it and get back to me?"

"Sure. I'll do that."

"In the meantime, if you hear any other information that we might need to solve this thing, I'd appreciate it if you'd let me know right away. I sense there's some hostility between you and Chief Rogers. I understand your hesitation to share your knowledge with him. I hope we can have a better working relationship."

He got to his feet, knocking a small lamp off of the table, and shook her hand. He gave her his business card with different numbers and emails on it so she could reach him at any time.

"It was nice meeting you, Chief Griffin. I hope we'll have answers for all of this before you have to leave Sweet Pepper."

Stella bumped into John and Walt outside on the sidewalk as she left town hall. They were standing next to the Cherokee.

"Did you and Agent Whitman have a nice conversation?" Walt asked with a grin. "John and I were putting up some money on him asking you to wear a wire next time you go to dinner with the old man."

"I probably wouldn't tell you if he did," Stella replied. "But we had a good conversation about Chum and Eric. I think the TBI has some leads they're not sharing with us. It sounds like this goes way back, before Eric was killed.'

"Really?" John was immediately interested. "Care to share those thoughts over lunch?"

"Not if it meant starving to death," she told him with a smile. "I know you'll take whatever I say back to Chief Rogers."

"He's my boss. You don't understand what it's like to have the state come in and take over a case. They do what they want and find the answers they want. They don't care if it's good for Sweet Pepper or not."

"Maybe I'll leave before it's over and Agent Whitman will want to take *you* into his confidence because you're the new fire chief. Until then, I'm not saying anything."

"I don't know what you're talking about, Stella. I don't plan to take your place."

"Funny that you don't know about the plan. Everyone else does." She was suddenly tired of playing all the games. She wanted to go to the cabin and see Eric. "I have to go. I'll see you later, Walt."

"Mind if I catch a ride back with you?" he asked after grinning at John. "I had to leave my truck in the shop. It's always something."

Stella agreed to take Walt home. He lived outside of town in the Big Bear Springs community. They stopped and picked up lunch at Scooter's on their way out.

Walt was eager to hear what Eric would have to say about everything Stella planned to tell him when they got back to the cabin.

It wasn't going to be easy telling Eric the truth about all of it, especially after having seen him alive and passionate about his beliefs on TV. Maybe he wouldn't be surprised that someone had killed him because he'd made himself a target. He'd never mentioned that he'd been working with the TBI.

"Did I mention that I found something interesting in all those Impalas I've been looking through?" Walt asked as they drove up Firehouse Road.

"No. I didn't hear you volunteer that information at the meeting either."

"This is for you and me and Eric. I'm done with those others. I know if they can find a way to hang this on me, since I was police chief at the time, they will. You and me want to know the truth for Eric's sake. That's all that matters now."

"Okay. What did you find out?"

"Shu Carriker had an Impala. Sounds interesting, doesn't it? I was thinking maybe me and you could take a ride over there and see if his wife still has it. I sat up with her a few nights after he went missing. I think she'll talk to me. What do you say?"

Stella was barely listening. She was staring at a "For Sale" sign that had been put up outside the cabin in her absence.

It looked as though the town had decided not to wait until she left. Maybe it was a way for them to work around the problem with Bob Floyd. If they sold the property, anyone could take down the cabin.

"Looks like Eric might be moving," Walt commented. "So, what do you think about taking a gander at that Impala?"

It was as hard as Stella had thought to talk to Eric about what she'd learned. She was glad her parents and Doug weren't there. She didn't think she could hide the fact that she was speaking to someone they couldn't see.

Walt followed the conversation between the two as best he could while he ate two hot dogs with chili and peppers, and French fries.

"I was working with them," Eric admitted. "I thought it would help me keep the fire brigade going."

"And you're the one who's always telling me that I'm a firefighter, not a cop," she accused. "What were you thinking?"

"I was desperate. Why do you think I wanted to warn you off? I'm standing here, dead. I wish I had it to go back and do over."

"What's he saying?" Walt asked.

"That he was crazy to get involved in an undercover investigation," she answered in her own interpretation.

"I didn't say that," Eric protested.

"You might as well have," she replied.

"I think the TBI is doing all of this because you were killed, buddy," Walt said to him. "I don't think they had anything until we found you in the firehouse."

"And Shu Carriker was in my coffin." Eric shook his head. "All these years. No wonder I couldn't rest in peace."

Stella told Walt what Eric had said. He almost choked on his hot dog, laughing.

"You're taking this better than I thought you would," she said to Eric.

"Is that why you brought Walt back with you? So you wouldn't have to tell me by yourself?"

"I don't like talking about you being dead. I can't imagine what it must be like for you talking about *yourself* being dead."

Eric grinned wickedly. "You may be overthinking how I feel about it. Women *are* more emotional than men."

"Oh yeah, right. Women aren't any more emotional than men. We just don't bottle it up. I've seen terrible things working the last ten years as a firefighter—stuff that would curl your hair. You're the one who got all moody because we found your bones in the firehouse and started cooking all the time so you could avoid thinking about it!"

"Are you saying it's good or bad that I cook?"

Stella told Walt what Eric was saying, as soon as he'd stopped laughing over Stella's defense of women.

"You think cooking might bring your door?" Walt asked his friend.

"Door?" Eric looked at Stella. "What's he talking about?"

"There's a popular belief that spirits see a door or tunnel and that leads them to the other side," she explained. "You haven't seen anything like that? How about a white light?"

"I woke up sitting in my rocking chair," Eric told her. "I don't know how long I'd been sitting there. It was like I'd been asleep. I tried to remember what had happened and then I tried to leave the cabin. There was no door, no light—definitely no tunnel."

Stella told Walt. "What happened when you tried to leave the cabin?"

"I ended up at the firehouse. I tried to leave the firehouse and ended up back here. I think I went back and forth for a long time. Then I finally got the idea. Only now, I can't go to the firehouse anymore."

. "And now the town put your cabin up for sale again." Walt snorted when Stella had related Eric's words to him. "It's a shame when a man can't even live in his own place. What do you think will happen if they tear it down?"

Eric didn't want to discuss what would happen. It was more because his pride didn't want him to try to make Stella stay because she felt sorry for him than anything else.

"What do you mean they put the cabin up for sale *again*?" Stella asked Walt.

"A while back, maybe twenty years ago, the town council tried to sell this place. No takers. They finally gave up. I think Eric did a good job scaring off any potential buyers."

"I think Bob was behind this," she said. "He's afraid to try to burn the cabin now, so this is his new scheme for getting rid of it."

"What do you mean he's afraid?" Eric asked her. "Why would he be more afraid now than yesterday?"

Stella gave him a condensed version of what she'd told Bob at the barbershop. Walt laughed, but Eric took it more seriously. "It's never a good idea to push an animal into a corner. Even a rabbit will come out snarling."

Stella, bewildered by that bit of folklore, repeated it to Walt who agreed with his friend.

"True enough." Walt changed the subject. "Are you going to talk to the old man, Stella? Can I eat the rest of your fries if you don't want them?"

"I wish you wouldn't," Eric said. "Let it go, Stella. Get out of it while you still can."

"Don't give up yet," she entreated. "We're close now, and we're going to find an answer."

"Is that a yes or no about the old man, or the French fries?" Walt asked, not hearing Eric's side of the conversation.

Stella slid the rest of her fries toward him. "Knock yourself out. I don't know yet about Ben. Let's go have a look at that Impala."

"Do me a favor," Eric said.

She looked into his amazing blue eyes, realizing that they were every bit as blue when he'd been alive. "Anything."

"Make sure you don't do this alone, and take some pictures of whatever you find. I'd like to see it."

"Sure." She turned to Walt who was finishing the last of the fries. "Eric wants pictures. Let's go."


Shu Carriker's old place was outside of town. There was a ramshackle group of buildings clustered around a house that had once been painted white, but was now a dirty gray after being ignored for many years.

The land around it was beautiful—a lush green valley stretching for acres along the river. Cows, chickens, and goats were wandering around with no fencing or barricades.

Most of the buildings were barely standing, some with roofs half gone, and others with only the bare frames of what had once been a barn or chicken coop.

Stella was a little nervous about driving across the bridge that spanned the river. She wasn't convinced it would hold the weight of a bicycle much less the Cherokee.

Walt assured her that it was safe. "They have a truck. They must get in and out to go shopping and whatnot. Go on. Don't be such a girl—or I'll tell Eric."

"If we go through the bridge and I die, I'm haunting *your* house." She gave the Cherokee some gas and it made it across the bridge. "I hope they never have a fire out here. The engine isn't coming across that thing."

Shu's widow, Thelma, and one adult son, both lived at the old homestead. They answered Walt's knock at the door together. Thelma peered over her son's burly shoulder.

"Yeah?" the man asked.

"It's Jack, isn't it?" Walt extended his hand to him. "You're the spitting image of your daddy. You're the youngest of the four, right?"

"What's it to you?"

"You probably don't remember me but I'm sure your mama does. I'm Walt Fenway. I've been here more than a few times as police chief. I tried to find your daddy when he went missing."

"Hi, Jack," Stella said with a smile. "How are you? The wall you repaired looks great."

"Chief Griffin." Jack nodded. "Why are you here?"

"We'd like to have a word with you and your mother."

"You can talk to me." Jack told his mother to stay in the house.

He walked out on the porch with Walt and Stella, closing the door behind him. They all walked carefully around a hole in the porch floor.

"What do you want? Nobody here called you. I paid my taxes this year."

Walt kept his tone friendly. "We're not here about taxes, son. We'd like to buy your daddy's old Impala. Do you still have it?"

"His Impala?" Jack looked confused. "What for? It's a piece of junk. It hasn't been driven since daddy left."

"We're collectors." Stella tried to help out, knowing Walt was making this up as he went along. "We collect old Impalas. There's good money in it, if it's the right one."

Jack's expression of anger and distrust melted away. "Sounds good to me. It's not drivable, but if you all want it, it's yours—for the right price."

He walked with them to one of the side buildings and pulled a threadbare tarp off of a black vehicle. The tires were flat. Weeds had grown into the car. The glass on the front and back had been shattered.

"I told you," Jack said. "Not much to work with. But you can have it for two hundred dollars. We probably have the title somewhere, if you're thinking about fixing it up."

Walt went right for the trunk. "You got keys to open this?"

"Probably." Jack's eyes narrowed. "Don't you want to see the engine?"

"Nope." Walt looked around the narrow enclosure. He picked up a rusted tire iron and applied it to the lock on the trunk. "This will do just fine."

Stella moved back there with him when the trunk popped open. Sunlight filtered through the rotting wood showing a large amount of what looked like dried blood in the trunk. There was also a piece of moldy red fabric, a glove, and a single boot.

Tucked in one corner, near the taillight, was a small transistor radio.

Stella's lips tightened when she realized that Ricky *had* to be part of this now. She was willing to bet the radio had belonged to him.

"This is it," Walt muttered, his voice filled with anger and sorrow. "This is where those jackals put Eric when they took him out of the silo. Who knows if he was alive or dead when they stuffed him in here? I hope they both burn in hell."

Stella put her hand on Walt's shoulder to steady him and then she took out her cell phone. "This is going to make a big difference. That's all we can do for him now."

As soon as she'd called Agent Whitman, she started taking pictures of the trunk and the rest of the car.

"You aren't really going to show Eric all of this, are you?" Walt asked. "I don't know if he really wants to see it. There's only so much a man can stand."

"Hey! What are you doing back there?" Jack came around the side of the car. "Is it worth the two hundred or not? If not, get the hell off my property."

Walt charged at the young man, knocking him to the ground. "Your daddy was a no-account killer who took the life of my best friend. This car is going to prove that. So unless you want to get in my way on this, I suggest you go back and get behind your mama's skirts."

Stella thought his technique was a little over-the-top, but she'd witnessed much worse in situations with Chicago police officers. It was hard to look at the trunk, knowing what had happened. She finally took the last picture and turned away.

Walt might be right about showing the photos to Eric. She'd have to make that decision later. In the meantime, the sound of approaching sirens, coming over the bridge, made her realize the scene would shortly be swarming with police and crime scene people.

Chief Rogers was the first one there. He slammed his car door and frowned at Jack Carriker as he ran by him to get to the house.

"I hope to God you didn't find anything important out here," he snarled at Walt and Stella. "You have no warrant. Anything here is totally useless. Good work, you two."

# Chapter 21

〜〜〜〜〜〜

While Chief Rogers yelled and cursed, Agent Whitman arrived on the scene and took a look at the trunk of the Impala. His laid-back manner made Chief Rogers look like a blustering fool.

"Excellent work." He smiled and shook Stella's hand. "I'm glad we talked about checking out the car. We'll have to wait for forensics to tell us if the blood and these items belong to Chief Gamlyn, but the story fits."

Chief Rogers was even more furious. "What are you talking about? There's no search warrant. This stuff can't be used as evidence."

Agent Whitman pulled a document from inside his coat pocket. "I think the DA will find everything in order."

"How'd you get this?" Rogers demanded. "Don't tell me she *told* you she was coming here. You would've been here too."

"As a matter of fact, Chief Griffin and I discussed the importance of finding the Impala this morning after the meeting. I obtained the search warrant after she left my office.

Clearly, she didn't need it before she found the evidence as the family member allowed her to inspect the car. We're covered as far as legality is concerned."

Rogers swore. "If that don't beat all. She lies, and you swear to it."

"What might be more interesting, Chief Rogers, is how you *knew* to come out here." Agent Whitman's tone was light and affable. "Chief Griffin called *my* cell phone to report her news. I have a feeling she didn't call *you*."

"I heard you all were out here. I thought you might need some backup." Chief Rogers was clearly on the defensive. "I can see you don't. I'll expect to see some kind of report about this, Whitman. You are a guest in my jurisdiction. Don't abuse my hospitality."

Chief Rogers scowled at each of them in a threatening manner and then went back to his car, spinning his tires in the dirt before leaving them behind.

"I don't think Chief Rogers was happy with this scenario," Agent Whitman said. "And I'd appreciate more of a heads-up next time. But I think you've found the jackpot here. I'll have the car towed somewhere safe and a state crime scene team will check it out."

"Sorry," Stella apologized. "I probably should have called you sooner. I'm not a police officer, but I am familiar with how things work."

Walt apologized too. "I know how things work and that's why I *didn't* call first. I didn't want to get out here and find the Impala missing."

Agent Whitman didn't seem upset. "All's well that ends well, Mr. Fenway. I'm curious about how you came to find the car. I looked through the same DMV records that you got. I didn't see this car listed on those records."

"I thought about it after I heard that Shu Carriker was buried in Eric's coffin. I remembered him having this old Impala. Good guess, huh?"

"Very good guess." Agent Whitman shook his hand. "It pays to know the area. Now if you'll excuse me, I'm going to call for help."

Zane called Stella to tell her that he'd clocked Chief Rogers going close to one hundred miles an hour after he left the Carriker farm. "What did you do to him this time, Stella?"

"Not much," she replied. "I think he wanted to put me in a trunk and close me up though."

"I'm meeting with him myself later. I hope he's over it by then."

Stella was curious. "What's up?"

Zane explained that he'd talked to John Trump about seeing an older black pickup riding close to a blue truck hauling a trailer on the day Deputy Chum was killed.

"I didn't think anything of it and road rage happens. I didn't actually see the blue truck go off the road. I was keeping an eye out for fires, not that kind of thing."

"Don't worry about it, Zane. Just tell him what you saw. I'll stay away from him until after he talks to you."

He laughed. "And I won't tell him we're dating. That way he won't take whatever you've done out on me."

Stella dropped Walt off at his cabin in Big Bear Springs after she left the Carriker farm. There had been a fire that had all but destroyed the cabin last year, but she couldn't tell it now. Everyone from town had come out to help rebuild the cabin on one long weekend. If anything, the structure looked better than it had before.

"Come on in back and we'll have some hard cider," he invited. "I know I need some. You must too."

"Sounds good, thanks." Stella opened the door to the

Cherokee to get out and her emergency pager went off. "On second thought, I'll have to take a rain check on that cider, Walt. Duty calls."

"Okay." He closed the passenger side door. "Think hard on it before you show Eric those pictures, huh? I don't know if I'd really want to see them if I was in his shoes. See you later. Be safe."

Stella turned the Cherokee around and switched on the siren when she reached the end of Walt's narrow drive.

She knew Walt was right, in some ways, about not showing Eric the pictures she'd taken. It seemed unnatural for him to see the place he might have died. He was probably better off not remembering any of it. Those memories could only bring him pain.

On the other hand, he deserved to know the truth, and that was what he was asking for. It might be difficult to handle, but she thought she'd want to know what really happened if she was in his place.

She didn't think he'd be happy with less either. And she'd learned an unhappy ghost could be a pain in the butt.

Walt's cabin was only about ten minutes from the firehouse. For once, Stella got there before anyone else.

Kent was on communications that day. "The call is from the Sunset Beach community over on Sweet Pepper Lake. The caller said it's a house fire and no one appears to be home. Most of those houses are vacation rentals, so it wouldn't be surprising. Can I drive the pumper?"

Stella saw Tagger hop out of his friend's pickup. "Suit up. We'll have Tagger on communications while we're gone. I haven't been up to the lake community since I took my first tour of Sweet Pepper. This should be interesting."

The first thing that Stella had noticed about Sunset Beach, and its hundred or so luxury cabins and houses stretched around it, was that there was only one road going in and out. The road circled around the lake and was barely graveled. There were large ruts in it and very little shoulder area. It was fine for everything but large trucks—like the ones they were bringing in.

She'd talked to the town council about it, but it was a private road, not maintained by the town. Still, it was part of the fire brigade's jurisdiction. That meant the town could wash its hands of it, but she still had to deal with whatever problems came up because of it.

Stella was surprised at finding the road so badly maintained. It was her understanding that most of the cabins around the three-mile lake were pricey, some worth millions. They were rarely used by the people who owned them. The cabins were rented out by the owners with routine chores performed by a local service.

"Where are we going, Chief?" Ricky asked as he ran into the firehouse.

"Where the rich folks live," Tagger said after speaking to Kent. "Well, they *could* live there if they wanted to."

JC whistled sharply as he tugged on his boots. "Better wear your best gear, brother. Don't want to disappoint them."

Ricky laughed with him—until he saw Petey. They hadn't spoken since they'd kissed.

"Hi, Petey."

"Hi, Ricky." She didn't even look at him before she opened her locker and started taking out her gear.

"Going to Sunset Beach," he told her.

"That's nice."

Ricky smiled at her hopefully but she didn't look up from what she was doing.

Stella was dressed and had her stopwatch out, observing her group.

Kimmie and David Spratt arrived with Sylvia. Hero ran in from the back of the firehouse—Stella knew where he'd been—and the two dogs barked and jumped at each other, obviously happy to be together again.

Royce Pope had caught a ride with John. Banyin called in that she was at the doctor. Bert Wando came in with Allen Wise. There was no sign of Marty, no call or text to explain why he wasn't there.

Stella didn't dwell on it as everyone got ready and climbed on board the two trucks. This was it for Marty, as far as she was concerned. She had a list of a few other people she could call to take his place. It was a small list, but she felt sure she could find one other person to make up her minimum quota.

She climbed in the front of the engine/ladder truck with Hero and Ricky, and the fire brigade set out for Sunset Beach.

"I suppose it's wishful thinking that they took care of this road after I sent the homeowners association a letter," Stella said to Ricky. "If they haven't made any changes, I don't know if we can even get up there."

"She wouldn't even talk to me, Chief," Ricky said mournfully. "I called her and texted her a few times. I never heard anything back."

Stella didn't pretend not to know who he was talking about. "She's dating someone, isn't she?"

"Yeah, but come on—we had a special moment. At least *I* thought it was special."

"Aren't you with someone else too?"

"No. Marcy broke up with me. I thought Petey and I were perfect."

Stella smiled, feeling old and wise. "Sometimes firefighters get close because of what they do. It might seem like love, but it's only the experience. It usually doesn't last from what I've seen."

Ricky shook his head, the little curl on his forehead moving back and forth as he navigated the fire engine through Sweet Pepper's narrow streets with the siren blazing.

"I know what I felt, Chief. Petey felt it too. She's probably scared."

"Maybe." It wasn't Stella's place to disagree about affairs of the heart and she usually didn't get involved.

It happened sometimes between firefighters, like it did in any other profession. She wasn't worried about it—unless it caused a problem with performance.

They went east out of town and followed the old highway until they reached the cutoff for Sunset Beach. The lake was visible before the turn, glistening in the sun. There were a few boats out on it, their white sails fluttering in the breeze.

"No such luck," Ricky said as he turned on the bad road. "I think we can get up there, but it's gonna be rough."

"Take your time," she said. "I mean it, Ricky. I don't feel like dropping off the side of the mountain into the lake today. Do the best you can."

She radioed the same advice to Kent in the pumper/tanker. She realized he had more experience getting a large vehicle in and out of tight spaces since he was an over-the-road trucker but she'd rather say it than be sorry she hadn't.

The engine had plenty of power to pull up the steep road. The wide tires made it through the deep ruts but had to straddle the edges of the road to keep going.

Stella looked for smoke but didn't see any in the cloudless blue sky. There was no smell of it either when she opened her window.

The road flattened out at the first cabin but didn't widen. There was even less gravel and more potholes. The engine went up and down through them. Stella knew it was probably hard on her people riding in back. She didn't like the situation and hoped John would fight for something better if the town made him fire chief after she was gone.

"Do we have an address?" Stella asked.

"215 Half Moon Road." Ricky looked at the GPS. "We're right here. I don't see anything."

The only thing Stella saw was a man standing at the foot of his driveway. The cabin behind him rose up three stories above the lake. She was sure the view was fantastic, but if there was a fire, she saw no sign of it.

"Park here," she told Ricky. "Let's see what's going on."

They walked up to the man, who was dressed in a blue-and-white striped seersucker suit with a blue bow tie. He had a thick head of white hair and was leaning heavily on a cane.

John reached Stella before she spoke to the man. "That's Barney Falk—he was the state rep for a long time from this area. Be careful."

She nodded. "Mr. Falk. I'm Fire Chief Stella Griffin. Did you call in an emergency at this address?"

Falk pushed the top of an old stopwatch. "I've had this stopwatch since I was in high school on the track team, Chief Griffin. Let me tell you, I could've run up here faster back then than you got here today."

Stella glanced at John. He shrugged.

"We made good time up here, Mr. Falk," she assured him. "What's your emergency?"

"My emergency, young woman, is that the insurance company has raised the rates on my home because of inadequate fire protection. What are you doing to improve your response time?"

# Chapter 22

～～～～～

S tella didn't like confrontation, especially with the people she served. She didn't back down from it either.

In this case she felt justified explaining her take on the
situation to the former local representative. "Mr. Falk, being
a former legislator, you should know calling in a bogus
emergency request for services is illegal. Perpetrators can
be subject to fine, imprisonment, or both. In this case, you
cost the people of Sweet Pepper some money on their taxes
for nothing."

Falk smiled at her like a predatory fox. "Sue me."

Stella pretended that she didn't hear him. "I've made
several recommendations that the road coming into Sunset
Beach be updated. Not only is it dangerous, but you have
no second exit from the community. The road isn't ade-
quately maintained by your property manager. It should be
turned over to the state or the town for maintenance. I'm
going to make a further recommendation to the state and
town that the Sweet Pepper Fire Brigade be relieved of
responding to calls here until the road is repaired."

"You go, Chief," Ricky muttered on her left side.

"Careful, Stella," John whispered on the right.

"Well, you just think you have this all figured out, don't you, Chief Griffin?" Falk said. "I believe you'll be hearing from my attorney. And let me leave you with this thought—if anything happens to one of these cabins because of your irresponsible behavior, you could be liable for criminal prosecution. Good day to you."

The old man turned and limped slowly back to his home. Stella led the way back to the vehicles parked alongside the road.

"I know you're Ben Carson's granddaughter," John said, "but Barney Falk isn't a good man to rile up. Better watch your back."

"It'll be *your* problem when I leave. You saw what the road was like. If this had been an emergency, it's likely we would've lost one of these homes. He was right. It took us too long to get up here."

John shrugged. "You know me being the next fire chief isn't carved in stone. They asked me. We talked about it. It doesn't mean it's going to happen."

Stella searched his handsome face. "Do you want the job?"

"No. Not really. The council is concerned that Petey and Ricky are too young and inexperienced for it." His eyes focused on hers. "I want you to stay and keep doing what you do. You're good at it and you aren't held back by all our taboos. I don't know what I would've said to Mr. Falk, but it would've ended with 'sir'."

She was surprised by his words, though honesty had never been one of their problems. "Thanks for the vote of confidence. I'm sure it will all work out, one way or another. Don't take the job if you don't want it."

John smiled. "Stella—"

They both realized that everyone was listening to what should've been a private conversation. Stella sent the team back to their places on the trucks and they looked for an open area large enough to turn around.

"John is gonna take over when you leave?" Ricky sounded angry. "I should've known they wouldn't care who you said should be in charge."

"Don't give up so easy. John doesn't want the job. He wants to be police chief. You and Petey might have to fight for what you want. Show them how good you are."

"Yeah. Right, Chief." Ricky managed to get the engine back down the treacherous mountain road after turning it around. "I don't think anyone's going to listen."

Stella didn't answer. She was leaving. The best she could do was make recommendations, which she'd done. She couldn't look over the town council's shoulders to make sure they followed them.

The whole group was subdued when they got back to the firehouse. Cleanup went smoothly and everything was put away for the next call.

But it felt like it was the end of something. There was none of the cheerful chatter or good-natured teasing that usually went on.

Stella made sure everyone understood the situation and that it wasn't their fault. They'd done their job, in record time. The problem with the road into Sunset Beach would have to be addressed.

When she got back to the cabin, her parents and Doug were back from sightseeing. They told her all about their experiences in Sevierville and Pigeon Forge and she told them about the fire brigade's annoying call.

"I wish I would've been there," Sean said. "Men like that need to be taken down a peg or two so they can relate to the rest of us."

Stella took a deep breath and twisted her hair into a pony-tail. "I guess it's not my problem. The next chief will have to deal with it. I've done what I can."

She told them about her and Walt finding the Impala they were looking for.

She was looking at Eric the whole time she spoke. His face was set in grim lines. She was still trying to decide if she should show him the pictures she'd taken.

"Dad invited us out to a barbecue tonight for dinner," Barbara told her. "It's one of the fund-raisers for the Sweet Pepper Festival. It also happens to be where the candidates for the next Sweet Pepper Festival Queen are introduced. Are you planning to go?"

Since there were hundreds of events leading up to the festival, Stella had crossed this one off of her list. "I don't think so, Mom. I'm beat. You guys go. I'm sure there will be lots of food and music."

"And there will be a former Sweet Pepper Festival Queen attending," Sean said. "Your mother told me she was the festival queen when she was seventeen. Wouldn't you like to see a picture of her?"

Stella smiled. "I'm sure she was pretty in her gown and crown. What was your talent, Mom?"

Her mother blushed. "I twirled a flaming baton. I think the music was something from the Doobie Brothers. Everyone was shocked by my taste in trashy music."

That made Sean and Stella both laugh. Doug wasn't sure who the Doobie Brothers were.

"Are you sure you don't want to go?" Barbara stroked Stella's hair. "Or we could stay here with you. We don't have to go."

"No. You guys go. I'm going to have a quiet supper, take a shower, and go to sleep. It's been hard today. I don't think I want to see anyone."

"Okay. We're going to change," her mother said. "What do you wear to something like this now?"

"I'd recommend jeans," Stella said. "The picnic tables at the VFW Park will rip anything else to shreds."

After her mother and father had gone to their room, Doug offered to stay home with Stella. "I don't think this sounds like somewhere I want to go. I'd rather stay here with you."

Some brochures Sean and Barbara had brought back with them from their sightseeing, blew off the table. The door to the back deck opened and closed—but only after the brochures hit the floor.

Doug looked around, his face a little pale. "It's *him*, isn't it?"

"I thought we settled this." Stella frowned at Eric. "There is no ghost."

"I don't believe you. I heard what you said to that man in the barbershop. This place is haunted. And I don't think the old fire chief wants me here."

Eric grinned. "He's more perceptive than I thought."

"He wants me to go out, doesn't he? Can you hear him, Stella? Should I stay in town tonight?"

"No one, including a ghost, is going to hurt you here, Doug," she promised. "I don't think I'd be very good company tonight. I think you should go and have a good time."

Doug looked around again. "Jeans, you say?"

She smiled and nodded. "I'll see you later."

After her parents and Doug were gone, Eric immediately appeared. "Were you able to get those pictures? Did you get them developed? I'm not sure how the digital aspect works. I see people talking about it on TV, but that's about all I understand."

Stella sighed. She was hoping he'd forgotten about it and she wouldn't have to make the decision. It seemed she didn't have much choice unless she wanted to lie to him about the pictures. She decided he'd been lied to enough.

"I hope you're ready for this." She took out her cell phone and plugged it into her laptop. "It isn't pretty."

His broad chest puffed out and he raised his head. "I've seen my share of bad things. Not as much as you, I'm sure, since you probably have as many fires in Chicago every day as Sweet Pepper has in a year. I think I can take it."

"I wouldn't say that many." She clicked the camera image on her laptop to download the pictures she'd taken. "And that's different. I'm sure I'd be more emotionally involved if my mother was killed in a fire. In this case, *you're* the victim."

He sat down beside her at the table. "Just show me the pictures. I'm a ghost. I don't have mental health issues."

The pictures came up on the screen and Stella looked at them with Eric as a slide show. "I'm sure there's enough blood in the trunk to safely say that Chum was right. You were put in the trunk after someone shot you in the head."

"You mean after Shu Carriker shot me in the head," he reminded her.

"Maybe. That bothers me. It's a small thing—but if Shu shot you, he'd want to get you and him out of there right away. Let's say he had an accomplice—the second mystery man Chum saw taking you out of the silo. Why did Shu go back inside right before the roof collapsed? It doesn't make any sense and yet his remains were found in there and mistaken for yours."

"Who knows? Maybe he dropped his gun and didn't want it to be found. It could've been anything. That looks like my glove and my boot in the trunk. I don't think anyone wanted to set Shu up for killing me, if that's what you're thinking."

"It couldn't have been a gun. It, or something left of it, would have still been in the silo." She shrugged. "Unless it was lost when the rest of the silo was demolished. Since there was no real investigation into what happened, anything is possible."

"Don't be so hard on them, Stella. Maybe today people investigate everything. Back then, if it looked like a duck and it quacked like a duck—we didn't investigate to see if it *was* a duck."

She smiled. "It's nice that you can be so forgiving about it."

"Those people were my *friends*. I never questioned once whether they would lay down their lives for me. I don't believe now that they didn't do the best they could at the time. Anyone can look back and see what they might have done."

"Okay." She rubbed her eyes so he wouldn't see the tears in them. "Maybe someone was trying to set Carriker up. How about shutting him up? Maybe when it was over, someone killed him and tossed him in the silo while it was still hot. They knew the coroner wouldn't get the remains for a few days. It's been a good cover-up for forty years, and kept everyone from trying to figure out who killed you."

Eric turned his eyes from the laptop screen to Stella's face. "You could be right about that."

Hero had come home with Stella. He lifted his head to start barking as Eric told Stella that someone was there. She looked out the window and saw her grandfather's black Lincoln pull into the yard with Bernard at the wheel.

"What does *he* want?" Eric asked. "I thought he was supposed to be at the barbecue with your mother."

"I don't know, but no cute tricks, please," Stella warned as she went to open the front door.

"Why not?" Eric grinned. "I have to practice so I can scare off potential buyers."

"Stella!" Ben greeted her with a hug as he reached the top of the porch. "Nice to see you. I take it you aren't going to the barbecue with your folks."

"No." She smiled at him and ushered him inside. He declined coffee or anything else. "But you already knew that, didn't you? That's why you're here."

He took the seat Eric had been sitting in. "I confess. I saw them get out of the rental car at the park and you weren't with them. I came here to talk with you privately about a few things."

"Okay." She sat at the table too. Eric perched on the stairs behind them. "What's up?"

"I got a call from an old friend today."

"Let me guess—Chief Rogers? Or was it Barney Falk? I've had a long day of making people angry."

He laughed. "Yes, you have. You seem to have that effect on some people. I got an interesting call from Bob Floyd as well. Did you really threaten him with a ghost?"

"I do what I have to. He tried to set the woods on fire to get rid of the cabin."

"You're a chip of the old block." He chuckled. "I also heard about you and Walt finding that old car. I guess that means Shu Carriker killed Eric Gamlyn. What a pity."

Eric growled a little and started toward them. Stella stared angrily at him and mouthed a warning.

"Were you involved in that, Ben?" she asked. "Did you pay Shu Carriker to kill Eric Gamlyn?"

# Chapter 23

"**P**ardon me?" Ben wasn't used to that kind of direct-ness.

Stella could see the shock in his face. He'd said many times that she was like him—to a point. He seemed to like that they shared a characteristic, but didn't expect it to be turned on him.

"People say Shu Carriker worked for you. They say if he killed Chief Gamlyn, you told him to. Something about getting thirty million dollars from the state? I guess that was about the same time you did those upgrades at the pepper plant."

For an instant, Ben let down his guard and Stella saw the ruthless face of a man who always got everything he wanted, done his way.

Eric saw it too and was immediately at Stella's side. *No way the old man was going to hurt her, not in his house.*

Ben suddenly relaxed and smiled. The other man was replaced by the affable grandfather he wanted her to know. "My very dear granddaughter, we've talked about this before. A man in my position is hated and feared on a regular basis. I lay off a dozen people—the story is that I kicked them down the stairs personally. Believe me—I couldn't have accomplished all the terrible things people gossip about in my lifetime, even with Shu Carriker's help. Surely you must have realized that by now."

She partially agreed, but she also wanted a real yes or no answer, not rhetoric. "Did you tell Shu Carriker to kill Eric Gamlyn or not? It's an easy question to answer."

His smile widened. "You're not wearing a wire, are you?"

She stared at him, tapping her finger impatiently on the wood table.

"No. I did *not*." His face was suddenly serious. "Shu did odd jobs for me before I made him manager at the plant. He left without a word of explanation and I hired someone else to take his place. I never saw him again. Chief Gamlyn died *after* that, I believe. If Carriker was involved, it was not at my behest. I respected Gamlyn. There was no reason for me to have him killed—if I indulged in that sort of conduct—which I have *never* done."

"Yeah. Right." Eric wasn't happy with his words. "He respected me right into the grave. I'm sure he did the same thing to other people."

Stella ignored him. "And the thirty million dollars that went missing when the county took over the fire service here?"

"There are records for the money that was spent on the plant."

"Gone in a fire," she told him.

"Then my accountant has them, as do the state and federal governments," Ben continued patiently. "Why do you always believe the worst of me? Why aren't you asking me about the millions in charity I give away every year?"

"I don't always think the worst of you. But I don't believe a man of your power got to his position and held on to it without a fight. Sometimes innocent people get hurt in that fight."

His sharp eyes pinned her to the chair. "Are you asking these questions for the TBI? I heard you're involved in their investigation, although for the life of me, I can't imagine why."

"I'm not wearing a wire and I don't work for the TBI. I'm asking these questions for *me*. I'm involved because I see some of myself in the old fire chief. No one should have to go out like that. Our job is dangerous enough."

"I see."

"So do you have any idea who killed Eric?"

"No. I'm sorry. It was a long time ago."

"What about Mace Chum?"

"Who?"

"Deputy Mace Chum. Come on. I know you've heard about it, Ben. It happened on the way out to your place. He was shot in the head."

"Of course. Sorry. I have a lot on my mind. I don't know any more about it than I've read in the newspaper. You probably know more than I do. And before you ask, I didn't have him killed either. I can't imagine who would want to hurt that poor man."

"Even though he still kind of thought you killed Abigail?"

He rubbed his jaw. "You don't pull your punches, do you? History has a long shadow here in Sweet Pepper. I didn't know *anyone* still thought that."

Stella sat back in her chair. If he was lying, he was the best liar she'd ever seen. Not that she was an expert, but usually people did something that gave them away. He was uncomfortable with her questions, no doubt, but his answers were smooth and sincere.

Was it all so long ago that his emotions weren't involved? Or didn't he ever get his hands dirty?

Or maybe—he was telling the truth.

"Sorry. I had to ask."

"I understand."

"You didn't come here to be grilled." She smiled at him. "You came to warn me?"

"Yes. About Barney Falk. He said you're an arrogant young woman and he's glad you're leaving town."

"Well, I guess I did *something* right today."

His lips twitched but he didn't laugh. "Barney is not a man to toy with, Stella. I'm not saying you should apologize. From what he told me, you were doing your job. Try not to confront him though. He could make your life miserable."

"Thanks, but since I'm leaving soon, I'm not too worried about it. He'll have to deal with John Trump then."

"Is that who they've chosen to replace you?" His shaggy gray eyebrows went up. "No one told me. I guess we'll see. I'm sure Captain Trump would be appropriately respectful. I wish you wouldn't go, Stella. You've been like a breath of fresh air. You remind me so much of Abigail, and your mother. It's almost like having her back in my life again."

"Even when I accuse you of murder?"

"Ha!" He got to his feet in a sure, quick movement for a man his age. "You've got fire in you—and it's not only that red hair. You don't play it safe. I admire that. We need more people like you in this world."

"Thanks." Two spots of red tinged her cheeks.

"I should be going now. It wouldn't be right to leave your mother alone at the pepper queen ceremony after I invited her. Why not come with me? They're doing a special presentation for the former queens tonight. You mother was one of them, you know."

"I'm too tired, Ben. Being arrogant and fiery for a whole day takes a lot out of you. I'm going to bed early."

"All right." He hugged her again. "Don't dare leave Sweet Pepper for good without telling me, young lady."

"I won't."

She saw him to the door. No sooner was he outside in his car than the whole cabin started shaking.

"What the—?"

"He says nice things about you and you get all wishy-washy," Eric complained. "He probably had me killed. Why can't you see him for what he is? Why are you so blind?"

It was a familiar theme. Stella could decide not to date John so she wouldn't have to hear it—evicting Eric was much harder.

"I'm not blind," she argued. "I'm trying to be rational and look at the facts. We can't convict people because of hearsay. We have no real proof that he's responsible for what happened to you."

"How much more proof do you need?"

"I don't know, Eric," she raged back at him, despite the continued shaking of the cabin. "How much proof does it take? Maybe you should go and ask Shu's ghost about it."

Eric's image blinked and then was gone.

Stella took a deep breath and let it out slowly. Without another thought, she went in her room, put on a swimsuit, and climbed into the hot tub on the deck. She closed her eyes and let the hot water bubble around her.

The sound of an owl (Eric had told her that was what it was) soothed her frayed temper. The mountain got quiet as most creatures went to sleep for the coming night.

"I'm sorry," Eric said after a while.

She didn't open her eyes or reply.

"I shouldn't have said those things to you."

"No. You shouldn't have."

"You shouldn't have told me to go find Shu Carriker's ghost either."

She pushed her wet hair back from her face and looked at him. "You're right. I'm sorry too."

"You really don't think Ben had it in for me?"

"I really don't know. The only way we can find out is to continue following the evidence."

"I was certain of his involvement in getting rid of the fire brigade. That's why I agreed to work with the TBI. Finding out that I was murdered made me feel he had to be part of that too."

"Maybe I see it differently because I'm an outsider." She shrugged. "He looks as much like a bad guy as a lot of other people."

"If you're talking about Ricky Senior, you're wrong."

"Eric, I'm sure that was Ricky's radio in the trunk of that car. It was covered with *your* blood. That seems to be a lot more proof than rumors about Ben hiring Shu to kill you."

"There's a good reason for that radio being there." Eric defended his friend. "And I distinctly remember seeing Ricky walk away from me and head out of the silo. He didn't shoot me."

"Maybe not. I'm betting he knows who did. I think he might have been one of the two men Chum saw carrying you out. We'll find out tomorrow when I talk to him."

Eric rocked silently in the chair for a few minutes. "Do you think there's really a light or a door or something that I was supposed to go through after I died?'

"I don't know. People seem to think so. I've often heard that sometimes souls can't leave until they take care of something important to them. Maybe someone had to find your bones and figure out who killed you before you could go. Maybe you don't remember *exactly* what happened, but you've always known it wasn't the death you'd expected."

"So when we figure out who killed me, I might disappear for good?"

She smiled at him as she got out of the hot tub. "There's as much chance of that as anything else. I've seen movies where that happened. My grandmother on my father's side says that ghosts sometimes get revenge on the people who wronged them."

"Both excellent sources of information," he said. "I think I'll look on the Internet. It's amazing how much is out there."

She yawned. "Knock yourself out. I'm going to sleep. We're practicing on ladders tomorrow—after I confront Ricky Senior with this new evidence."

"You didn't tell the TBI agent the radio belonged to Ricky, did you?"

"No. I didn't know for sure. I still don't. He's been a good friend to me, and to the fire brigade. I want to be the one to tell him."

"I wish I could come with you. Sometimes it's better being around people. Sometimes it reminds me of how much I've lost."

"I know it must be hard for you. Don't stay up too late on the laptop. I don't want Doug to get all freaked out seeing a ghostly face staring at the screen."

He laughed. "That sounds like an interesting trick to try."

"Don't you dare!" She yawned again. "Goodnight, Eric."


Stella didn't hear her parents and Doug come in from the barbecue that night. She was up early and left them a note about ladder practice. She got dressed and put her hair up under a Sweet Pepper ball cap.

Eric was nowhere to be found. She wondered where he went at times like that.

Hero was asleep on the rug by the fireplace. She'd either come back for him later or Eric would send him down to the firehouse. The big puppy whimpered a little in his sleep. She rubbed his back but he didn't wake up.

She climbed on her Harley to head down the mountain, ignoring the "For Sale" sign. It was foggy again that morning. Stella took the curves down Firehouse Road quickly. Her thoughts were on what had happened to Eric at the silo.

It seemed to her that someone, maybe Shu, had shot Eric while he was still inside. Reason unknown—possibly to keep him from stopping the county from taking over the fire brigade. Possibly because he was working for the TBI.

Shu and Ricky Senior carried him out and put his body in the trunk of the car. That explained the music from the radio inside, and outside, the silo.

She didn't understand why Ricky would participate in this undertaking. She believed Ricky was dedicated to Eric. This seemed to go against his nature. Yet the facts appeared consistent.

For whatever reason, they put him behind the wall in the old firehouse. It was a grisly fate, especially if Ricky was part of it. Why would he betray Eric that way?

*Maybe his own life was being threatened.*

The Harley kicked into gear as she reached the main road into town.

*And what about Chum?*

Shu Carriker either had a long reach from the grave or someone alive today had killed Chum. Was there something else that he'd seen that night at the silo forty years ago? He'd been holding back more that he could have told her that day at the firehouse.

*What was someone afraid that he'd tell?*

The only one who'd seemed threatened by Chum's last words to her was Chief Rogers. Maybe it was only that his pride was hurt because Chum hadn't come to him. Maybe it was something darker.

She remembered what he'd said to John that day at town hall about there being more competition for her grandfather's money. No doubt Don Rogers was hiding some secrets too.

Except for a few trucks bound for the pepper plant, the

road was mostly clear. Stella made good time getting into town, but it wasn't soon enough.

John and Officer Schneider were leading Ricky Senior out of the café in handcuffs while people stopped on the sidewalk to stare. Chief Rogers watched his officers walk their suspect down to the police station.

Stella parked her bike and went to see what was going on

"I guess you're not the only person in Sweet Pepper who can figure out what's happening," Rogers mocked her. "We've arrested Ricky Hutchins Sr. for the deaths of Eric Gamlyn, Shu Carriker, and Deputy Mace Chum."

# Chapter 24

~~~~~~~~~~~~~~

Ricky Junior came running out of the café. "What's going on, Chief Rogers? Why are you arresting my dad?"

"I'm sorry you had to see this, son." Chief Rogers put his hand sympathetically on Ricky Junior's shoulder. "Better get him a good lawyer."

Stella stopped Ricky as he lunged at Chief Rogers. "Not this way. You can't help your father if you're in jail too."

Ricky checked himself and nodded. "You know my dad didn't kill anyone. We'll get him a lawyer and sue for false arrest."

When he'd gone back into the café to find his mother and tell her what had happened, Stella pushed through the large crowd of people that had gathered. By nightfall, there wouldn't be anyone in town who didn't know the elder Ricky had been arrested.

Stella went to the police station to find John. She knew she had no chance of Chief Rogers letting her talk to Ricky. John might be able to help.

She didn't believe Ricky had killed Eric, but she thought

he was involved in *some* way. If he'd been one of the men who'd helped get Eric out of the silo, she wanted to know why.

Chief Rogers must have had some new evidence to arrest Ricky for Chum's murder. She could see how he could make the link between the radio in the trunk and Ricky—though she couldn't imagine how he'd found out about it. She could even see how he could think Ricky could be involved in Shu Carriker's death.

This was a bold move, probably calculated to cut the TBI out of the investigation.

John was at his desk with a fresh cup of coffee when she found him. He didn't have his own office, despite being the only Sweet Pepper police officer with rank. He sat outside Chief Rogers's spacious office.

Whether this was so he was handy for Rogers to call when he needed someone, or due to a lack of space, Stella wasn't sure. She wasn't sure how much he was willing to put up with to take over as police chief in twenty years or so. John had his own secrets that he hadn't shared with her.

He looked up at her and then covered an open file on his desk.

*Probably something to do with Ricky's arrest.*

"You guys have been busy already this morning. I think you know why I'm here."

He nodded. "Ricky Senior. I hate it too, but the facts don't lie."

"What have you got that's different from yesterday?"

"I can't talk about this with you, Stella. The chief is hot about getting this before Agent Whitman. You're part of the enemy camp. If I help you, I'm done here."

"I won't tell anyone, John."

"I can't take that chance. I'm sorry."

"All right. Can you at least get me in to see Ricky? I want to talk to him."

He thought about it as he shuffled papers on his desk. "I don't know. What do you want to talk to him about?"

"I don't think he killed anyone—least of all Chum. That's what this all hinges on, right? The other deaths are too old. You have new info about Chum."

"I can't tell you that." He glanced around the nearly empty office. "It will be a while before Ricky is processed. I suggest you come later with Agent Whitman. The chief can't keep *him* from visiting the prisoner."

"Thanks." She smiled at him. "I probably shouldn't have asked you. I know you have to stay on your side of the fence."

He frowned. "I wish I still *had* a side of the fence. I got the official word this morning. Chief Rogers and Mayor Wando said that they expect *me* to take your place when you leave. No offense, but I don't want to be fire chief."

"Did you tell them that?" Stella wasn't surprised since that rumor had been spreading for weeks. He'd wanted to ignore it.

"They made it clear that they don't care what I think. They *need* a fire chief. As a police officer, I'm replaceable."

"I'm sorry, John. I'd pick someone else to replace me, but there's no one else willing to take the job full-time."

"Thanks anyway, Stella. I'll be sorry to see you go."

"Even though I'm part of the evil Carson Empire?" She grinned to lessen the sarcasm.

"You're one part of that empire I'm going to miss."

"Trying to chat up the help?" Chief Rogers's booming voice hit them from across the room. "You stay away from Officer Trump, Ms. Griffin. Your feminine wiles won't work on him anymore. He knows where his bread is buttered!"

*Feminine wiles?* Stella didn't comment, but it was hard not to smile. She left Rogers gloating over his unexpected victory while John mourned the loss of his career aspirations.

As she was going out the door, Myra Strickland, whose family had started the Sweet Pepper Festival, stopped her. "How are those tour guide lessons going, Chief Griffin?"

"I know a lot more about the pepper business now."

*Should I tell her that I'm probably leaving town soon?* No doubt the other woman had heard the rumors.

Myra consulted her appointment book. "All of our tour guides will get together for dinner tomorrow night. We'll find out what everyone has learned. Have you been fitted for your tour guide vest?"

"No. I've been a little busy."

"We're *all* busy, Chief Griffin, but we must stay on schedule. I'll call Molly Whitehouse and tell her to expect you. Have you chosen your category for the recipe contest yet? You know we count on every person on the festival committees to submit a recipe for the contest."

Stella had totally forgotten that she needed a pepper recipe. "I'll take care of that right away. Thanks for the reminder."

Myra let her go. Stella saw Agent Whitman getting out of his car and went to talk to him.

"I suppose you've heard about Ricky Hutchins," Stella said. "Chief Rogers is still enjoying his triumph. I can't figure out yet what new evidence he has, but I'm sure he'll let us know."

Agent Whitman nodded. "I got the official phone call a few minutes ago. He said I didn't have to bother coming to help him. He had to know that wasn't going to happen."

He looked at the Daily Grind Coffee Shop next door. "Let's duck in here for a moment before we help the chief celebrate."

He insisted on buying Stella a mocha latte and had Valery, the owner, make him a triple-shot latte. They sat together outside at a café table on the sidewalk.

"I received the same information Chief Rogers did late

last night. A local pilot for the forest service gave him some information about Deputy Chum's death. He was flying over the scene when he saw the deputy's blue truck being pushed off the road by an older black pickup with a license plate beginning with 'SR'"

Zane hadn't told her he'd seen any part of a license plate. She was surprised, and wondered why he hadn't mentioned it.

Agent Whitman sipped his coffee and studied the high profiles of the Smoky Mountains that surrounded the town. "It was very foggy so the pilot could only read that much of the plate. He didn't actually witness the shooting. He didn't report it until Chief Rogers's people questioned him about it."

Stella knew Ricky Junior frequently drove a battered black pickup, though she'd never noticed the plate. For Chief Rogers to arrest Ricky Senior, the truck must actually belong to him and have the right license plate. She had to admit that it was a strange coincidence.

"He also arrested him for Chief Gamlyn's and Shu Carriker's deaths," she said. "Do you understand how those roll in with Chum's death?"

"We've thought since we came in on this that Deputy Chum was involved in the other two deaths."

Since he was being so forthcoming, Stella pressed on. "What made you think that?"

"It's common practice for a criminal to want to unburden themselves to the people they feel they've wronged. Deputy Chum couldn't do that with Chief Gamlyn, so he confessed to you. He also went by on his way out of town and apologized to the Carriker family."

"So you think Chum and Ricky Senior killed Eric and Shu."

He nodded. "And Ricky killed Chum before he could give it all away."

Stella thought about it. She still wasn't sure she believed

it. She might not be as astute at hearing confessions of guilt as Chief Rogers and Agent Whitman, but some things didn't make sense. She found it hard to swallow that Ricky had killed Eric.

"I'd like to talk to Ricky and hear the whole story. Do you plan to question him?"

"Of course." He finished his coffee. "You're welcome to join me. Your help has been invaluable solving three homicides. The state of Tennessee and the town of Sweet Pepper owe you a great debt."

Agent Whitman said he would call her when they could interview Ricky. Stella looked at her watch. It was still early, too early to go to the dressmakers for her tour guide outfit. She probably had plenty of time to head back to the firehouse and get going on ladder practice.

On the way back out of town, she thought about Ricky Senior. She really liked him, but how well did she know him? If he'd killed Eric and Shu, that was a long time ago. He might have been a much different person back then—though Eric and Walt probably wouldn't agree with that.

Looking at the facts—he was in the grain silo, maybe when Eric was killed. That was probably his radio in the back of the Impala. He'd lied to her about his involvement in Eric's death.

These could be unfortunate coincidences—or he may have killed all three men.

Sean and Doug were already at the firehouse when she arrived. Barbara had dropped them off and gone to town to have coffee with Ben. The rest of the group was straggling in.

She knew the constant training could be hard and didn't say anything about late arrivals. Showing up on time was more important when they had a call.

"Ladder practice?" Sean asked with a smile when he saw his daughter.

"Yep. I try to do it as often as I can. We're not great on the ladders, probably because we don't use them much during calls. I figure we should be prepared."

"Yeah." He laughed. "I've seen at least one two-story building while I've been here."

"There may not be high-rises, but my people need to be prepared."

"Don't get all defensive." Her father hugged her. "You're right. Sweet Pepper may not be Chicago, but it's best to be ready for anything."

There was a second floor on the firehouse. It was only used for storage and made a good place to practice with the ladders.

Stella had thought if the fire brigade ever had to have full-time members, it would be a good place for them to sleep. That was a long way in the future, if ever.

Stella looked at her group as Bert Wando came up in his letter jacket and waved to her from the back. Hero and Sylvia sat on the sidelines with Tagger, watching the proceedings.

Last time they'd practiced with ladders, Hero had decided to get involved. He and Sylvia had run up and down the rungs barking. It made for a funny, but not very effective, practice.

"I know none of you like the ladders." Stella was already getting started as John parked his car and joined them. "But we have to keep working with them. We don't have a lot of tall structures in Sweet Pepper, except for trees. However, if there had been a fire at the three-story cabin at the lake, we would've needed this practice."

Ricky Junior pulled up in his father's old Chevy. She was surprised to see him there since he was trying to help his father. Stella went on, explaining why they all had to put on their gear to make the practice feel more like the real thing. She didn't always require that much for practice sessions.

"We're going to suppose someone is trapped upstairs and the structure is on fire. Each of you will have to climb the ladder and bring the victim down in a safe manner. We've practiced this before, so I expect a little speed. Any volunteers to be the victim?"

Tagger's hand went up. "Me, Chief. Pick me. You know I like to be the victim."

"Okay. Tagger it is." Stella thanked him and he went inside. "Petey, you're up first. Get in your gear and let's go. Everyone else, suit up. Your turn is coming."

Ricky held back as everyone went inside. "Just wanted to let you know I could be called away, Chief. Mom is talking to a lawyer in town. She may need me there if she gets to visit Dad."

"I understand. Thanks for coming, anyway. How's your mom holding up?"

"Okay I guess. It's a lot to take in. They impounded my truck to look for blood or some such. I wish I knew why Chief Rogers thought Dad could do something like this. He loved Eric Gamlyn. Everyone knows that. And he didn't hurt Deputy Chum either."

Since Stella had her own doubts about Ricky Senior, she didn't venture an opinion. "Let me know if there's anything I can do."

Ricky went inside to change as Walt Fenway's old truck chugged into the parking lot. Stella grinned. It didn't sound any better after it had been in the garage. He got out and she watched him come toward her in a determined way, even ignoring the excited pleas for attention from the dogs.

"Is somebody going up that ladder?" he asked.

"Everybody goes up the ladder," she replied. "We call it ladder practice."

"Glad I was a cop and not a fireman." His tone was a little brisk.

"What brings you by?"

He snorted. "Ricky Senior is in jail. You got a minute?"

Stella looked at her father. Sean waved her on. "Go on. I've got this."

"Thanks, Dad. I'll only be a minute."

Walt and Stella walked away from the practice area and where Tagger was sitting with the dogs.

"So you told Whitman and Rogers about Ricky's radio in the back of the Impala? What were you thinking, Stella?"

# Chapter 25

"You had to know they'd go after Ricky right away," he continued. "Now we might never know the whole story. There's some rational explanation for it. Ricky didn't kill Eric. My old buddy would be turning over in his grave over this, if he had one."

"I didn't tell *anyone*. I went to talk to Ricky about the radio and Chief Rogers was taking him out of the café when I got there. You should know me better by now. I wouldn't share with Don that way."

Walt glanced away, still angry, but now without her to direct it at. "Well that beats all then. What made them pick him up?"

She told him about the partial plate and Zane's account of the black pickup riding close to Chum's blue one. "They've tied the whole thing together. Even Whitman believes Ricky did it. He's going to let me go in when he interviews him. When I ask him about the radio in the Impala, it's going to be icing on the cake for Whitman and Chief Rogers."

"Ask him anyway," Walt shot back. "He didn't do it. Ricky can't shoot well enough to hit a moving target. I know that much. I've been hunting with him. And there's no way on this green earth he'd hurt Eric. They were like brothers."

"I know. I know." She ran her hand around her neck in frustration. "But he's involved in this somehow. I don't know how yet, and I can't ask him without making him sound even guiltier. I don't know what to do."

Walt nodded. "I'm gonna look into this black truck thing and see what I can find out. Be careful if you see Ricky. Don't make things worse than they already are."

"I will." She looked into his worried eyes. "You know the story of Cain and Abel, right? They were brothers too."

"I'm telling you, Stella, Ricky didn't do these things. And I'm sorry if I'm a little angry. It's frustrating being out of the loop sometimes on things that matter. Not that I'd want to go back to that life."

"I know. It's okay. Ricky's your friend."

His voice was gruff when he said, "Just let me know what he says, will you? I wish I could see him."

Walt stalked back to his truck and gunned the engine. Stella went back to ladder practice. She hadn't missed anything. Petey was starting up the ladder to save Tagger from the imaginary fire.

Her father was timing Petey. "Just remember—fast is good—safety is better. You have to get up there and get back down in one piece."

Petey nodded, but didn't stop climbing.

Tagger kept yelling, "Help I'm burning," as loud as he could.

Sean nodded at Petey as he and Stella watched her. "Has she done this before? She doesn't look like she could get a child back down the ladder with her. I'm not sure if she can bring Tagger down by herself."

Stella smiled. "Looks can be deceptive. Just watch her."

Petey reached the second-floor window and dove inside, headfirst. She got Tagger (who was supposed to be unconscious, but kept crying out for help) across her narrow shoulders and came right back down the ladder with him.

Spontaneous applause broke out from the rest of the group. Tagger took a bow before he went back upstairs to be rescued again.

"Guess you were right." Sean looked at the stopwatch. "Not bad time either. I wouldn't have believed it."

The rest of the fire brigade took their turns going up the ladder. Everyone did a good job, except for Kimmie, who had a hard time getting Tagger across her shoulders, and finally had to give up.

At that point, the dogs ran up the ladder with their leashes dragging behind them.

Banyin shrugged. "Sorry, Chief. I wasn't prepared for them to dart off like that."

"That's okay," Stella said with a laugh. "We were done anyway. Everyone can change and we'll meet inside to talk about it."

Banyin didn't go up the ladder, for obvious reasons. Her husband had actually come to the firehouse to make sure that his pregnant wife didn't try it. He never got out of his car, though he waved and left when practice was over.

Petey had been the fastest, no surprise there. Ricky was only a few seconds behind her. Stella told everyone else they were going to have to schedule more ladder practice to get those times down.

She told Kimmie she needed to lift weights to add some muscle. "Tagger is about one hundred and fifty pounds. You could have to lift more weight than that. You're going to have to work up to it."

Kimmie sniffed and wiped her eyes. "We can't all be Petey, Chief." Her husband, David, put his arm around her shoulders. "I might not be able to bring someone down a ladder, but I *can* hold the hose."

"But what if Petey isn't there the day we need you to climb a ladder and bring a pregnant woman back down with you? It's important that all of you keep growing and maintaining your skills. You can do this, Kimmie. I know you can."

Kimmie nodded, too emotional to speak. Hero and Sylvia licked her legs.

"That's about it," Stella said to the group. "If any of you know of someone else who could take Marty's place on the fire brigade, let me know. Thanks for coming out today."

Stella noticed that she had a missed call from Molly Whitehouse and sighed. She was going to have to go and have that vest fitted to be a tour guide at the festival.

She told her father she could drop him and Doug in town on her way.

"I don't understand why you don't tell them you won't be here for the festival," Sean said.

"Because I'm not leaving yet." She'd suddenly made up her mind. "I may be here in October. If not, I'll find someone else, around my size, and show them how to do it. They need the help, Dad. What did you always tell me about community service?"

"I wasn't talking about Sweet Pepper, honey." Sean got in the Cherokee with her. "I want you to come back with us."

"I'm not leaving until I know what happened to Chief Gamlyn." She started the engine as Doug closed the door behind him, silent as father and daughter argued.

"You're a little obsessed with this thing, don't you think?" Sean said. "The guy has been dead for a long time. Let it go. It's not gonna bring him back."

Surprisingly, it was Doug who ended the debate. "I don't know. It may be obsession, but no police officer rests until a crime against another officer is closed. It doesn't matter how old it is, or if you knew that person. It's supposed to work that way to keep us all safe."

Sean gave Doug a disgusted look but didn't say anything else on the subject. Stella smiled at Doug in the rearview mirror and then drove them into Sweet Pepper.

Stella parked in front of town hall and checked her phone. No word yet from Agent Whitman about the interview with Ricky.

Doug went on to the café, where they were meeting Barbara, giving them some time to talk.

Sean hugged Stella and apologized when they got out of the Cherokee. "I'm sorry, darlin'. I miss you and I want you home."

"You probably only miss the Harley." She grinned at him, making light of the serious moment.

"Probably," he agreed, following her lead. "I'm thinking about taking it across the country again."

"Talk to Mom about that yet?"

"I'm getting her a little sidecar."

They both laughed at that idea. Barbara wouldn't get near a motorcycle.

"Seriously," he said. "I'm not trying to tell you what to do or how to live your life. If you think this is the right place for you, I guess you should stay."

He looked around Main Street and then back at his daughter. "Do you?"

Stella followed his gaze along the narrow street where colorful new banners for the Sweet Pepper Festival were being put up and shops bustled with tourists.

"I would've said no a year ago, Dad," she said honestly. "This place kind of grows on you, I guess. I like being the fire chief. I feel like I'm creating something important here—not just working a job. I don't know yet what I'm going to do. Some days I still feel like a stranger in a strange land."

"I understand." Sean frowned. "You know whatever you decide to do, your mother and I will support you."

Barbara came out of the café with her father at that point. Both of them were laughing, their arms around each other.

Sean took in the picture they made, standing on the sidewalk together. "Who knows? Think the fire chief might have room for a new recruit?"

"I'm sure she would, but it doesn't pay, you know. That's what 'volunteer' means."

"Not a problem. I'm married to the pepper heiress."

They both laughed at that too. It seemed too weird to be true.

"She won't stay," Stella predicted. "At least not yet. Maybe when you retire."

He kissed the side of her head. "Fair enough. I won't say anything else about what you're doing. It's your decision. Just be happy."

Stella watched him join her mother and Ben. Doug came out of the café with a biscuit and a coffee to go.

*Could Sweet Pepper be my home?*

There were a lot of reasons to stay. There were as many reasons to go back to Chicago. She wasn't sure how to make the decision. She'd never expected to live anywhere except where she was born and raised.

Molly Whitehouse texted again about the fitting for her tour guide vest. Stella decided to walk the few blocks, mostly uphill, to her shop.

She walked past the Sweet Pepper Bed and Breakfast as Flo Ingle, the owner, was putting letters in her mailbox, which matched the colorful Victorian gingerbread house. Her blond hair was teased up high on her head, as always, and she wore her usual pink dress.

"Good morning," she sang out when she saw Stella. Her blueberry-colored eyes were full of questions. "I know you've heard about Ricky Senior by now."

Stella nodded. "I was there."

"Don't tell me you think he's guilty. Because there's no way anyone will ever convince me that he killed *anyone*—much less Eric Gamlyn. Those two were like brothers. What in the world is Chief Rogers thinking? He's *not*. That's the problem."

"I haven't known Ricky as long as you," Stella said. "He doesn't seem like a killer to me, but sometimes people make mistakes."

*"Mistakes?"* Flo's pink face turned red. She put her hands on her ample hips. "Mistakes are when you put too much pepper in with the brownie batter—not killing someone and hiding their body for nearly half a century. I can't believe *you'd* think he was capable of something like that."

Stella liked Flo. She was one of her first friends in town and had been one of her mother's friends growing up.

Even if Ricky was guilty of the charges against him, Flo wouldn't believe it. Maybe if Stella had known him longer, or he hadn't already lied to her about the silo fire, she might be more inclined to agree with her.

"I like Ricky. I don't want him to be guilty of anything," Stella said. "I hope none of it turns out to be true. I'm sorry, but I have to go. Molly is waiting for me."

Flo's face immediately cleared of her annoyance and she smiled. "I'm sorry to take it out on you. I've been stewing all morning and you're the first person who knows what's going on that I've seen. You go on to Molly's. I've heard you're a tour guide this year for the festival. That's too bad. You were a brilliant recipe judge last year. You would've loved my new recipe this year. Of course, I don't know how you could've given it better than a blue ribbon like you did my recipe last year."

Flo hugged her and hurried back to her guests in the old house. Stella continued on her way to Molly's shop.

The little bell tinkled when she pushed open the door. She was surprised to see so many people waiting to see the little seamstress. Stella wasn't there more than a few minutes when she learned that the town's hatmaker, Matilda Storch, was under the weather after having gall bladder surgery. Molly was working on festival hats with Matilda's assistant as she also worked on dresses and costumes.

Stella waited her turn to have her red vest fitted, glad she didn't have to wear one of the huge hats as she did last year. She knew hats were important to the people involved in the festival, but it was hard to do anything while you wore one. She'd thought last year that her neck was going to need a brace as she got in and out of the Cherokee with Matilda's lavish creation.

Valery Reynosa, owner of the Daily Grind Coffee Shop, waited patiently with her, already wearing a red dress with tons of ruffles. Her hat was also red, with ruffles cascading from it. This year's theme was South America.

"I know," Valery said as Stella eyed her dress. "It's over-the-top, but what can I say? It brings in the tourists. I hope they don't want me to dance. I'm not good at dancing."

Stella reassured her. "It looks really good on you. You've got the coloring for it. Bright red isn't great on me. And I don't dance either."

Valery smiled. "It's all to keep the festival going, right? That's the important thing."

Molly's mouth was full of pins as she did some work on a bright blue dress that was very similar to Valery's. Stella didn't know the lady wearing it, but she was giving Molly a hard time about the skirt being too short.

The birdlike dressmaker kept nodding and talking around the pins in her mouth as she acknowledged her customer's complaints.

"I heard they arrested Ricky Senior this morning," Valery said. "He seems like such a nice man. I guess I haven't known him that long. It's hard to imagine that I was talking to a murderer every day for the last two years."

"That's crazy talk," Lucinda Waxman said from behind them.

She was one of the grandes dames of Sweet Pepper. Her granddaughter, Foster, had been the festival queen last year—as had Lucinda and her daughter, Charlene, before her.

"Ricky never hurt anyone in his life. Chief Rogers is showing off because that man is here from the TBI and he doesn't want to be upstaged. I've already told the town council that Chief Rogers should be taken out of office for this."

Again, it was the people who had known Ricky his whole life who couldn't believe he'd killed anyone.

It was possible, Stella thought, that the truth was somewhere in between. She knew Eric was going to feel like these people, the way Walt did, about the matter. She hoped the truth, one way or another, would come out during the investigation.

Her cell phone buzzed and vibrated. Agent Whitman was ready to question Ricky Senior. It seemed the fitting was going to have to wait.

# Chapter 26

S tella ran breathlessly into the police station in town hall twenty minutes later. The fitting she thought was going to have to wait, couldn't wait, at least according to Molly.

Stella had been pushed to the front by the crowd at the dress shop before she could leave. Her red vest was filled with pins in unlikely places. She'd chafed as Molly had told her to keep still.

The rest of the women in the room, who were waiting for hats and dresses, gave her some unpleasant looks, but the fitting was over quickly. Stella was pushed back through the crowd and out the door.

"He's in the conference room." Sandy Selvy pointed in that direction. "Poor man must be dying of thirst. They wouldn't even let me give him coffee and a doughnut when the rest of them had one. As if Ricky Senior could hurt a fly."

Stella didn't stop to debate the issue. She followed Sandy's finger to the conference room. Chief Rogers was waiting, like a guard, outside the closed door.

"Where do you think you're going?" he asked her.

"I think I'm going in with Agent Whitman to question Ricky."

"This doesn't concern you, Ms. Griffin. The fire department doesn't dictate justice in this town."

"Chief, I'm going in there. Don't make me get Whitman out here to override you. That would be even more embarrassing than just moving aside."

They stared at each other like kids in school—seeing who could outlast the other. Stella didn't know what made Chief Rogers back down before she did.

He suddenly moved aside. "Be my guest." His voice reflected anything but that courtesy.

"Thanks." She opened the door and walked inside, closing it carefully after her.

Agent Whitman was already questioning Ricky. He looked up at her and nodded at one of the chairs around the table. There was another agent with him, and a woman recording everything that was said.

Stella took a seat and listened.

"I know from talking with Chief Rogers that you've denied shooting Deputy Mace Chum, Mr. Hutchins," Agent Whitman said in a pleasant tone. "I'd like you to tell me about that. Do you want your lawyer present?"

Stella agreed with Sandy—Ricky Senior looked terrible. The whole ordeal had taken its toll on him. His face looked gray and his mouth was set in a grim line. His usually laughing dark eyes were dull and scared.

"I don't need a lawyer. I don't know what else I can tell you, Agent. I didn't shoot Mace Chum—or anyone else. I wasn't on the road when Mace was killed. As I told Chief Rogers, I was in the café with other people who will vouch for me. I have an alibi for that day."

It was the way he said *that day* that bothered Stella. She felt again that there was a kernal of truth here somewhere about what had happened, if not to Chum, then to Eric. Agent Whitman wasn't asking the right questions.

"But you know who was responsible for Deputy Chum's death," Whitman persisted. "Was it an associate of yours? Did you pay someone to shoot the deputy?"

Suddenly Ricky's face changed. He grinned as he gazed at Stella. "I swear I didn't shoot the deputy. Or the sheriff, for that matter."

Stella smiled, knowing he was talking about the old Eric Clapton song. She believed him when he said he didn't shoot anyone. What part *did* he play in all of this?

Agent Whitman looked confused about the reference to the sheriff and searched through his notes before he continued. "Let's go back to where this started. You were involved in the deaths of Shu Carriker and Eric Gamlyn. Mace Chum was your accomplice in those deaths. Can you explain what happened that night forty years ago?"

The ready grin faded from Ricky's face. "I would rather have died that night than ever hurt Eric."

"But something happened that night at the silo fire that no one but you, and Deputy Chum, knew about, didn't it?" Stella butted in even though she knew Whitman would probably ask her to be quiet. "You and I have talked about this before."

Ricky hung his head. "Yes."

"And you lied to me when we talked, didn't you?"

"Yes."

Stella glanced at Whitman. He sat back in his chair and waved her on.

"So tell me again what happened the night Eric died." Stella waited silently, hoping the answer wouldn't be as bad as everyone feared. *Come on, Ricky. Tell me the truth.*

Ricky took a deep breath. "I lied because I've been lying for forty years, since it happened. I didn't want to go to prison. I wanted to be with my wife and start a family. I suppose I've done all of that. It's time to tell the truth."

Agent Whitman sat forward in his seat again.

"You're right about one part of the charges against me," Ricky said. "I killed Shu Carriker. It was an accident. I only meant to get him out of the way. I didn't mean for him to die. I wanted to haul him into the police station to face charges for killing my friend, Eric Gamlyn."

Agent Whitman looked a little less than satisfied with that response. He seemed as though he might tell Ricky so, but Stella jumped in. She wanted to hear the whole story. She knew Eric would want to know the truth too.

"Start at the beginning," she coaxed with a pleading look at Whitman to hear him out.

"We've come this far, Chief Griffin," Agent Whitman said. "You've got the floor."

Ricky focused on Stella. "Most of what I told you was true. I *was* in the silo and Eric came in for me. He gave me his face mask. I saw Shu Carriker come up behind him. I couldn't imagine why he was there. We all thought he was gone for good."

He paused and drew a breath. "Before I could say something, Shu pulled out a gun and shot Eric in the back of the head."

Hearing Ricky describe the moment of Eric's death was painful. She could imagine the look of surprise on his handsome face as the light went out of his brilliant blue eyes. All the plans and dreams he'd had were gone with him.

"He fell to the floor in the silo," Ricky choked out as he sobbed. "I think he died right away. God, I *hope* he died right away. I can't tell you what it was like, seeing him go down that way."

Stella wiped tears from her eyes. That might be one reason Eric couldn't remember anything about his death. She was so relieved that it wasn't Ricky who shot Eric. She knew Eric would be too.

"Then what?" Her voice trembled, but she'd come too far to stop now.

"I was shocked. *Horrified.* I didn't know what to do. All I could think was that Shu might shoot him again. Eric was on the floor, burning debris from the roof was falling all around us. Shu bent over him with his gun. I picked up a piece of wood that was on the floor and hit him hard with it. He collapsed next to Eric. I grabbed his gun."

It was as if they all took a collective breath after the terse retelling of Eric's and Shu's deaths. The woman recording the conversation wrote something in a black notebook. Whitman shook his head but didn't say anything.

"Was Shu dead?" Stella tried to decide what questions should be asked. She was glad Whitman was letting her take the lead—she didn't know if Ricky would have admitted this otherwise—but she wasn't an interrogator.

"I don't know." Ricky clasped his hands tightly together, his eyes unfocused, as though he were still seeing the terrible event so long ago. "Suddenly, Mace Chum was there in the silo too. He said to help him get Eric out before the roof collapsed. I didn't know what else to do. We got Eric out of there."

Stella saw him lick his lips and got up to pour him a glass of water from the sideboard. He thanked her and she sat back down. The man couldn't go on speaking without something to drink. Whitman still didn't comment.

Ricky drained the glass and then went on with his story. "I planned to go back for Shu as soon as Eric was safely outside. But as we walked out the back door, the roof collapsed. There was no going back into that inferno."

"Which was why Shu's remains were in the silo after the fire," Stella muttered, mostly to herself.

"Yes," Ricky responded.

"What happened then, Mr. Hutchins?" Agent Whitman seemed to be finished with Stella's brand of questioning.

"Chum said to help him put Eric in the back of Carriker's old Impala. I thought we should get the medics, but when I put my head against Eric's chest, there was no heartbeat. He had no pulse."

Ricky wiped away tears that continued to stream down his cheeks. "I thought Chum knew what he was doing. He was a deputy. He checked too, and shook his head. Eric was dead."

They had to pause for a moment for Ricky to regain his composure enough to speak.

"Chum said we had to take Eric somewhere else or we'd be blamed for killing him, and for Shu's death. He was a sheriff's deputy. He knew the law. I was eighteen. I believed him because I was terrified."

"I understand you were young and scared, Mr. Hutchins," Agent Whitman said. "But it's hard for me to believe you fell for that."

"I didn't know what to do. My best friend was dead— with a bullet in his head. I was responsible for Shu's death. I knew that. I'm not saying what I did was smart or rational."

Ricky took a deep breath, his broad chest rising and falling with the movement. "So I did what Chum told me. We drove to the firehouse, hollowed out a place in the wall, covered it with a piece of sheet metal, and left Eric there. God help me."

"That's not possible," Whitman objected. "The smell would have given it away."

"The fire brigade never went back there after Eric died," Ricky explained. "They put the gear away and parked the trucks that night. We didn't know how to go on without Eric. Two weeks later, before we could figure it out, the town closed down the fire brigade, and the county took over. They never used the firehouse. It was a long time before the building was rented out for something else."

"Okay." Agent Whitman took a few notes. "I think that's enough ancient history. Let's talk about Deputy Chum's death. You and he had a secret you'd shared all these years. A secret that could've put you both in prison. Suddenly, he started going out and telling everyone. He was leaving town. You still planned to live here. That must have made you angry."

"I didn't know anything about Chum talking to Stella until after he was dead," Ricky said. "Why would I kill him? The damage was already done."

He had a good point, Stella thought, still reeling from the description of what Chum and Ricky had done. If Ricky was telling the truth, he hadn't killed Eric but he'd concealed his death all these years.

She wished she'd realized, as Whitman and Walt Fenway had, that what Chum had told her was tantamount to a confession. She obviously didn't think like a cop. Maybe that was a good thing.

The other agent whispered something to Whitman.

Agent Whitman nodded and then spoke to Ricky. "One more thing before we take a break, Mr. Hutchins. What part do you think Deputy Chum played in the silo fire incident?"

"I think he was there with Shu Carriker to kill Eric. That's why he had the keys to Shu's Impala and a plan already in place. I've had a long time to think about this. Chum didn't just show up, like he told Stella."

"Did you and the deputy ever talk about it afterward?" Whitman asked. "Did he ever confess to you why he wanted to kill Chief Gamlyn?"

"We never spoke of it, sir. He never confessed anything to me. He didn't even come to tell me he was leaving the day he was killed. We all knew there was money involved when the county wanted our fire brigade closed down." Ricky looked directly at Stella. "Ben Carson wanted that to happen. I'd say he got his wish in the only way he could, by killing Eric Gamlyn."

# Chapter 27

～～～～～～～

Stella leaned against the Cherokee in the sun outside the town hall. She was in no hurry to go back to the cabin and tell Eric what his good friend had admitted to doing.

He would be furious and brokenhearted. The cabin would shake and Eric would probably vanish, as he had when her grandfather had been there.

Ricky's testimony would be compelling against Ben Carson, if there was ever a trial. Whether that would happen with a forty-year-old case was another story.

Without Mace Chum's confession to setting up Eric's death with Shu Carriker—and the plot behind it—they really had nothing.

It was possible Agent Whitman could follow up on it and try to take Ben down, but it seemed unlikely to her. Ricky's testimony would strengthen what everyone had already believed to be true about Eric's death. She knew her grandfather wouldn't care.

Stella quickly found out that standing on the sidewalk was a bad way to go unnoticed. Ricky Junior and Lucille came out of the café and pushed her for information. Not bound by any feeling of confidentiality, she told them what Ricky Senior had confessed.

"That can't be true," Lucille cried. "He would never do such a thing."

"Don't worry, Mom," Ricky said. "We'll fight this. Was Dad's lawyer in there?"

"No," Stella said. "He was alone. He said he didn't want a lawyer. He wanted to tell what happened."

Ricky raged. "This is stupid. They can't get him for what happened to Deputy Chum. He was at the café."

"They have him for what happened forty years ago. I'm sorry, Ricky."

That conversation brought out several other people who wanted to know what had happened. It made Stella regret her decision not to leave right away. She hadn't minded telling Ricky Junior and his mother what was going on, but she didn't plan to share information with people from the café and the barbershop.

"I have to go," she finally said, getting in the Cherokee. "Let me know if I can do anything to help."

Before she left, she tried calling Walt to let him know what was going on. There was no answer at his home or his cell phone. She decided she'd put off telling Eric long enough. She might as well go back to the cabin.

Eric was back from wherever it was that he went when he disappeared. He was singing show tunes from old Broadway musicals—his favorites were *Hair* and *Jesus Christ Superstar*. Hero watched him work in the kitchen.

"I have a great recipe in mind for the contest this year," he said as Stella walked into the cabin. "I came up with the idea for candied stuffed peppers. We'll take a whole pepper, clean it out, dip it in a glaze, and then fill it with something sweet. Maybe a chocolate mixture. Or maybe we should dunk the pepper in chocolate and then fill it with a marsh-mallow mixture. What do you think?"

He seemed so happy that she hated to say anything about what had happened that morning. Still, he was bound to find out. Either Walt would tell him or he'd see it on TV. At least he'd hear it from her this way.

Eric's smile had disappeared by the time she'd focused on him again. "What is it? Did you ask Ricky about what happened?"

"Chief Rogers arrested Ricky for your murder before I could talk to him."

The cabin shook a little with his anger. "That's ridicu-lous. Ricky couldn't kill anyone. He always had my back."

"That's true, to an extent, Eric. Let's sit out on the deck and I'll tell you what he said."

They looked out over the river and rocked as the sweet, cool wind blew down from the Smokies. Stella told him exactly what Ricky had confessed to. Eric didn't get angry again. He stared blindly out at the trees.

"Are you okay?" she asked when she was finished.

"Yes. At least I know what happened." His gaze came to meet hers. "Thank you."

"Ricky might not have had anything to do with what happened to Chum. I suppose he'll go to prison for Shu Carriker's death. He might serve some time for covering up what happened to you."

"I suppose that's possible."

She put her hand on his. It was like a projection—her hand went through his, leaving only that strange feeling of static electricity lingering. She knew he could be solid when he wanted to. She wished she knew the trick of being able to touch him when *she* wanted to.

"You can talk to me about this," she said. "You don't have to keep it bottled up."

"It doesn't matter. It's not like it will affect anything. It doesn't matter how I feel about it."

"Of course it does. You still have feelings. You get angry and excited—mostly angry." She laughed a little to try to ease the tension. "You have to be angry now, but the cabin isn't shaking."

"I'm not angry." He got up and walked to the rail that rimmed the deck. "I was a fool to think I could push the world to be the way I thought it should be. The world pushed back."

"Okay. So your feelings are hurt. Ricky betrayed you. He knew what happened and didn't say anything. We might never have found your bones, except for the fire."

He turned and faced her, his arms folded across his chest. "And would that have been such a terrible thing? I wish it hadn't happened. The truth does me no good, Stella."

"We're back," her mother's voice called out as she entered the kitchen. "Stella?"

Stella glanced in that direction. When she looked back, Eric was gone. She sighed. Sometime she was going to have to ask him if she couldn't see him but he was still there, or if he had a secret hiding place.

"Out here," she told her mother.

Barbara, Sean, and Doug all joined her on the deck.

"What's that you're working on in the kitchen?" Barbara asked as Hero continued to bark at Doug.

"Quiet, Hero," Stella said. "It's the contest recipe for the festival. Something about stuffed peppers, except they're sweet. Don't ask me yet. I'm not really sure."

"I didn't know you'd learned to cook while you've been here." Barbara sat down where Eric had been.

Doug and Sean disappeared back into the den to watch TV. Stella knew that her father had told her mother she was thinking about staying in Sweet Pepper.

"I guess I've been inspired by peppers." She wondered what her mother would have to say on the subject.

"I guess you have." Barbara looked into her daughter's face as only a mother can. "Your father said you're thinking about staying here."

*There it was.* "I said it had some benefits. And that I like being chief."

"You could be chief back home. You're already up in rank, and you have years to go."

"There are too many people in front of me. I won't see chief in my lifetime. I'm sure Dad told you the same thing."

"He did," Barbara admitted. "But it's more than your job, Stella. It's your life and your home. You never thought about moving before."

"This is different. I kind of like it here. I know I wasn't supposed to. It just happened."

Barbara took her daughter's hand in hers. "I know you better than to think you'd be swayed to stay here because of the Carson money."

"You're right about that. If anything, that whole family legacy thing would be something that would drive me away. I'd be staying despite that."

"Then what is it? Yes, you'd be fire chief, but at substantially less money than you make as a captain in Chicago. Is it the man you're dating?"

Stella thought about Zane. "No. I like Sweet Pepper. I like the mountains. I don't know. I feel like I should stay—sometimes. I don't know yet. I haven't made up my mind. I thought you should know."

"You don't have to go back the same time we do. Ignore your father. You wouldn't want to fly back anyway. You've got the Harley."

"It's not Dad." Stella grinned. "Well, not *only* him. Everyone else is constantly asking me how much longer I plan to stay."

"Don't make a rash decision," her mother counseled. "Take your time. Once you give up your job, it will be hard to get back."

"That works both ways," Stella assured her. "They want to make someone fire chief here who doesn't want the job. That's not good either."

"Never mind that. Make the decision for yourself."

"I will, Mom." Stella was suddenly inspired, thinking about their lives. "You know how you went to Chicago and found your life? Maybe I'm doing the same thing, but backwards from the way you did it."

"Maybe." Barbara smiled but there were tears in her brown eyes.

"Don't worry so much about me. Whatever I decide, it's not the end of the world, is it? Let's go have some lunch. I'm starving."

"I've wanted your father to try Scooter's Barbecue," Barbara said. "How about that?"

"Sounds good. Let me take Hero out for a few minutes and we'll go."

Barbara agreed, going to tell Sean and Doug where they were eating. Stella put Hero's leash on and left the cabin for a short walk in the woods.

Eric kept his place, perched on the deck rail, watching Stella and Hero walk around the trees that led down to the river.

*Did that mean Stella was staying in Sweet Pepper?*

Eric was almost too scared to think about it. He'd convinced himself that he could handle her leaving. It was too painful to let himself think it could be true—that she might not leave.

Lunch was good at Scooter's. Petey was there waiting tables. She switched with one of the other waitresses so she could have Stella and her parents.

There was more barbecue, hush puppies, and fries than
there normally would have been. Scooter Mason, a large bald-
ing man wearing a greasy apron, came out to shake hands
with Sean, Barbara, and Doug and then insisted the meal
was on the house.

"You make sure you don't take our fire chief home
with you, Barbara," he said jokingly. "We like her where
she is."

"I don't have a plane ticket, Scooter," Stella told him.

"Good." He called for Petey. "Get these fine people some
banana puddin'—and don't spare the whipped cream. I'll
see you all again, I hope. Thanks for visiting."

Stella had never seen so much banana pudding or whipped
cream on one plate. "I don't think we can eat all of that," she
told Petey as four dessert plates arrived.

"That's why they make doggy bags, Chief," Petey said.
"Scooter said not to skimp. Enjoy!"

Most of the banana pudding was going back to the cabin
with them, along with some hush puppies and extra barbecue that Doug couldn't eat.

After the rigorous practices they'd had recently, Stella
had given the fire brigade the day off—unless an emergency
came up.

Instead, she took her parents and Doug to Cades Cove,
a historic park in the Great Smoky Mountains National Park.
It was a lot of driving, but the scenery was worth it.

They walked through what was left of an old town where
the residents had been forced to move to create the national
park. There was a church and cemetery, some old home-
steads, and they were even lucky enough to see some deer
and a few black bears along the way.

Sean and Barbara enjoyed the adventure. Doug slept
through most of it, jumping up when they all yelled, "Look
at the bears!"

On the way back from the park, they stopped at one of

the usually crowded whitewater rafting spots on the river. "The water is low because it's been dry this year," Stella explained.

"We used to come down here when we were kids," Barbara said. "When I could sneak away from the mansion anyway. My father didn't like me going out at all. He would've pitched a fit if he'd known I was here."

"It sounds like fun," Sean said. "Why was Ben afraid for you to be here?"

"He was always worried I'd get hurt. There were a few accidents every year. I think because I was an only child, my mom and dad were a little overprotective."

"Tell me about it." Stella rolled her eyes and laughed. "My mom and dad were the same way. Still are, come to think of it."

"Not my parents," Doug chimed in. "With eight of us in Catholic school, I think they were hoping to get rid of one or two of us."

They all laughed at that and Stella punched redial on her cell phone to try Walt again. Still no answer.

"Where does he live?" Sean asked. "I don't want our last night here to be filled with you trying to call your friend every five minutes. Maybe we could stop by his house."

Stella put her cell phone away. "You're leaving tomorrow?"

Barbara nodded. "It's been fun, but we have to get back. And since I can see you have a decision to make about staying here, I think I should go. It's been a nice visit."

"You've decided to stay then?" Doug asked.

Stella shrugged and turned on the Cherokee's engine. "I'm not sure yet. Walt doesn't live too far off the main road on the way back to the cabin. I'll stop in there. Then no more cell phone until you guys leave. What time is your flight?"

"Nine forty-five tomorrow morning," Sean said. "That way we'll be back home by lunch and have some *real* food."

"Okay. But you're not keeping me from making a decision about Sweet Pepper," Stella told them. "I can decide what to do with you here too."

"We know," Barbara said. "We should get back. We know you'll make the right decision for you, one way or another."

"If you stay, the Harley comes home," Sean said. "No pressure."

"Thanks." Stella navigated the Cherokee past the dry riverbed as it curved and crossed under the road.

She turned off on Walt's rutted road about twenty minutes later. Everyone held their door handles and made grunting sounds as the SUV bounced up and down through the runoff ditches and rocks.

"What a place. Not much money in retiring as police chief here," Sean said when they finally stopped in front of Walt's rebuilt cabin.

"The view in back is worth all the trouble getting here. He wouldn't want to mess that up by building a real house," Stella replied. "That, and Walt's famous hard apple cider. If he's here, we'll have some."

There was no sign of Walt, or his battered old pickup. Stella looked in the kitchen window and saw a coffee cup on the table. He may have recently left, or he'd been gone for hours—there was no way to know without going inside. She wasn't feeling that desperate yet.

"Probably nothing," she told her passengers. "I left a note on his door. He's in and out all the time. He usually can't find, or can't figure out how to use, his cell phone."

"It's bothering you anyway," Sean said as she got back in the vehicle.

"I'm used to having him at my beck and call, I guess. He could be out hunting or fishing, for all I know. He was a little cryptic about proving that Ricky Senior wasn't guilty when I saw him at ladder practice yesterday. I'm sure I'm worried about nothing."

# Chapter 28

Walt's disappearance continued to bother Stella as she and her parents got ready for the tour guide's dinner that night.

Myra Strickland had been kind enough to extend an invitation for the dinner to Sean and Barbara. Stella probably wouldn't have gone otherwise since they were leaving the next morning. Doubtless, Ben had something to do with the invitation.

Stella wore red and black. Her red sweater was a light knit that had seashell shapes worked into it. Her black dress pants tapered down to her black, heeled boots.

She thought about putting her hair up but decided against it. The thick red strands had something against being pinned up. Maybe it was because they spent so much time under a helmet.

Barbara wore a royal blue dress that complemented her naturally rosy complexion. Sean wore a white shirt and blue sport coat. They didn't match exactly, but Stella smiled and took a picture of them with her cell phone before they left the cabin.

Doug had decided to stay home and eat the rest of the hush puppies and barbecue that had been left from lunch. "You guys have a good time. I want to hang out and see if I can catch the Cubs on TV this evening."

"Don't even think about polishing off the banana pudding," Sean warned. "It better be here when I get back."

Doug laughed. "If it disappears, the ghost probably ate it. It wasn't me."

Stella tried to look around the room in an inconspicuous way. She hadn't seen Eric since she got back from Cades Cove. She hoped he wouldn't take Doug's remark as a reason to do some ghostly prank. She had a feeling that he wasn't too far away.

They took the Cherokee to town. Stella tried calling Walt again as soon as she reached the main road. There was still no response.

She saw John as he was coming out of the police station at town hall. He was heading for his patrol car, probably on duty that night.

"I'm going to stop for a minute," she told Barbara and Sean. "I'll be right back."

She pulled the Cherokee next to the patrol car and got out to walk around and talk to John. They had plenty of time to get to dinner at Myra's old Victorian home. Maybe John had seen or heard from Walt today.

"Chief." John nodded when he saw her. "Something up?"

"Probably not." She glanced at her parents' interested faces looking out at them. "I haven't been able to get in touch with Walt all day. Have you seen him around?"

"No. But I've been busy helping the game warden. He had some illegal hunting going on. Was there something in particular you needed Walt for?"

She explained what Walt had said at ladder practice about proving Ricky was innocent. "I was at his place earlier today. It was hard to say if he'd been home or not."

John shrugged. "I'm sure you're right. It's probably nothing. I think sometimes he wanders around the mountains for a few days at a time. Maybe that's what he meant about proving Ricky was innocent. Walt says he does his best thinking when he's off by himself. Did he mention anywhere or anything in particular he thought was going to help Ricky?"

"No. It's probably nothing."

"Want me to check on him?"

"That would be great, if you have time. You know him and his haunts a lot better than I do. I have the tour guide dinner tonight."

"I thought you were leaving Sweet Pepper with your parents."

She evaded his gaze by watching two people walk by on the sidewalk. "Maybe."

He smirked. "Are you staying, Stella?"

"I don't know yet, John. I'll decide soon. I know it affects you too. I'm sorry the decision has been a long time coming."

He moved closer to her. Stella was *very* aware of her parents watching.

"That's okay. I hope you stay—for more than one reason." A flirty smile played on his lips.

"Oh? Something besides you not wanting to take my place as fire chief?"

"Maybe. I'm not sure yet."

"I'm still a Carson, John. Nothing is going to change that whether I'm here or in Chicago."

"I know." He gently touched the side of her face. "I'll check on Walt. See you later. Enjoy the tour guide dinner. They had me do that a few years back. Never again."

"What are you doing this year?"

"Recipe judge—hot and spicy category."

"I thought all the categories were hot and spicy."

"Some more than others, Stella." He touched a finger to the brim of his hat in a short salute. "Goodnight. I'll call if I hear anything."

The tour guide dinner boasted most of Sweet Pepper's list of important people. The whole town council turned out with Mayor Wando and his wife, Jill. Of course, Bob Floyd and Nay Albert were there.

The two least seen council members—Danielle Peterson and Willy Jenkins—were there too. Danielle was a retired schoolteacher who always wore bright red to complement her dark skin and red glasses.

Willy owned Beau's Bar and Grill. Stella had never seen him without suspenders over a Beau's T-shirt. He looked more like a bouncer, with powerful arms and a wide chest, than a local business owner.

Danielle spent five minutes gushing over how much she liked Stella and what a great job she'd done for the town. She wasn't from Sweet Pepper and enjoyed community services, always angling for the town to get more.

Willy knew Barbara from high school. He paused to give her a big bear hug as he worked the room, giving out free beer cards with every handshake.

"Barb, your daughter is amazing," Willy said. "I hope she stays. Odds at the bar right now are on her staying, but it changes every day."

Sean laughed at that. "What kind of odds are those?"

"Five to one she stays," Willy replied. "I can get you in on that, if you like. Anything for Barb's husband."

"I'd better not." Sean glanced at his wife's frown. "My wife probably wouldn't like it."

"Both of you have a free beer on me anyway." Willy handed each of them a card.

"I think it might be rude to bet on your own daughter," Stella said when he was gone.

"I didn't bet anything," Sean reminded her. "I think that woman over there is trying to get your attention."

It was Molly Whitehouse. She was there with all of the tour guides' vests. They gathered in one of Myra's bedrooms and put on vests, like bridesmaids getting dressed before a wedding.

Stella's vest fit her fine. Everyone waited until they were all ready to go back out into the crowd. Myra had reminded them that this was kind of a dress rehearsal for the real thing when they would be directing visitors around town during the festival.

The idea was that they would all go out at the party and start randomly telling people about the history of Sweet Pepper, how the peppers were grown and bottled, as well as geographical information for navigating around town.

More than half of the eighteen tour guides were young women—most looked like they were still in high school. They giggled and said crazy things as they took each other's pictures with their cell phones and complimented each other's hair.

*No wonder John said he wouldn't do this again.* Stella was fairly sure she would be on that list too by the time this was over.

"Okay now." Myra got their attention. "I have this whistle that belonged to my dear dead husband, the late mayor, who began this festival. I'm going to blow it, and you'll all circulate around the room and begin telling one part of your story. When I blow it again, you'll switch to another group of people and begin telling a different aspect of what you know. Ready?"

*As I'll ever be,* Stella thought.

"Go!" Myra blew the whistle.

Several people were so startled that they dropped or

spilled the drinks they were holding. Stella went to the first group she saw without a red-vested speaker and began talking about growing peppers, as she'd learned from Mackie Fossett.

The whistle blew and she moved on to the next group, which included her grandfather, his wife, Vivian, and Zane. She started talking about bottling the peppers.

"Doing great," Zane said with a laugh when Myra blew the whistle again. "Hey, you wanna hit Beau's tonight when this is over?"

"No," she said breathlessly. "My parents are still here. Maybe tomorrow."

The next group included Mayor Wando and his wife, with Nay and Bob.

*Tough crowd.*

The mayor did what he could, but Bob and Nay were not exactly on Team Stella. As she left them when the whistle blew, she heard Bob complain that doing this was demeaning for the fire chief.

Stella ignored him and went on to the next group, until Myra finally called a halt to the tour guides' speed session. She was relieved to find her parents and go into the buffet supper that was waiting for them.

"Did that change your mind about staying?" Barbara laughed. "You should try being the festival queen. There were so many embarrassing moments that I still cringe when I think of them."

They found a table in Myra's lovely landscaped backyard. Live music was playing from a string quartet situated in the gazebo. Fairy lights adorned all the bushes around the perimeter. The smell of pine and fried chicken filled the night.

Ben and Vivian joined them, filling the table for five. It was easy to see the strain between Vivian and Barbara as conversation went back and forth between them.

Eventually, when they were done eating, Sean asked Barbara if she wanted to join the dancers already on the flat green lawn. Barbara got to her feet at once.

Ben watched them for a moment as Vivian excused herself to go gossip with Jill Wando at the next table.

He turned to Stella. "Terrible news about Ricky Hutchins. I'm sure no one can believe it."

She agreed. "I don't believe he killed Deputy Chum. He admitted to his part in Eric's death. I think what happened with Shu Carriker should be considered an accident, or even self-defense."

"I don't know. The courts go hard on people who keep secrets."

"You heard that Ricky accused you of putting Shu up to killing Eric."

He nodded. "Of course. When in doubt, blame a Carson."

"Aren't you worried they might all rise up with pitchforks and torches one day and drag you out of the mansion?"

"You have quite an imagination, Stella." He laughed hard at her scenario. "As I told you, I had no reason to want to see Eric Gamlyn dead. I didn't hire Shu to kill him. Maybe Shu was still angry that Eric wouldn't let him join the fire brigade. I don't know. As for Mace Chum, maybe he had his own vendetta. It was a long time ago."

"What about the money—the thirty million dollars? I wonder if the TBI will try to track that down." Stella studied his impassive face.

"You know, money like that is hard to keep up with. It could've gone almost anywhere. And after all this time, I'm sure it's been well spent." He got to his feet. "I'm going to talk with a few friends. I suppose I'll see you at the airport with your parents tomorrow. Goodnight, Stella."

She watched him for a few minutes as he talked with Barney Falk. If he had anything to do with Eric's death, she felt sure no one would ever know. The old man was too crafty and cunning. The fact that he'd compared her to himself wasn't necessarily a compliment.

Stella's cell phone vibrated. It was John. "No sign of Walt anywhere, so far. I'm sure he's out in the woods or something. How's that dinner coming?"

"You could've warned me about the routine they put you through."

"And ruin the surprise? Talk to you later."

*Brief and to the point.* John wasn't worried about Walt. Everything was fine.

*Probably.*

The dinner ran late, but Stella had her parents home by nine.

Doug was asleep in front of the TV. It appeared that Eric had left him alone while she'd been gone. Stella woke him and switched off the TV. Only as Doug stood up did they both realize that he was naked under the blanket that had covered him.

Doug gulped, turned red all over, and snatched up the blanket he'd hastily dropped on the sofa. "I swear I didn't mean this to happen, Stella. I was wearing clothes when I went to sleep. I don't know how it's possible . . ."

His clothes were nowhere to be found around the sofa. He wore the blanket upstairs, where he finally found them—neatly folded on the bed.

"Real mature," Stella said aloud downstairs to her ghostly housemate.

Eric's laughter followed her out on the deck as she sat down in a rocking chair.

"So you're staying?" Eric had promised himself that he wouldn't mention it when he saw her. It was a promise he couldn't keep.

"You too?"

"This isn't idle curiosity. I have something at stake here. If you know, tell me."

"I don't know. Not yet anyway."

"You're not leaving with your parents."

"No. I was never leaving with them. You shouldn't listen to so much gossip. They're leaving in the morning. I wouldn't fly back anyway. I'd take the Harley."

"You'll never get all the new stuff you've bought since you got here in the saddlebags."

She smiled. "I'm sure they had UPS when you were alive."

Hero wandered out of the den to lie at her feet. He looked up at her hopefully to see if she might be about to go for a walk in the dark woods. When she didn't move, he lay his head down on the deck and went back to sleep.

The night grew even quieter after Stella's parents had said goodnight and closed the bedroom door. Eric and Stella had spent many nights like this on the deck, talking about life, death, and the world around them.

The little owl that lived in the tree by the deck, hooted mournfully as the moon rose over the mountains.

"He sounds lonely tonight," Stella said to Eric. "Do owls live with their families?"

"I think so. The young ones have probably already left the nest," he whispered.

"What about his mate? She must have stuck around after they raised their family."

"Maybe she's enjoying ladies' night out somewhere," he joked. "Or it doesn't always work that way. Sometimes you're alone."

"You'll be alone again if I leave."

"I know."

"What will you do?"

"What I did before. At least death has left me in my home. I look at the mountains. I listen to the rain. I dream about the past. When there's electricity, I watch TV."

"I could stay. You wouldn't be alone."

"Only if you decide it's what's best for you," he cautioned. "I'm dead, Stella. One way or another, I'll always be alone."

She sighed and decided to go to sleep. It was a long drive to the airport in the morning. She took her cell phone out of her pocket and plugged it in for the night. A green light flashed letting her know she had a message.

There were no words in the message—just a picture of a bloody boot.

"What is it?" Eric looked over her shoulder.

"Walt's in trouble."

# Chapter 29

"How can you tell?" Eric wondered.

"This is his email and I've looked at his ratty old boots plenty of times," she explained. "I'll have to drive down the mountain and call John."

"Can you tell where he is from his email?"

"No. It doesn't work like that. I'm not sure I recognize the place from the picture either." She zoomed in on it. "Maybe a barn of some sort? Do you recognize anything?"

Eric came closer until his head was beside hers. His nearness created a frisson of energy. It tickled her ear and made her shiver.

Stella smiled and rubbed her ear. "You're like a zap of static electricity, you know that?"

He turned his head and kissed her cheek. "How did that feel?"

"Disturbing." She turned and looked directly into his bright blue eyes. "What do you think? Barn wall?" Her voice was a little breathless.

"Could be. Or an old cabin. Definitely hand-hewn lumber. See the irregular sizes and depths." He touched the phone screen and it went blank. "Sorry."

"That's okay. Electronics don't like you, but they recover." She put down her phone. "I have to go."

"I know. I wish I could go with you, though I suppose I wouldn't be much help."

Stella had already changed into the shorts and T-shirt she planned to sleep in before her parents went to bed. "I hate to wake them, but I can't go out like this. Who knows what Walt has gotten himself into?"

"Allow me."

She watched Eric melt right through the bedroom door and hoped her parents wouldn't wake up and see him going through her clothes drawer. Not that they'd shown any ability to see him—but this would be a particularly bad time.

A moment later, he was back with jeans, a T-shirt, socks, and boots.

"Underwear?" she asked hopefully.

"Sorry." He grinned. "I couldn't find any. They must be mixed up in the clothes bag from the laundry that you never empty until it's time to wash again."

"Thanks anyway."

"I could borrow some from your mother."

"That's okay." Stella managed to get into the tightly packed kitchen pantry and change her clothes. She left her parents a note on the table.

"Be careful." Eric waited by the kitchen door for her as she put on her boots.

"Always."

He raised one brow. "Don't get cocky. If Walt is hurt, it might involve Chum's killer."

"I said I'll be careful." She put her hand on the doorknob. "Don't worry. I'll be fine. No one expects the fire chief to get involved in what should be police activities."

"There's a reason for that."

Eric was very close to her. She smiled and kissed his cheek. For once, as she touched him, he was solid, almost alive. He must have anticipated her move. "What did *that* feel like?"

"Sweet. Warm. Human."

"I'll be back."

He watched her get into the Cherokee and drive back down the mountain. Hero whimpered and Eric let him outside for a while. The puppy never left the fifty-foot perimeter outside that was under his control. The lonely old screech owl in back hooted again.

"I know how you feel, old son."

The cell phone was working again by the time Stella had reached the main road. She called John and met him at the firehouse. They looked at the email from Walt together, as she and Eric had.

"Maybe he took one of those random pictures you don't mean to take and accidentally sent it," John said.

"Or he's trying to get help."

"You think he's in trouble?"

"I think so. I've thought so all day. You have too, haven't you? This picture was sent early this morning. Because of the crazy mountain interference, I just got it. I tried calling him again while I was waiting for you. Still no answer."

"This isn't much to go on." He didn't deny that he was also worried about Walt. "He didn't say anything to you about what he was looking for to prove Ricky's innocence?"

"No. I've gone over and over it in my head. He didn't say anything specific."

John sighed heavily as he leaned on the top of his police car, staring at the image on the phone. "This could be anywhere, Stella. I don't know how this can help us find him."

"Couldn't you get someone to track his cell phone since we think he might be in trouble?"

"Sure. It might take a while, but the county could do that."

"That's someplace to start anyway." Stella stared out at the night around them, barely able to make out the shapes of the mountains. "What could he have been thinking, John? You've been friends with him for a long time. I told him the police had picked Ricky up because of the report from the forest service. Where do you think he'd go from there?"

"I think I'd look for another black pickup. Maybe a local truck with 'SR' on the plate."

"You think he knew someone like that?"

"I don't know," John admitted. "It's just a hunch."

"He was down at the county DMV looking up Impalas from the 1970s," Stella said. "It wasn't on the list, but that's how he remembered that Shu Carriker had an Impala."

"Okay. Let's take a look at his cabin. Maybe he got more records than he told you. Get in. I'll drive. We'll get there faster."

Stella was about to defend her mountain driving record when a call came through for John. There were two wrecks, no injuries, near Myra's home.

"Probably someone with too much to drink leaving the tour guide dinner," John remarked after taking the call. "I have to do this first, Stella. At least they don't need the fire brigade."

"I'll go over to Walt's and see what I can find. Meet you there."

"That's it, right? Don't leave without me if you find something. You're only the fire chief."

"I know. Although I'm beginning to think Chief Rogers should deputize me." She climbed into the Cherokee. "I'll see you later."

Just to prove to herself that she could make good time on the curvy roads, Stella checked the clock before her trip to Walt's.

Everyone was always saying she drove too slowly, but that was to be expected from someone not used to the back roads and steep inclines. She didn't think she was any slower than they were—just more careful.

She looked at the clock in the Cherokee when she reached Walt's cabin. Fifteen minutes. That didn't seem too bad.

She got out and locked the vehicle, another thing Ricky and the others laughed at her about. No one in Sweet Pepper ever locked up. Most of the shops and restaurants left their doors unlocked as well, despite the police asking them to lock up when the day was over.

For her, it was a habit after growing up in the city. She couldn't imagine not locking her doors, except at the cabin, where Eric took care of the whole breaking-and-entering risk. She'd actually feel sorry for anyone who tried it there. They'd get more than they bargained for.

Of course, being the ex–police chief, Walt's cabin door was locked. There were chinks in some of the walls that she could put her hand through, but he had still locked the door.

Stella picked up a rock and broke one of the windows to let herself in. She'd have to get that fixed for him, but finding him as quickly as possible felt like a priority. She didn't want to wait for John or a locksmith.

Once inside the rustic old cabin, she could tell that Walt hadn't been back for a while. The coffee cup she'd seen earlier had green fuzz growing on the bottom. It was still on the table, in the same spot she'd seen it earlier.

It looked to her like Walt had been gone for going on three days—considering it was already almost one a.m. She'd been willing to believe he was out hunting or poking around, until she saw his email. Now she thought he was hoping to be rescued.

She focused on finding the DMV records he'd printed out. Unless he'd guessed where he should go, he'd probably found an answer in those documents.

The pages were splayed out across the large old stump he used as a coffee table in his living room. These were covered in coffee rings and had a few food stains on them, but she was able to read them.

She sat in his torn brown leather chair, as he would have, and started looking through the documents. Several times she paused as she heard noises like mice—or maybe snakes—in the walls around her. She hoped it wasn't scorpions.

Stella wished Eric was there. It was hard to imagine her life without him anymore. She knew it was ridiculous. He was dead. Nothing she could do would bring him back.

She didn't care. He was a large part of why she wanted to stay in Sweet Pepper. She didn't want him to be alone again.

Of course, there was also John. He was important too. So were all of her fire brigade members. *Her fire brigade.* No wonder Eric had fought so hard, ultimately giving up his life, to keep his group together. She understood the attachment.

Ricky, Petey, and the rest had become like her family. It was even different than her family at the fire station back home. These people she'd handpicked for the group. There weren't many of them, but they worked well together. That meant something to her.

"There you are."

She found some scribbled notes on one of the pages. She couldn't tell what Walt had written, but she could read the typed listing. Beside the information about the Impala was a listing for a black 1984 pickup, license number SR 1357. It was registered to Thelma Carriker.

"Walt probably found this and went after Carriker," Stella

said to John's voice mail on his phone when he didn't answer. "I know I said I wouldn't leave here without you, but I'm going to see if I can find him. Maybe you can come and find me."

She also left a message for Agent Whitman whose voice mail said he was in Knoxville until the next morning.

She looked at the phone for a long minute, trying to decide if she should call Chief Rogers. It wasn't a difficult decision. She slipped the cell phone back into her pocket and took the DMV list with her, without calling him.

It was only about another twenty minutes to the Carriker farm. There were no streetlights down the long, twisting, gravel road that led there. The farm was dark too—no outside or inside lights that she could see.

Walt could be anywhere on the property, including the farmhouse Jack shared with his mother. Her memory of the place told her that all of the buildings seemed to be made of that same rough lumber that Eric had pointed out in the picture. She wasn't sure where to start looking.

Jack had a shotgun, maybe more weapons too. All she had was her cell phone.

She suddenly recalled that Ricky had said Jack was at the firehouse on the day Chum had come to talk to her. Had he heard what the deputy had said?

With a plan forming in her brain, she slowly drove the Cherokee into the long, rutted dirt drive. No house lights came on. She took the flashlight out of her emergency kit and got out to look around.

There was no sign of Walt's old pickup in the yard. It could be in one of the dozens of outbuildings with him. The shack they'd found the Impala in had been big enough to hold more than one vehicle. He could be there, or in one of the other buildings.

Reminding herself that help could be coming right

behind her, Stella proceeded to start searching the buildings closest to the house. It was so dark, even the flashlight beam had little effect. There seemed to be skittering, slithering sounds coming from everywhere along with crickets, frogs, and owls.

She wished she could yell for Walt. Even if she could, he might not be able to hear her. She glanced around. How hard could it be to locate a grown man and a truck?

Two whole buildings and three black snakes later, she wasn't so sure. She wasn't even certain she could find all of the outbuildings she'd seen when she'd been there during the day, looking at the Impala.

There were still no lights from inside the house and no sounds from that area. She hoped Jack and his mother were heavy sleepers.

Stella stumbled on some lumber hidden in the darkness and cursed softly, hoping no one had heard her. Something sharp had gone in through the bottom of her boot. *Probably a nail.* It stung, but she didn't stop to check it.

"Who's there?" Walt's voice was more raspy than usual as he called out of the darkness. "Stella? Please tell me that's not you. Or you've got the police with you."

She shone the flashlight toward the sound of his voice but there was nothing. "Keep talking. I can't see you."

"That's because Jack shot me in the leg and dragged me into this old storm cellar."

Stella followed the sound of his voice and found a hole in the rocky ground close to the house—*too close*. She glanced up at the dark shadow of the house again. No one seemed to be stirring.

The flashlight picked out rough stairs carved out of rock leading into the cellar. Carefully, she lifted what was left of the wood door that covered the opening. The light immediately flashed on Walt's dirty, gaunt face.

"Are you alone?" he asked in a bare whisper.

"Yes. But John is on the way."

Walt swore with much more colorful accents than Stella had when she'd run into the woodpile.

"I didn't mean to send you that picture," he complained. "It was supposed to go to John. He wouldn't have come out here alone."

She went carefully down the stairs and put down the flashlight so the beam was pointing into the small cellar. "Well, next time, resend. I'm the only one who got the message, and that took a while. You're lucky I came at all."

Walt continued to complain while she untied him. She wished she'd brought a knife to cut the thick, rough rope that bound him. Eventually, he was free and she helped him stand.

"Not that I'm ungrateful." Walt groaned from the pain in his injured leg. "You're a sight for sore eyes."

"You're welcome." She put his arm around her shoulders and put his weight on her as they went slowly up the stairs. "Let's get out of here."

"Sounds good to me."

As they reached the ground level, a bright light shone in their faces and a shotgun clicked.

"Well, what have we got here?" Jack Carriker asked. "Chief Griffin. I don't see a fire. What brings you out here tonight?"

# Chapter 30

~~~~~~~~~

"You might as well let us go," Stella said. "The police are right behind me."

Jack laughed. "You know, they always say that in the movies. They don't mean it, but they say it. How stupid do you think I am?"

"Plenty stupid," Walt said. "Bad enough you killed poor Chum. You're just like your murdering father. Did Ben Carson put you up to this?"

"The old man had nothing to do with it." Thelma Carriker joined her son with another gun in her hand. "That deputy was going around saying my Shu killed the old fire chief. I wasn't letting him get away with that. I didn't care if he was going to another *country*. Jack took care of him, didn't you, honey pockets?"

"I told you not to call me that in front of anyone," Jack complained. "But since you're out here, you kill her and I'll finish him. We can bury them in the cellar tonight."

Walt laughed. "You don't have the guts. Why didn't you kill me when you shot me in the leg? It's one thing to drive up and shoot Mace Chum where he couldn't face you. It's another to look someone in the eye and do it."

Stella wished he'd keep his mouth shut. Her eyes searched the road that ran by the farm, praying for headlights to show up. *What was keeping John?*

"Look." She hoped to gain some temporary control over the situation. "I'm not kidding about the police being right behind me, Jack. I'm the fire chief. I'm not armed. I wouldn't come out here without knowing there was backup."

Thelma looked at her son in the dim light coming from the porch. "Let's take our chances, boy. If they can't find them, they can't say we did anything."

"Don't tell me what to do, old woman," Jack sassed. "I said we should shoot them. Go ahead. Shoot Chief Griffin and I'll finish up old Walt here."

Stella rationalized that it looked as though she and Walt might die before John could get there. No point in standing there, waiting for it to happen.

Jack was right in front of her. His shotgun barrel held toward her head.

"Look! There they are now! I told you they were coming." Stella pointed toward a set of headlights coming toward the farm.

"Where?" Jack turned his head to see what was going on.

Stella took a quick step and put her knee into his groin. He doubled over with a groan and she grabbed his shotgun, but not before Thelma's shotgun went off, the sound of its retort echoing through the quiet night around them.

The kickback from the gun pushed Thelma down hard on her butt. Walt limped over to the woman and jerked the shotgun away from her. "I swear, Thelma, you should've known better."

Thelma started crying and rolled over next to her son. "Jack? Are you okay, honey child?"

"Leave me alone," the object of her affection snapped. "I'm dying here. Call an ambulance."

The headlights Stella had pointed out, and used to advantage, went by the farm without stopping.

John, Chief Rogers, and Agent Whitman weren't more than a few seconds behind. Their vehicles pulled into the driveway, sirens blaring and lights flashing.

John ran from his car, his gun drawn as he took in the scene. "Everyone okay here?"

"I need an ambulance," Jack said. "And I want to sue Chief Griffin for assault."

Walt started to sway and Stella propped him up with his arm around her shoulders.

"We need an ambulance," she told John. "Walt's been shot—blood on his boots in the picture." She grinned at him.

"I'll call for that." John took her hand and scanned her face in the bright glow from the police car's headlights. "You sure you're okay?"

"If you're talking to *me*, I sure could use some hard cider about now," Walt said. "Never mind that ambulance. I've shot myself worse than this cleaning my gun."

Chief Rogers stepped in at that point, demanding to know what was going on. Agent Whitman had his own questions. Stella was there long after the ambulance had come for Walt and Jack. Thelma was handcuffed in the back of John's police car.

It took a lot less time to explain everything to her parents and Doug when she got back. Sean had been up, rummaging around for a snack, and had seen her note on the table. Both he and Doug said she should have woken them and taken them with her.

Stella smiled at Eric who was sitting on the stairs as she told the story. She'd made her decision about leaving Sweet Pepper. All that remained were the details.

\*   \*   \*

"Did you say we're stuffing these peppers with sweetbreads?"
Stella asked Eric as she looked inside the hollowed, candied
pepper shell.

"I said we're stuffing them with sweet *bread*," he
corrected as he stuffed the first batch of peppers with the
mixture from a large glass bowl. "This is fruit bread.
Remember, you bought the candied fruit for it? I baked the
bread yesterday while you were at practice. Now we're stuffing the peppers with it. At least I am."

"Sorry. I was picturing, you know, insides stuffed in the
peppers. I know what sweetbreads are."

He laughed at her. "That's amazing from a woman whose
main diet is Pop-Tarts and Doritos. Are you stuffing the
peppers?"

"Yes." She made a face as she picked up a handful of the
bread mixture. "It looks pretty in there. I hope it tastes good."

"Try one. Then you'll know."

"Not that it matters." She put her first stuffed pepper on
a cookie sheet lined with baking paper. "It has to go in today.
As long as people don't get sick eating it, it's going as is."

"Just try it. It's good."

"Easy for you to say—you don't eat." She did as he
advised and was pleasantly surprised. "*Mmm*. You're really
good at this. I shudder to think what I'd be taking to the
festival if I had to come up with ideas by myself."

"So do I. Now, stuff."

They worked in companionable silence for a few minutes.

Stella didn't regret her decision not to leave Sweet Pepper.
It had been difficult to tell her parents that day they'd left in
August, but she still believed it was the right decision. She'd
had a long time to think about it when she drove back to
Chicago, packed up most of what she owned, and sent it to
the cabin.

Some of her things had stayed behind in her parents' attic. No matter what, her space in the cabin was limited. She'd respected that fact and was happy with the result.

Stella hadn't brought any furniture back with her. She liked Eric's old stuff, but the deer antlers had to go. He'd given her a hard time about a few things but they'd compromised in the end and it had all worked out.

Eric had seemed surprised when she'd returned, despite her telling him that she would. She knew when she'd seen his face again, after being gone most of the month of September, that she'd done the right thing.

"How are you going to transport these?" He held up a tray of finished peppers. "We really need something with sides to keep them in place."

"No problem." She whipped out a box of plastic wrap. "They won't go anywhere once I wrap them up in this. And it won't stick to them either. My mom said last night that she swears by it."

That was another addition Stella had to make. She'd put in a landline phone so her mother could keep in touch, apparently at any time of the day or night since she'd called after eleven last night to ask about the festival recipe.

"She likes to talk on the phone," Eric observed. "She must really miss you."

Stella shrugged. "I'm sure she'll figure out ways to come down all the time. A free place to stay and a wealthy father makes that very attractive."

"Someone's here." Eric glanced out the window. "Ricky Junior. Did you miss practice today?"

Stella wiped her sticky hands on a wet towel. "Like I'd schedule a practice on the first day of the festival. It must be something else."

Ricky Junior knocked on the door and it opened before Stella could get there. He looked at it and smiled. "Was that the ghost or do you need to get your door fixed?"

"Maybe both," she said. "With Jack out of the picture, I guess I need to find a new handyman."

She was glad to see a smile on Ricky's face. While his father had been going through his court proceedings, Ricky had lost his ready smile and unique sense of humor. He'd even started driving more slowly.

"Would you like to try a stuffed candied pepper? They're good."

"No thanks. I'm here to let you know that I have to quit the fire brigade, at least for right now. I'm sorry, but my mom needs me a lot more at the café. I can't get to all the practices and promise I can show up for calls."

Stella had been expecting this—and dreading it. She depended heavily on Ricky to help with the vehicles as well as driving the engine/ladder truck to calls. "I understand. I hate it, but I understand. How's your dad holding up?"

He shrugged. "About like you'd expect. He doesn't complain, but he's lost a lot of weight and he looks really bad. I hate that he carried that secret around about Carriker and the old fire chief for so long. Things like that eat at you. I guess it was a relief being able to talk about it, but jail's no picnic, you know?"

She smiled at him. "You're always welcome back when you can."

He scuffed his tennis shoe on the wood floor and looked away for a moment. "Not like you really need me anymore. Now that you're not leaving and the town council gave you that ten-year contract, you can always find another driver."

Stella did something she normally didn't do—she hugged him. "I'll miss you. Let me know if you need anything."

Ricky looked as embarrassed as Stella usually did when someone from the fire brigade hugged her. Maybe it was rubbing off on her.

"I won't keep you anymore. You better get these peppers up to the festival for judging. Don't make Theodora or Elvita come and get them. It can get ugly, Chief. I'll see you around."

Stella watched him leave, feeling Eric looking over her shoulder. "I *knew* this was going to happen. I don't have any idea who can drive the engine now. I've got Kent on the pumper. I need someone with big truck experience on the engine too."

"You'll find someone," he said. "In the meantime, the kid was right. You better get these to the festival. Go and win us a blue ribbon. And good luck with the tour guide thing too."

Stella put on her black pants and white shirt, topping it with her red vest. At the last minute, the festival committee had added a red Sweet Pepper ball cap as part of the costume. She put her thick red hair up in a ponytail and let it hang out of the back.

"How do I look?" she asked with a big smile on her face.

He looked at her quickly and then looked away. "You look great. Just don't let anyone take pictures."

"Thanks for the encouragement."

Eric watched Stella pack the peppers into the Cherokee. He'd told her she could park closer to the cabin and he could have helped her with the trays. She'd declined—it was bad enough to have things moved inside by an invisible hand. She didn't want to see her picture in the paper with boxes of peppers moving *outside*.

# Chapter 31

~~~~~~~~~~

The Sweet Pepper Festival was crowded, as it was every year. Hundreds of vendors hawked their wares to thousands of tourists under deep blue Tennessee skies. There were caramel apples, knitted hats, and hand-turned wooden bowls. Anything and everything someone might like to buy.

Downtown Sweet Pepper was wall-to-wall people wandering up and down the streets, filling the shops and restaurants, spending plenty of money. It was no wonder Mayor Wando stood in the middle of blocked-off Main Street in  his traditional top hat and tails welcoming people to town.

Everywhere Stella looked there were peppers. There were pepper flags flying from every house, every shop. Farmers sold the gold, green, and red fresh peppers along the streets in special stalls. Little kids wore pepper costumes and adults wore pepper-shaped hats. The sun gleamed on the freshly painted pepper water tower over it all.

Stella took her post at Main and Center streets, about a

block from the main festival areas. It wasn't long before she was answering questions about everything she'd learned about peppers. It was surprising how many people wanted to hear her talk about growing and distributing peppers.

She was ready for them.

It took ninety days to grow a Tennessee Teardrop pepper, Sweet Pepper's specialty. They were one hundred thousand to two hundred thousand degrees on the Scoville heat index, which had been created to let people know what they were about to put into their mouths. Sweet Pepper grew five thousand bushels of peppers in a good year.

The peppers were bottled in the factory on the hillside (here she was supposed to point and suggest tours of the packing facility). The company was started in 1840 by Charles Carson. The peppers were shipped from there across the U.S. and to twenty-six countries around the world.

By noon, she was exhausted and her mouth felt like it was filled with cotton. Relief came when Lucinda Waxman's granddaughter, Foster, came with her bag lunch and a big glass of sweet iced tea. Stella thanked her and then gulped half of the sweet tea in one swallow. Normally she wasn't a fan of sweet tea. It was too sweet for her taste. It was delicious after a morning of answering pepper questions.

She sat on the old-fashioned bench near the antique streetlight at the corner and ate quickly while there was a lull in foot traffic.

She'd barely finished when a call came in on her cell phone and her emergency radio. She knew Tagger was handling calls that day. He was the only one who didn't care if he went to the festival.

Stella ran to the Cherokee, glad the peppers were gone from her front seat. For a moment she panicked, wondering who was going to drive the engine.

She hadn't had time to contact anyone about taking

Ricky's place. She'd never driven anything bigger than her motorcycle before she came to Sweet Pepper. She was still getting used to the size of the Cherokee.

As she raced back to the firehouse, she mentally went over all of her volunteers' applications that had been submitted before they had started with the fire brigade.

It had been easy to tag Kent for the pumper/tanker since he'd had experience driving a big rig. Her thoughts took her to JC's application—he'd driven a cement truck for several years before going to work for the pepper plant.

Lucky for her, JC was already in his gear by the time she got there. Most of the volunteers were either arriving or changing their clothes. Tagger had already opened the big bay doors.

"The fire is at the old meatpacking factory near Frog Pond," Tagger told her as she walked inside the firehouse. "Our records don't show a company being in there, Chief. It must be something new."

She nodded as she took off her shoes and vest while she was walking toward the locker area. "So we don't know what we're going into?"

"Sorry," Tagger said. "I'm still calling around, trying to get some info about it."

"Let me know right away if you figure it out."

Stella saw JC and pulled him to the side of the locker area. "Ricky quit this morning. Do you think you can drive the engine?"

He didn't hesitate. His broad, dark face was intent. "Sure. Is that where you want me?"

"Yes. Thanks. I'll meet you there. Tagger has the keys. Go ahead and start it up."

JC seemed surprised but didn't ask any questions until the group was ready to go and the engine was leading the way with him, Hero, and Stella in the cab.

"Ricky quit because of his dad, didn't he?"

"Yes. He may come back. I don't know right now. Are you okay with driving?"

"Sure." He grinned, showing even white teeth. "I only gave up driving the cement truck because the company I worked for went out of business. There aren't a lot of jobs around here that don't involve peppers, you know what I mean?"

Stella liked JC. He handled himself well at calls and during practice. He was always willing to lend an extra hand. He also managed to drive the engine smoothly, and at a good speed.

The old meatpacking factory was a shabby two-story brick building that sat on the side of the highway, about ten minutes from the firehouse. There were no cars in the overgrown parking lot. Stella assumed no one was working there, or the building was being used for storage. It didn't look as though anyone had been there for a long time.

"Any information on what's inside?" she asked Tagger on the radio.

"Nothing, Chief. Maybe it was kids in the empty building. I don't know yet. I have a call in to the county."

"Thanks. We're here now. Let me know if you get any information."

Stella got out of the engine with Hero at her heels. She had Petey use the heat sensor to pinpoint the location where the fire was burning.

The few windows in the building had been boarded up. There was no way to see inside. There was plenty of smoke coming out of it, but no sign of fire outside.

"Looks smack in the center of the building," Petey said. "I guess we assume no one's inside?"

"For now." Stella told everyone to be careful. "I think this place is empty, but let's not take any chances."

"What's the cargo?" Royce wiped sweat from his face.

"We don't know that either. We'll have to use the aerial

ladder on the engine to get the water inside," she said. "We'll have to vent the roof, no matter what."

"I'll go up, Chief," Petey said. "Where's Ricky?"

"He had to quit," Stella said tersely. "Let's get moving."

There were odd noises coming from the building. It sounded like crispy cereal in milk. There were snap, crackle, and pop noises as they stood outside getting their gear together.

JC was raising the ladder above the roof. Petey was ready to climb. No one had argued with her about going up there.

They were hooking the hoses up to an old water hydrant that the county had probably put in for the meatpacking facility, when John arrived in his police car.

"Sorry I'm late, Chief." He was still putting on his bunker coat. "Festival traffic. What have we got?"

Stella explained the situation to him. "Let's move."

"Where's Ricky?" John looked around at the shorthanded group.

"He quit this morning."

Royce and Kent had to use the axes to get through the loading doors as Petey went up the ladder. At that moment, the materials stored in the old plant became clear—a dozen large fireworks burst out, showering the crew with multicolor sparks. Hundreds of them stored inside started going off, loud booms accompanying each set catching fire.

Kimmie and David shouted happily and pointed at the display like children. Sylvia and Hero growled at the light show and crouched down on the concrete, where they were waiting to see if they were needed.

Stella barked out a warning about the fireworks. "Keep your heads low in there!"

Bert Wando pushed Kimmie aside as a heavy burst of red sparks almost hit her. Allen Wise yelled at everyone to be careful.

Stella reinforced the warning on the radios. "This might look pretty, but it's dangerous. Stay on your toes."

Petey reported her movements on the radio. "I'm going to crack the roof open and you can have someone start the water up here."

"Watch yourself," Stella warned. "We have exploding fireworks coming out of the building."

"Really? Cool." Petey laughed. "Don't worry, Chief. I'll be careful."

Stella shook her head. Firefighters needed to take exploding fireworks seriously. She'd seen some places go up in Chicago that way. It was no joke.

She had John and JC standing by with a two-inch hose as soon as Petey gave the signal. Kimmie was still giggling as the fireworks began to shoot into the sky. A crowd of cars had already begun gathering in the parking lot and along the side of the road. People were sitting in the backs of their pickups and on car hoods to watch the show.

"Tagger." Stella called him on the radio. "Get me some police backup out here. We have civilians who think this is a free fireworks show."

"Will do, Chief."

Before Petey could get to the roof, a larger group of fireworks, probably the bigger, aerial bombs began going off. A portion of the roof blew off, sending heavy showers of sparks up into the sky—and knocking Petey from the ladder.

Stella saw her fall and reacted quickly by heading toward the ladder as she called for an ambulance and medical team. To her surprise, Kimmie was one step in front of her, already working her way up the ladder to the roof.

"Are you going to let her go?" John yelled above the noise of the exploding fireworks.

"We all have to face our fears sometime," she told him. "Kimmie has to know she can do this."

"Yeah, but Stella—"

"Not up for discussion."

Stella kept her gaze on Kimmie's rapidly moving form. She was poised at the bottom of the ladder to assist her if the other woman needed it. She radioed Kent and Royce to make sure they were all right inside the building.

"Not really much of a fire, Chief," Kent said. "These fireworks are kind of lighting themselves off right now. We're hitting them with as much water as we can. It's like dominoes in here."

"Keep going," Stella said. "Be careful."

She could make out Kimmie's movements as she reached the roof and approached Petey's inert form. Without hesitation, Kimmie got Petey up across her shoulders and started back toward the ladder.

Stella raced up to the roof to help Kimmie with her burden.

"I can take her, Chief," Kimmie said breathlessly. "Let me do this, please."

Stella stepped off on the rapidly deteriorating roof. Kimmie went down the ladder with Petey across her shoulders until she met JC at the bottom.

"Okay," Stella said to John. "Let's get that water up here while there's still a roof."

John, JC, and David manned the bigger, three-inch hose on the platform, setting it up so that it would spray onto the roof where Stella directed. Large portions of the roof had been destroyed from the inside as still more aerial bombs went off.

The group finally had to take another hose up the ladder for a more direct effort. Stella and Kimmie held the two-inch hose in place until the booming fireworks stopped.

By that time, the ambulance was there for Petey. Sweet Pepper police, along with county police, were directing traffic and asking civilians to leave the parking lot. There were hundreds of cars and trucks.

Even the Smittys came out from the *Sweet Pepper Gazette* to take pictures, unheard of during a festival.

Stella walked through the smoky, old building with John as they all worked to make sure there were no more hot spots. It was hard to say where the fire started without a more thorough investigation.

"Looks like we got it all," she said. "I want to know who agreed to let someone store fireworks here without a permit."

"Top priority for tomorrow," he promised. "These old places outside the town are hard to keep up with."

"Tell Petey that," Stella muttered. "She could've been killed up there."

"You were right about Kimmie," he admitted. "I wouldn't have believed it."

"Sometimes you have to have a little faith."

# Chapter 32

~~~~~~~~~

Petey was injured but she'd recover. Stella had waited, with all the fire brigade members, at the hospital with Petey's parents until the doctors were sure about her.

"She's got a broken arm, some cracked ribs, and a fractured collarbone," the emergency room physician told them. "She'll be here a day or so and then we'll have her home. She probably won't be up to many fires for a while, Chief Griffin. But she'll mend."

Stella thanked him and gave everyone else the good news. "She's kind of banged up but she'll be okay. I'd say we have Kimmie to thank for that."

"That's right," Royce shouted.

He and JC lifted Kimmie up on their shoulders while she laughed and cried at the same time.

"First drink at Beau's is on me," Stella said. "Let's get back to the firehouse and get everything cleaned up. You guys did a great job out there. I'm proud of all of you."

"Me too," John said. "I think we need a few more warm bodies, Chief. We never replaced Marty. Now Banyin and

Ricky are gone, and Petey will be out for a while. I'd say we need to recruit."

Stella agreed. "Agreed. But not tonight. I'll see everyone back at the firehouse."

The group took the pumper and the engine back to the firehouse to be cleaned and readied for the next call. All the gear was cleaned and put away before the weary band of firefighters got into their individual vehicles and left the parking lot.

Stella's phone rang before she could leave. It was Theodora.

"I'm so sorry you were called away from your tour guide duties, Stella. But don't worry about a thing. We'll look for you tomorrow."

Stella thanked her, not quite sure what to say.

"I have the most marvelous news. Your recipe for stuffed candied peppers has won the blue ribbon in the most creative recipe in your division. Congratulations!"

"That's great." Stella thought about how excited Eric would be when he heard. "Thank you for telling me."

"Well, needless to say, you've fit right into our hearts here in Sweet Pepper. And now you'll always be in our tummies too."

Stella knew everyone would be waiting for their free drink at Beau's, but she had to take a few minutes and tell Eric the news before she joined them. She hopped on her Harley, gunned the engine, and was gone.

The sharp turns going up the road had become so familiar she didn't even mind them in the twilight as she had when she'd first come here. The sun was fading behind the mountains, casting long shadows into the trees that surrounded the road.

She stopped dead as she reached the cabin, the Harley's tires screeching under her.

Bob Floyd was standing next to his white SUV, the "For

Sale" sign that had been up was in his hands. There was a large truck with a bulldozer coming off of it.

"What's going on?" she demanded after parking the bike. She could see Eric standing at the window. "What are you doing up here?"

"I'm about to clear *my* property," Bob said. "I'm willing to give you time to get your things out of the cabin and then it's going to be rubble."

# The Sweet
# Pepper Difference

〜〜〜〜〜〜〜〜〜〜〜

Sweet Pepper, Tennessee, is famous for its peppers! We grow
them by the bushel and then pick and pack them right here
for the most flavorful pepper you've ever eaten! For more
than 180 years, the hottest, sweetest peppers in the world!
Come visit us in October for our Sweet Pepper Festival!

## Know Your Peppers

Because knowing the strength and taste of the peppers you
use with your foods can make or break your meal, it's best
to know your peppers!

The featured pepper is the cherry pepper. These peppers
are also known as pimento peppers. These little cuties are
heart-shaped, about four inches long and three inches wide.
They are very mild, scoring about five hundred on the Scoville heat index, hardly a hot pepper at all. Cherry peppers
are primarily used for the red part inside stuffed olives.

# Recipes

~~~~~~

### HOT/SWEET PEPPER RELISH

5 green or red bell peppers (sweet)
5 jalapeño peppers
1 medium onion
1½ cups distilled white vinegar
½ cup sugar or sweetener
2 teaspoons mustard seed

Wash the bell peppers well and trim to remove stems and seeds. Clean and cut stem ends from the jalapeño peppers. Peel, core, and wash the onion. Cut the peppers and onion into large pieces. Coarsely grind the peppers and onion together.

Add the ground peppers and onion mixture to vinegar, sugar, and mustard seed in a large pot. Bring the mixture to a boil over high heat. Reduce heat and cook at a low boil for about 30 minutes. Stir often to prevent scorching.

Refrigerate the relish in airtight containers. The relish can also be frozen for future use.

*Makes about 2 quarts.*

# BACON-WRAPPED BANANA PEPPERS

**20 banana peppers**
**3 packages cream cheese, softened**
**20 slices bacon**

Preheat oven to 350.

Slice the banana peppers to open a side of each one. Remove all seeds.

Fill each pepper with cream cheese and then wrap each with a slice of bacon.

Place the peppers in a baking dish. Do not layer.

Bake for 1 hour or until the bacon is crispy.

*Serves 5 people.*

# RED PEPPER FUDGE

**5 cups of sugar**
**2 sticks butter or margarine**
**1 can evaporated milk**
**6 ounces unsweetened baking chocolate**
**1 jar marshmallow creme**
**2 teaspoons vanilla extract**
**1 tablespoon red chili powder**

Bring to a boil the sugar, butter, and milk. Heat until the mixture begins to reach the soft-ball stage. Melt the chocolate separately. Combine the chocolate and the marshmallow cream. Add the vanilla and the red chili powder. Fold the two mixtures together. Pour into a pan lightly sprayed with cooking oil to prevent sticking. Allow to cool until firm.

*Serves 6 people.*

*Ex–cemetery tour guide and reluctant medium Pepper Martin is dying for a break from communicating with the no-longer-living. But returning a legendary Wild West star's ghost to his hometown is proving one killer of a road trip . . .*

FROM
## CASEY DANIELS

# WILD WILD DEATH
*A Pepper Martin Mystery*

Her job has been cut, she's low on cash, and her detective sometime-boyfriend refuses to even *talk* about her ability to see the dead and solve their murders. So Pepper is most certainly down for a vacation to get her spirits up. But when her cute scientist friend Dan is kidnapped, Pepper soon stumbles upon another deadly mystery that brings her to New Mexico. And she's after a clever murderer . . .

## PRAISE FOR
## THE PEPPER MARTIN MYSTERIES

"There's no savoring the Pepper Martin series—
you'll devour each book and still be hungry for more!"
—Kathryn Smith, *USA Today* bestselling author

"Entertaining . . .
Sass and the supernatural cross paths."
—*Publishers Weekly*

penguin.com
facebook.com/TheCrimeSceneBooks
caseydaniels.com

M1095T0412

Becca Robbins is happy to help research a farmers' market and tourist trading post—until she has to switch her focus to finding a killer…

## AN ALL-NEW SPECIAL
## FROM NATIONAL BESTSELLING AUTHOR

## PAIGE SHELTON

# Red Hot Deadly Peppers

**A Farmers' Market Mini Mystery**

Becca is in Arizona, spending some time at Chief Buffalo's trading post and its neighboring farmers' market to check out how the two operate together. She's paired with Nera, a Native American woman who sells the most delicious pecans—right next to a booth with the hottest peppers money can buy.

When Nera asks her to deliver some beads to Graham, a talented jewelry maker inside Chief Buffalo's, Becca is grateful to get a break from the heat. Little does she realize that the heat's about to get cranked up even more—because Graham has been murdered, and she's the one who finds his body. She soon discovers that Graham was Nera's cousin, and that her uncle was recently killed, too, after receiving a threatening note. Becca begins to think the murders may have something to do with the family's hot pepper business. Now she must find the killer, before she's the one in the hot seat…

### Includes a bonus recipe!

paigeshelton.com
facebook.com/TheCrimeSceneBooks
penguin.com

33029098441918

ISBN 978-0-425-25245-1

## GETTING WARMER

Fire Chief Stella Griffin is working to solve the mysterious death of her predecessor, Eric Gamlyn—who also haunts her cabin. Yet the more she learns, the more burning questions she must answer. Just as Stella thinks she has a lead from Deputy Chum, someone snuffs her hopes—and the lawman.

Adding fuel to the fire, Stella's parents soon arrive—with her ex-boyfriend—hoping to persuade her to return to Chicago. Now Stella is torn between the life she left behind and uncovering what happened to her ghostly friend. But she'd better think fast or more than her investigation could go up in flames...

### Praise for *That Old Flame of Mine*

"Dark family secrets, a delicious mystery—and a ghost! What reader could ask for more?"
—Casey Daniels, author of the Pepper Martin Mysteries

"So difficult for me to put down and even more difficult for me to have it end." —Cozy Mystery Book Reviews

jjcook.net
penguin.com

ISBN 978-0-425-25245-1

5 0 7 9 9

9 780425 252451

$7.99 U.S.
$9.99 CAN